# KNIGHT TAKES QUEEN

## LUCY LEROUX

Knight Takes Queen © 2021 Lucy Leroux

❀ Created with Vellum

# TITLES BY LUCY LEROUX

**The Singular Obsession Series**
Making Her His
Confiscating Charlie, A Singular Obsession Novelette
Calen's Captive
Stolen Angel
The Roman's Woman
Save Me, A Singular Obsession Novella
Take Me, A Singular Obsession Prequel Novella
Trick's Trap
Peyton's Price

**The Spellbound Regency Series**
The Hex, A Free Spellbound Regency Short
Cursed
Black Widow
Haunted - Coming Soon

**The Rogues and Rescuers Series**
Codename Romeo
The Mercenary Next Door

Knight Takes Queen
The Millionaire's Mechanic - Coming Soon

**Writing As L.B. Gilbert**
**The Elementals Saga**
Discordia, A Free Elementals Story
Fire
Air
Water
Earth

**A Shifter's Claim**
Kin Selection
Eat You Up
Tooth and Nail

**Charmed Legacy Cursed Angel Watchtowers**
Forsaken

# CHAPTER ONE

Caroline Wentworth took out her pen, hyper-aware of her father's ghost hovering behind her. He watched with sullen disapproval as she prepared to sign away his legacy.

"I'm going to need these in duplicate," her attorney murmured, pushing two sets of papers toward her. Though she didn't let her emotions show, Amare was adept at reading between the lines. He knew how difficult this was, even if no one else appeared to.

"I will also need you to initial here," he said, pointing out the spaces in the middle of the contract. When she was done, Amare quietly gathered the papers, putting them in his briefcase. "I'll send these out right away."

"Thank you," she replied, hoping he didn't hear the hoarse quality of her voice.

Straightening, he hovered for a minute. "You should take the rest of the day off. The spa retrofit is almost completed. You should get a massage...maybe a facial."

Caroline's smile felt a little stiff. "I'd love to, but I have just enough time to grab a coffee before my next meeting."

Amare blinked, then glanced at his watch. It was half-past three. "You scheduled another meeting for this afternoon?"

"I did." *And there's no way in hell that I'm canceling it.*

"Oh." He fumbled with his suitcase closure, clearly wondering what could be so urgent that she'd scheduled *another* appointment.

Caroline wanted to jump up and down, shouting, *Yes, there are more important things!*

But she didn't. Caroline would never raise her voice to Amare, or anyone. That would have been unseemly, and she had been raised never to shame the family name.

Wentworth women didn't get angry. They were never disheveled or sweaty in public. Their hair was always styled, and they wore heels and hose. While most were college-educated, a Wentworth woman devoted her time to doing good works after graduation. They sat on various charity boards, and supported their brothers, husbands, or fathers, so these men could get on with the family business.

But Caroline was an only child, and her father had been gone over a year, carried away by a previously undiagnosed heart problem. His death had left the Wentworth hotel chain teetering on the verge of bankruptcy. Hampered by debt and with the livelihood of thousands on the line, Caroline had stepped out of Gene's shadow, devoting her every waking minute to pulling the business back from the brink.

Caroline had slashed the overhead, streamlining spending at all of their locations, had ruthlessly shut down unprofitable areas, and expanded their conference centers, actively courting professional groups to have their meetings at the hotel. At over half their locations, she'd stopped running their restaurants. Instead, she'd partnered with outside groups, bringing them in to run newer and better options in their place.

But that hadn't been enough. For the chain to survive, Caroline had been forced to sell three of their properties, including the original Wentworth Hotel in Charleston.

After being offered a fraction of their value shortly after Gene's death by an American investor, Caroline had courted a prominent Saudi Arabian hotel conglomerate interested in getting a foothold in the American south. The money from the sale had slashed their debt to nothing, and it was now funding renovations on the remaining five properties. Not only that, but thanks to her negotiations, the Saudi group was retaining the majority of the original Wentworth employees. Only a small fraction of upper management personnel had ended up without a job. Most of those people had already been snapped up by other hotels.

That last was a detail everyone seemed to overlook, especially the hack writers at the various trade magazines who covered news of the sale. They had made it sound as if Caroline had put entire families up on the chopping block, when, the reality was, she'd done everything humanly possible to save every job she could.

Her father would have been the first to say it hadn't been enough, not if it meant sacrificing their flagship hotel. Caroline had been born at the Charleston hotel, delivered by a doctor who'd stayed there every year for his anniversary.

*He still will.* The hotel would reopen under the new management before August when Doctor Sam and his wife of forty-five years came back for their annual pilgrimage. She simply wouldn't be there this time.

*Which is fine.* It wasn't as if she spent her birthday at the Charleston location anymore. She'd hadn't even celebrated it in the last five years. Caroline had been too busy doing damage control at their other locations.

*Except for the birthday before last...*That was when she'd been celebrating getting engaged.

*Don't go there,* Caroline ordered herself. She needed to focus on the work ahead. That included ongoing renovations at three of their hotels, rebranding them as miniature resorts by expanding their spa and leisure options. The recently re-christened Worthington Luxe, her current headquarters, had the most work done. The location was closed to the public in preparation for a grand re-opening in just over a week.

It made her stomach twist just thinking about it. Caroline had gambled a great deal on the success of the Luxe.

The hotel was spacious without being so large that overhead was a burden. The location, beachfront property on Coronado Island in San Diego County, was beautiful with plenty of parking. On paper, there was no way to lose, but Caroline had grown up in the hotel business. Success was never guaranteed. This location had a fair amount of competition from neighboring hotels—including the local landmark, the Hotel Del Coronado.

Hiding her tension, Caroline said goodbye to Amare, stopping to check her appearance in the full-length mirror in the adjoining bedroom suite. After freshening her lipstick, she swiftly redid the French twist that was part of her signature look. When she was done, her makeup was flawless, and not a strand of hair was out of place.

Despite that, she still looked tired. The evidence of this week's sleepless nights was written all over her face. Reaching for her cosmetics, she dabbed a little concealer under her eyes before washing up and straightening her suit jacket with rough hands.

*I can do this. The worst part of the day is over.*

Leaving her rooms, she checked in with the facilities manager regarding a problem with the boilers, then consulted with the concierge about a large group checking in together the day after the grand re-opening.

"The new chef also asked you to pop in when you get the chance," Janet, her assistant, informed her after they went over her schedule for the next few days.

Caroline glanced at her watch. "I have just enough time for that and a cup of coffee."

"Oh, I can get you the coffee," Janet said, always ready to drop everything to make Caroline's life a bit easier. "

"That's not necessary," Caroline said with a stiff smile. "Just make sure Marcy finishes organizing that whale-watching tour for the Dole group."

Caroline retreated before Janet offered her condolences. Except for her assistant, most of the staff had probably forgotten it was the anniversary of her father's death. However, every single one knew it was the day she'd officially sold three of their hotels.

Aware that everyone was watching her, she cut across the lobby to the kitchens. Her heels sounded like gunshots on the marble floor.

*Things won't be so awkward once the hotel has guests again.* Once the hotel opened, the routine would be established, order restored. In the meantime, she and her staff had a million things to do to get ready.

Trying not to rush, Caroline met with the chef, then one of the receptionists, and squeezed in a few minutes of conversation with the head gardener. She grabbed a coffee, then rushed back to her office with only five minutes to spare.

The representative from the Lahore Fertility Clinic waited in the hall. With her first genuine smile of the day, Caroline hurried to meet her.

"Hi, how are you?" Lilia asked, reaching out to shake.

"I'm great," Caroline said, pumping the woman's arm with a little too much enthusiasm. She looked over her shoulder, spotting Janet, her assistant, coming up the corridor.

"Why don't we step inside my office?" Caroline asked, ushering Lilia inside before her assistant spotted her.

"Caroline!"

Drawing the door partially so only her upper body was sticking out, Caroline tried her best not to swear aloud.

"What is it?" she asked, pasting on what she hoped was an innocent expression.

"Sorry to disturb you, but there's a man from the FBI here," Janet said, checking her tablet. "His name is Agent Rivera. He'd like to speak with you."

Caroline blinked. "An agent? You know what, never mind." She pointed behind her. "I can't see anyone at the moment. I have an important meeting."

Frowning, Janet held up her tablet. "But we just went over your schedule. There's nothing on your calendar."

"Yes, I know." Caroline closed the door a little more as Janet tried to peek behind her. "I forgot to put it on there."

Janet's brow puckered. "You took a meeting *after* Mr. Bankole?"

"*Yes.*" Caroline coughed, trying to soften her tone. "I did. And I have to get it, so why don't you tell the man to see Mr. Shepard? Keaton is here today, right?" she asked, naming the head of security, a man who'd been working for the Wentworth chain since her father's early days.

"He is, but Agent Rivera was, um...*firm*...about speaking to you. He said it was important."

"I can come back if you're busy," the fertility rep said from behind her.

"*No,*" Caroline insisted, waving at the woman to sit back down. "This will only take a moment."

Caroline turned to Janet. "First things first—I want you to call the local FBI office and check this man's credentials—"

Janet fished a piece of paper out of her pocket. "He showed me his badge. Plus, he gave me this card..."

Caroline held up a hand. "Business cards are extremely easy to fake. I just ordered a new set for myself last week. Please call the office from a number you find yourself, *not* one he gives you. If it checks out, then take him to speak to Keaton. Walk him over to security yourself if you have to. I'll be calling it a night after this, so I'll see you tomorrow. Thank you and good night!"

After closing the door behind her, Caroline apologized to Lilia. "Sorry about that."

"Not a problem," the rep said, opening her satchel. "I have all the paperwork as requested. You can sign now, or, if you'd prefer to take your time, I can leave them so you could go over them at your leisure."

"I'll sign now," Caroline said with determination. She picked up her pen with eagerness this time. "Your office emailed me the contract template, so I had ample time to review the details. I'm all set."

After signing her second life-altering contract of the day, Caroline listened as Lilia gave the spiel on the next steps—from choosing a sperm donor to the possibility of in vitro fertilization should Caroline change her mind about using her own egg to conceive a child. Lilia also explained the particulars of preliminary genetic screening.

"I know that's not what you discussed with the doctor," Lilia said, retrieving a DNA testing kit. "But many women like to keep that option open in case something turns up in your genetic screen. That's not going to be an issue given how detailed a family background you gave—no red flags there. But we always mention it, just in case."

"I understand," Caroline murmured, turning her chair to face Lilia as the woman came around with a long cotton swab in a little vial. After passing it over the inside of Caroline's cheeks, the nurse-practitioner-turned-fertility-liaison packed up.

Lilia zipped up her bag, but then paused. "If you have any questions, feel free to call the office anytime to speak to one of our doctors. I understand you're going for our premium-level service, where our donor exclusivity clause kicks in."

"Yes," Caroline replied, weaving her fingers together. "It's particularly important to me that the father of my child isn't...um, how do I put this? That he isn't *popular*."

Flushing at her inane remark, she passed a hand over her face. "I just meant that sperm donors are one of those cases where being a favorite is a bad thing," she finished awkwardly.

"I understand completely," Lilia said with a laugh. "There are those crazy tales of a single donor fathering dozens of children, or a hundred in one case. But that would never happen at our clinic, even with our standard service. Then there is the fact you've chosen our most exclusive option, which gives you access to our highest tier of candidates. Once you pick your premium donor, he goes off the market, never to be used again."

"That is some comfort," Caroline said, sitting back in her chair. "I'd strongly prefer my future child not have dozens, maybe hundreds, of half-siblings running around, possibly in the same future dating pool. You hear these horror stories..."

Gracefully, Lilia waved her hand. "Again, that's not an issue with the Lahore group. Our donors have gone through almost as many background checks as our staff. It's rigorous *AF*."

This time, Caroline's laugh was genuine. "You don't have to do the hard sell. I've already signed the papers."

It felt almost as if she were buying a custom-made car or something equally expensive. *A custom car would be cheaper.*

"So, what happens if a premium donor goes to another clinic behind your back?"

"We sue the crap out of them!" Lilia laughed. "Just kidding—except not really. Our premium donors *do* sign contracts prohibiting them from donating to another facility during the period we are actively advertising their genetic material. If they don't get snapped up during that time, they are welcome to go elsewhere. If they do, we destroy their sample. In most cases, this isn't an issue because we headhunt our donors aggressively, approaching premium candidates after a highly selective search. We don't take walk-ins."

She patted her bag. "The legalese in the contracts they sign would discourage them from even considering going to another facility."

"Oh." Caroline nodded, cringing internally at the phrase *'advertising their genetic material'*. "Everything is so well thought out..."

The rep beamed. "That's why we're the number-one fertility clinic on the West Coast. We don't leave anything to chance. Now, we usually advise our potential moms to wait for the genetic screen but since you chose the premium package, you'll be able to access your donor list as soon as the contracts clear our legal department."

Caroline fiddled with the pen. "Great. So, will that be on a website?" she asked, picturing the password-protected couture shopping website her cousin had signed her up for.

"Actually, we've found the most secure method to be a hard-copy version. You'll receive a binder—"

"Once the contract, i.e., my payment, clears," Caroline finished.

Obviously, Lilia knew better than to answer that. She simply chortled, repeated the standard assurances, and then handed over a business card before taking her leave.

Once she was gone, Caroline collapsed in her chair, sinking into the plush leather cushion as if she were boneless.

She had done it. The papers were signed. Caroline was going to be a mother—and she was doing it on *her* terms.

Still reeling from the sheer magnitude of what she'd done, she stayed in her prone position until a stray thought made her snort aloud.

*If selling three of our hotels didn't make Daddy turn over in his grave, then this definitely would.*

Ever so slowly, Caroline forced the corners of her lips up in a ghost of a smile. Then she started to cry.

# CHAPTER TWO

Isaac Rivera stared down at the mousy brunette who worked as Caroline Wentworth's assistant.

"I told you that I need to speak to *her*, not that fossil you have working security."

He crossed his arms, leaning against the wall across from the dragon lady's office door. "I just flew across the country for this, so I don't care how late it is. I'm not budging until I talk to her. We both know she's still here."

They'd watched a middle-aged Hispanic woman in a blue suit leave the office not five minutes earlier.

Janet cast a nervous peek at the door. "Yes, but you see, it's just not the best day."

Isaac grunted. "Most aren't," he said with a shrug.

Granted, now that his divorce had hit the one-year mark, things weren't as grim as they had been once upon a time. He was no longer a blood-sucking vortex of doom, at least according to Ethan, a friend from the office. It helped that Isaac was dating quite a bit now, or at least he had been until his workload got too heavy.

The case he was here pursuing had been keeping him up late for months, but he'd finally gotten a big break. And Caroline Wentworth was mixed in this up to her Cartier-covered neck.

The mousy assistant seemed to be getting desperate now. She wrung her hands, glancing at the door. "If you come back tomorrow, I can work you into her schedule."

"Nah, I'm good," he said, not about to get chased away by a half-pint gatekeeper.

The assistant gave the door one last desperate glance. "It's, um, just that today is the anniversary of Mr. Wentworth's death."

*Well, fuck.* Isaac didn't move, but a red flush started to creep up his neck.

"That's Caroline Wentworth's dad—the former CEO of the chain."

He held up a hand. "I got it," he said, jaw tight.

"So, will you come back tomorrow?"

He sucked in a deep breath. "Unfortunately, I can't do that. As I said, this is important. And I get that you're required to run interference for your boss on what is obviously a tough day, so tell you what—we can pretend you didn't see me waiting here."

Janet's lips drew into an awkward grimace. "Ex-excuse me?" she stammered.

He flicked his fingers to the end of the hall leading to the main lobby. "If your shift isn't over, go meet with some other staff members...there were some painters who looked like they needed help."

The little woman planted her heels a little farther apart. "I'm sorry, I can't do that—" she began, but she stopped when a small commotion at the end of the hall claimed her attention.

A painter stood with a dark-skinned Hispanic woman dressed in one of the hotel's signature teal blazers. This one was a few shades darker than the others, which may have meant she was a manager.

"Janet..." The woman gestured frantically. "We had an accident with a paint can."

Panic flitted across Janet's face.

"It's okay if you have to go," he said smoothly. "I can wait here all alone...by myself."

The poor woman's expression tightened. Janet held up her leather-bound tablet, almost as if she were debating beating him over the head with it. Wisely, she put it down. "Please don't be here when I get back."

Isaac made a noncommittal noise that could pass for an agreement. It was all the little bird needed to fly away.

*Finally.* Peeling himself off the wall, Isaac took a step toward the door. He'd just raised his hand to knock when it swung open.

He'd seen a picture of Caroline Wentworth before. Jason White, one of the other agents in the Boston bureau, had forwarded him an article picturing Caroline with Liam Tyler, her ex-fiancé, who was Jason's brother-in-law.

The photo had been a candid shot with Tyler in the forefront and Caroline in a fancy skirt suit standing off to one side. They'd caught her staring down at her phone, a generically attractive blonde going about her day.

How she looked in that picture was nowhere near the reality. Isaac's brain stuttered as he took in the *real* Caroline Wentworth.

Dressed in a sleeveless peach silk blouse and white skirt, she could be summed up in one word—*luscious.*

Platinum hair, curves that defied gravity, and glowing golden skin were paired with the best damn legs he'd ever seen. With those blessings, her face could have been plain, even a little ugly. It would have evened things out. But this woman's face was worthy of a character on his mom's favorite Mexican soap opera, the one that featured only tens. Lush lips, high cheekbones, and perfect bone structure that gave a nod to some Nordic or Swedish ancestors.

Except Caroline Wentworth's eyes were rimmed in red, and that bitable little nose looked raw as if she'd been wiping it too hard with tissue paper.

She blinked up at him like a deer caught in headlights, craning to look past him at the empty corridor. "Who are you? Are you supposed to be here?"

He reacted far slower than he should have. Clearing his throat, Isaac fished out his badge and held it up. "Agent Rivera. I believe your assistant told you that I needed to speak to you."

Thick golden lashes screened her eyes, and Caroline made a visible effort to stand a little straighter. "I'm sorry, but I'm swamped at the moment. If you could explain your issue to our head of security, that would be great. If you'd like, I can call Janet, my assistant, to show you to his office."

Isaac slid his badge into his coat. "She's already offered. But this is a sensitive matter. I need to discuss it with you and *only* you."

The woman made a sound in her throat that would have been a growl had it not been so delicate.

"Look, it's not a good day. Perhaps if you come back tomorrow, I'll be able to find ten minutes. It will give Keaton a chance to verify your credentials. No offense, but I can't take a stranger at face value just because he flashes a badge."

He pretended to check his notes. "Your assistant did verify my credentials. But if it makes you more comfortable, you can speak to Jason White."

"Jason?" she echoed with obvious dismay. "From Boston?"

"Yeah, that's my field office. I work with White and his partner, Ethan Thomas, on occasion, but I flew out especially for this."

He didn't need the bureau's 'Reading Micro-expressions' course to know she was not happy. "Have you been there long?" she asked.

"A few years. I was at White's wedding to your ex's sister."

"I see." Her lips turned down.

*Fuck a duck.* Isaac wanted to kick his own ass. Mentioning his tenuous connection to Liam Tyler, her former fiancé, was the last thing he should have done. Why the hell had he said that?

*And there it is, genius—the shutters are down.* Caroline's expression had completely closed up.

"I'm afraid I don't have time for any additions to my schedule," she said crisply. "I have one week before this hotel opens to the public, and the renovations are eight days behind. If Keaton can't help you—"

"He *can't*," Isaac interrupted.

Caroline closed her eyes, inhaling a deep breath. "If that's the case, I can put you in touch with Sally Ines. She's in charge of security across the entire chain. Trust me, if Sally can't solve your problem, then it isn't going to get solved."

With effort, Isaac held onto his temper. *Remember that her dad is dead.*

"I'm sure Sally is a miracle worker. At some point, I will have to speak to her, but I need to talk to you is because there has been a direct threat to your person."

The thick fringe of blonde lashes fluttered, and wide blue eyes fixed on his. "Excuse me?"

"Someone wants to kill you."

*ॐ*

Caroline blinked up at the tall, dark, and dangerous-looking man. She started laughing. "Is that all?"

One of the man's dark brows rose—just one, like a thickly drawn question mark on his too-handsome face. "I don't follow. Isn't that enough?"

She lifted a shoulder, deciding to be honest. "Not really, no."

The man crossed his arms. "You're not taking this seriously."

Caroline couldn't seem to stop looking at the man's hand. His shirt cuff had ridden up when he moved, revealing the edge of an intricate tattoo that wrapped around his wrist.

*Huh.* Maybe he did undercover work. Undercover agents always got tattoos when they infiltrated the underworld, didn't they? Caught up in the idea, she continued to stare until he waved that hand in her face.

"Miss Wentworth, I don't think you understand the situation."

"Call me Caroline, please," she said before she could stop herself. She didn't want this man getting familiar, but her upbringing—the hospitality industry with a thick layer of regular southern manners on top—made it nearly impossible to be outright rude.

"Caroline, this isn't a joke. The threat is real. Someone wants to hurt you."

"They'll have to get in line," she said shifting her weight absently, wishing she had changed out of her heels before opening the door.

"Do you get threats that often?" he asked, brow puckered.

*Dear Lord, I am so tired.* "If I say yes, will you go away?"

His eyes widened.

Caroline's shoulders slumped. "I apologize. It's been a long day."

She raised her hands half-heartedly. "I don't know what to tell you. I'm a woman in a high-profile business. Since the news of the sale got out, there has been an escalation in hostile messages toward me. Some are probably death threats."

"Really?" His nose wrinkled as he leaned a little closer.

Caroline didn't know whether he was skeptical or going for a sympathetic air, but, either way, she was too tired to care.

"It's nothing new. People have said a lot of things about me over the years. I can handle it. I've been in the public eye since I was a teenager. I realize that makes me sound like Paris Hilton—I didn't mean it that way—but as I mentioned before, it's been a long day."

The agent raised his index finger. His lips parted as if in preparation for a lecture, but, in the end, he closed his mouth. "All right, I'll make you a deal. I will come back tomorrow if you agree to let me see you home. I will drive you there. You will not leave. And, in the morning, I will drive you back here. Then we will have a long talk."

He stood straighter, his shoulders seeming to increase in width by the second. The agent was starting to resemble a monolith, as if he were silently telling her that he wasn't going anywhere.

Frowning, Caroline grabbed her phone and pulled up her calendar. "I can see you for half an hour—that's an entire thirty minutes—before I see the linen vendor. However, I have to warn you that is going to happen incredibly early in the morning."

"The time doesn't matter, I'll be here. Now...about that drive home."

"Oh, the escort isn't necessary—"

The man's lips compressed. He took an aggressive step forward. "Look, lady, I get you had a tough day with it being the anniversary of your dad's death and all, but I am here because I want to keep you *alive.*"

Caroline jerked her thumb at the door at the end of the hall. "I meant you don't have to drive me home because I am living here during my stay in San Diego. I sleep here. I eat here. I don't ever leave…"

Her voice had climbed an entire octave by the time she was done. Blinking rapidly, she backed away and tried to swallow over the lump that had suddenly developed in her throat.

Agent Rivera swore under his breath, then scrubbed his face with his hands. When he spoke, it was in a much gentler tone. "I'm sorry. I misunderstood. It's….um…actually great news that you are sleeping here. Security-wise, that's the best-case scenario."

Caroline worked on holding herself very straight. "We can discuss that tomorrow."

"Right." He began to walk backward. "What time is your, er, sheet meeting?"

"Six sharp."

Agent Rivera closed his eyes. "Ah."

"If that's too early—"

"No," he interrupted abruptly. "See you at…six."

"Sharp."

He inclined his head in gracious defeat. "Bright and early."

When he continued to stand there, Caroline gave up, turning on her heel. She walked down the hall, taking the room's key card out of her pocket. When she turned around, Agent Rivera was gone.

*Sweet baby Jesus, finally.*

But then she remembered that, thanks to her vindictiveness, she had to see the man again in less than seven hours.

# CHAPTER THREE

Isaac resisted the urge to run out of the Luxe hotel. He made himself go to the security office to tell the supervisor not to let anyone who wasn't cleared by them into the private corridor where Caroline Wentworth worked and slept.

Since no unauthorized people were ever allowed back there, his point fell a bit flat. But he told himself it had been necessary regardless.

*I made her cry.*

Granted, Caroline had been crying *before* he spoke to her. *Seriously, how did I manage to do this on the first anniversary of her dad's death?*

He climbed into his rental car, then sat there for a moment. Then he banged his head against the steering wheel.

All those times his ex-wife had said he was an asshole had slid right off his back because he'd known she tended to blow things out of proportion, but this…he was going to have to fix this.

Not only was Caroline Wentworth a young and surprisingly *hot* workaholic, but she was somehow tied to the biggest case of his career. He needed her cooperation if he were going to bring Blackbeard down.

*I need more information.* Checking the time, he pulled out his phone.

He was tempted to call Ethan Thomas, but Jason, his partner, was the one who knew Caroline best.

The phone rang for ages, but Jason eventually picked up.

"I need to know everything there is to know about Caroline Wentworth," Isaac said without preamble.

"Isaac?"

"Yeah. It's me. Tell me about Caroline."

"*Okay...*" There was a long pause. "Oh yeah, I heard you were going out to the West Coast. This is related to your smuggling case, isn't it? Ethan mentioned you'd tied it to the hotel chain. I had no idea it was the Wentworth."

Jason was a funny guy, for an FBI agent, but he sometimes beat around the bush. "Well, it is."

"*Shit.* Sorry about your CI, by the way."

"Yeah, finding him like that was fucked up." Isaac sighed. His confidential informant had been in the bay for days. By the time his body washed up, he'd been unrecognizable.

And there was no way in hell he was going to let Caroline Wentworth go the same way. The god of hot, emotional, but still strong women would strike him dead.

"Hold on a minute," Jason muttered as a noise in the background came over the line. "I'm just back from dinner, and I'd like to have this conversation in private."

Isaac frowned as he registered movement in all the din. "Are you hiding from your wife?"

"Uh...no. Well, yes. I love Maggie to bits, but Caroline is a topic on which we don't agree."

"Yeah, I heard the details from Ethan," Isaac said, filling in what he knew. "Maggie thinks she's stuck up and superficial."

Maggie Tyler, Jason's wife, was a sweetheart, but now that he'd seen Caroline up close and personal, her comments were starting to sound like a case of female cattiness.

"As I said, I don't agree with my wife on this," Jason said. "Her perspective is a little skewed—mostly because Peyton, her best friend, was in love with her older brother Liam their entire lives.

She and her other brother Patrick love Peyton like a sister—hell, *I* love Peyton like a sister. But that meant Caroline was always fighting a losing battle for their approval. They're not real proud of themselves now, but Maggie and Patrick were allies against anyone Liam dated, up until he broke things off with Caroline to finally get with Peyton."

"Sounds like a soap opera." And he would know. Growing up with a single mom and two sisters, he never got to watch what he wanted. That was why he'd grown up watching shows with titles like 'Venganza de Amor' and 'La Esclava'.

"It was a huge mess," Jason agreed. "Especially for Caroline, because they had to stop a major hotel merger between the two chains when Liam called off the wedding. Honestly, she's a lot nicer than people give her credit for. She was always nice to me anyway. And Caroline had a hell of a time when her dad was alive. I don't know all the details, but I saw enough to make me glad I was born with boy parts. Girls from the South have it *rough*."

"Wait," Isaac grunted. "I thought that Liam guy married a man."

He was almost certain he'd heard something like that.

Jason snorted. "He *did*. He also married Peyton. It's what the kids call a thruple."

"Huh." Isaac processed that. "Well, good thing Caroline Wentworth got the hell out of Dodge."

Who the hell needed the stress of two partners? One had been enough for him. *Sometimes, it had been more than enough.*

"The end of the engagement was a shit show." Jason was in the mood to gossip. "More so for her. Caroline and Liam had been a hotel-world power couple for a while, and you know how those people are—they stick with the richer half after a breakup. Caroline's stock sank in their social circle when Liam ended things. But I heard it went back up after Liam's wedding…mainly because their old set decided Liam was a sexual deviant."

A corner of Isaac's mouth turned up. He wasn't one to judge who slept with whom, but having an older *and* a younger sister made him sympathetic to the dumpee under most circumstances. "Caroline is better off. Anyway, I just needed some insight on her. I kind of charged in like a bull into her Coronado hotel today."

There was a snicker. "Did she castrate you? Cause that's what I see Caroline doing to a charging bull."

Isaac scowled. "I thought you said she was nice to you."

"That doesn't mean the woman is a pushover," Jason pointed out.

"Well…I had shitty timing." Isaac checked his notes for her dad's name. "It turns out today is the anniversary of Gene Wentworth's death."

"*Oh.*" Jason harrumphed in sympathy. "How did that go?"

"She did *not* cry in front of me. There was some very pointed, *not* public crying."

Jason sighed loudly across the line. "Way to pile on."

"I will do better tomorrow," Isaac swore. "But this thing she's mixed up in is some serious shit. I can't handle her with kid gloves."

Jason was philosophical. "Just don't get her dead. She has a whole damn hotel chain to run and happiness to find."

Isaac snorted. "I'll do my best, Dr. Phil."

"Hey, I'm trying to help, man," Jason groused. "Also, I'd genuinely like for the universe to stop kicking that woman when she is down. So do what you have to do to protect her without making her cry tomorrow."

Jason hung up before Isaac could think of a snappy comeback.

Everything was going to be fine. Caroline was a grown-ass woman. Yes, she had been through some shit, but look at her now—she was handling it like a pro. Tomorrow, he would lay out his case and she would listen. Once she heard the cold hard facts—at six in the damn morning—she'd acknowledge there was a real danger, and he'd get the cooperation he needed to conduct his investigation.

There was too much at stake for him to allow any other outcome.

Opening his phone, he made a few notes, editing some of the details he'd jotted down beforehand about Caroline. He deleted 'stuck-up' and 'socialite' and inserted 'workaholic' and 'sensitive' with a question mark after it.

He also wrote down the names of her assistant and the description of the woman he'd seen leaving Caroline's office.

Janet hadn't known who the woman was. He got the impression Caroline didn't take meetings with people her assistant didn't know very often. Which meant she might be hiding something. Whether she liked it or not, Isaac was going to find out what it was.

# CHAPTER FOUR

Bleary-eyed, Isaac threw back the last of his triple-shot Americano so he could toss the Styrofoam cup into one of the discreetly positioned bins in the Luxe's lobby.

*Even the trash cans are sleek.*

He'd been to the Caislean Hotel in Boston a few times as Jason and Ethan's guest, so he wasn't a stranger to fancy hotels. But this place was something else.

Designed like a massive Mediterranean villa, it was painted all white, with columns everywhere. The palm trees and black-and-white marble tiled floor made it feel like a sprawling palazzo. And once the sun rose, the large lobby would be filled with light thanks to the floor-to-ceiling arched windows that would showcase the picture-perfect ocean view.

After doing more research last night, he'd read that Caroline had bought this place recently, taking the neglected property and refurbishing it. But from what he could tell, she'd hadn't gutted the interior, choosing instead a judicious retrofit that removed dated additions, polishing the bones of the place while seamlessly integrating modern amenities.

This place was going to make a killing when it opened. And it seemed the staff knew it. All around him, people were working, polishing, or painting things. Not a single one looked even the tiniest bit grumpy to be up so early in the morning.

*Bunch of freaks.*

Then one of the painters moved, and he caught sight of Caroline beside one of the men wearing the ubiquitous hotel uniforms the same color as the ocean.

The sun was pouring through one of the high arched windows, lighting up her perfect creamy skin and picking up threads of pure gold in her blonde hair.

*Well, shit.* Blood rushed out of his head, heading south like it was trying to beat the traffic. *Stop. Remember it's six fucking AM.* That was way too early for a hard-on.

The self-reproach didn't help much.

Caroline wore another sleeveless silk blouse, this one a few shades darker than yesterday's off-white. That was paired with a powder blue skirt in the same family as the color worn by the staff. On anyone else, that ensemble would have looked bad, washing most white women out. But Caroline was tanned enough to pull it off.

Except that was an understatement. The curves under the simple outfit were pure gold, like the sun. Isaac wanted to touch her just to see how warm she was.

*Or bask like a lizard on top of her.*

Caroline finally turned, and the open expression on her face disappeared, settling into an expressionless mask.

That was hardly surprising, but somewhat disappointing given the raging hard-on he hadn't been able to quell.

Moving his satchel to cover his erection, he nodded in greeting. She returned the gesture, exchanging a few final words with her employee before pointing to the hall leading to her office.

His long legs caught up with her at the door, despite Caroline's rapid clip and significant head start.

"I've spoken with Janet and Keaton," she began after taking the seat behind the glass table she used as a desk. Behind were a double set of coral-colored bookshelves filled with elegant objects d'art, including more than half-a-dozen bottles that appeared hand-blown. "Both have independently verified your credentials."

"Great. Glad that's out of the way—"

"And now that I've had a bit of time to think about it," she interrupted, folding her hands on her desk and shifting uncomfortably, "I would appreciate it if you didn't discuss your business with the staff. Keaton and I both agreed it would be a bad idea to let you run amok, scaring people."

Isaac gave her a tight smile. *Don't make her cry,* he reminded himself. "This will sound harsh, but I'm not here to scare people. I'm here to tell *you* specifically that you need to be…"

"Scared?" she asked in exasperation.

"Concerned," he said slowly. "Aware and concerned."

There was that little growl sound again.

Caroline leaned forward. "Look, I've been in this situation before. When I was fifteen, my father had to do a round of cutbacks at one of the hotels. Despite that, he was determined to throw me a lavish coming-out party—a sweet sixteen. I received more than one threat afterward."

He knew some of what was coming up, but he didn't know the details. "You were threatened? Not your father?"

She shrugged. "One of those men continued to stalk me for a long time afterward. He broke into my rooms once, to wait for me after school."

Isaac stiffened, suddenly irrationally angry at a man he'd never met. "That's fucked up."

She blinked, seemingly surprised by the swearing.

He debated apologizing, but if his information were correct, he was going to be spending a lot of time around Caroline Wentworth. It was best if she got used to his foul mouth now.

"What happened?"

"It was fine," she added in a smaller tone. "One of the maids was in the hall. She hit him with the mop while screaming. He ran away."

"That was what, ten years ago?" Isaac consulted his notes. "Was it

Albert Perry or Jorry Smith? Because you had restraining orders against both during that period."

That was one of the reasons he'd slept like crap. Not content with Jason's summary, he'd spent a few hours doing a deep dive on all things Caroline Wentworth. And what he'd found made him pissed off. *A lot.*

Caroline frowned. "Um, it was a bit less than that. And the man who broke in was Albert. He ended up dying while on parole."

She broke off, tucking an imaginary stray hair behind her ear. "My point is that I've dealt with security issues before."

*The understatement of the year.* He cleared his throat. "I'm aware—I also know about the countdown clock."

Caroline had come of age during the first wave of internet depravity. Like some of her more famous contemporaries, she'd been singled out on one of those gross websites that counted down until her eighteenth birthday. That was when she became 'legal' in the eyes of American perverts everywhere. The European ones considered her fair game earlier.

He looked her in the eye. "I'm sorry you were sexualized at such a young age."

A line formed between her brows. Her nostrils flared delicately. "Uh…thank you?"

"I have sisters," Isaac explained. "If that had happened to them, I would have ended up in prison, not in the FBI. This is why I asked my boss to give me leave to discuss my case with you as frankly as possible."

Sighing, Caroline sat back in her plush leather office chair. "All right then. Please go ahead," she said, waving him on.

Isaac echoed her move, crossing one leg over the other for good measure. "For the last three years, I've been tracking a very dangerous man," he began. "He's a smuggler, one who transports anything and everything. He calls himself Blackbeard."

Feathery lashes fluttered over her sun-kissed cheeks. "Like the pirate?"

Setting his leg down, he leaned forward, his dark eyes boring into her light blue ones. "Don't let the cute nickname fool you—or, better yet, take it at face value. The historical Blackbeard was ruthless, leaving a string of bodies in his wake. The new one is no different. Wherever this guy does business, people die. His body count is at over a dozen people, and those are just the ones we know about."

Caroline's face was appropriately sober. "I see."

*Good.*

"Blackbeard is a specialist. He only does one thing—move contraband. Like the pirates of old, Blackbeard deals in anything that has value: stolen antiquities, drugs, counterfeit luxury goods—even people." He paused. "Sometimes, just parts of people..."

Her lips parted. "As in human organs?"

"Yes," he confirmed. "Rumor has it at least one mafia don in need of a transplant entrusted Blackbeard with the crucial delivery."

She fiddled with her pen, clearly unsure how to react. "I hope it was a kidney, something people have two of..."

He wrinkled his nose. "Pretty sure it was a heart."

Her head pulled back, a subtle withdrawing.

Isaac followed her, leaning forward as if drawn by a magnet. "This outfit takes great pains to maintain their reputation. Very few of Blackbeard's transactions have been seized. Most of the information we have was learned after the fact."

She set down the pen. "I take it his willingness to kill is part of how he keeps his shipments from being stolen or seized."

"He likes to make examples of snitches," Isaac confirmed. "People are afraid to talk."

Caroline inclined her head, but her eyes were unfocused as if picturing the worst.

"So, what makes you think this man has targeted me? I'm in the hotel business. I have nothing to do with shipping or importing. None of my hotels are particularly close to an airport. We don't even have a helipad. Aside from renting rooms for meetings and handoffs, which could happen at any hotel, I don't know what a criminal could do at the Wentworth."

"That's because you don't think like a criminal." Isaac's devious mind had come up with several possibilities. "For example, a vendor could take advantage of a contract to bring illegal goods in and out. I once worked a case where cheap T-shirts were soaked in liquid cocaine and then dried. They boxed these up by the hundreds. Once the boxes arrived in the States, the clothes were soaked in water, which was then slowly evaporated to recover the drug."

Her eyes widened, but he wasn't done. "I heard of another case down in Florida. Customs seized over five thousand of those mini hotel shampoo bottles. They were filled with pure liquid opium, an ingredient in several different drugs. I could go on and on. Suffice to say, there are quite a few possibilities."

Her mouth tightened, and he could tell she was marshaling her arguments against him. "But there isn't a connection to *my* hotel here, is there?"

Isaac took out his phone, then pulled up his agency-approved recording app. "I had an informant on the lower rungs of Blackbeard's operation. I was skeptical at first, but, after a few months, I was able to establish that his intel was good. Because of him, my colleagues and I were finally able to intercept one of Blackbeard's shipments. It was listed as electronic parts."

"What was it?" The fine gold of her brows had crept up a few millimeters.

He twitched up a pant leg before crossing one over the other. "Cats."

"Cats?" she echoed.

"Big cats meant to fill a private and illegal zoo for a drug czar." He pressed the play button on the third recording down.

The sounds of a busy dock filled the air. Then, a one-sided conversation began to play.

"It's all set at the hotel," his informant said. "But it wasn't easy. Wouldn't a cheaper place work better? They have less security."

There was silence as if he were listening.

"And the woman—that Wentworth bitch? Am I still supposed to follow her?"

Caroline straightened in her seat, visibly bristling.

Suddenly, the background noises increased, along with a layer of static, as if someone had turned up the volume on the recording. The response was tinny, as if someone had pressed the recording device to the speaker of a phone.

"Keep a close eye, but don't be obvious," a new voice said. It was so garbled that Caroline could barely make it out. There was a sentence she didn't catch, but then the static cleared, making the last sentence clear as day.

"The boss wants her gone, but it has to be at the right time."

Caroline flinched as the recording abruptly cut off. There was a minute of silence.

She held her breath, letting it out slowly. "I can see why you think this might be about me. But it doesn't necessarily mean I'm the woman they are talking about. They don't even mention the hotel by name. And it could be another woman with the last name Wentworth. I'm not the only one out there. I'm just the last of the Charleston Wentworth's."

A barely perceptible vibration tinged that last line. A less observant person would have missed it.

Isaac fished out a photograph from his folio. Isaac had taken the time to print it out, but he'd been hoping he wouldn't have to show it to her. But he did it anyway—a physical picture always had more impact.

Caroline stared down at the man in the photo. It wasn't a photo of the corpse currently laid out in the Savannah PD morgue. No, this was an ID picture, the uniform that of a worker at the Wentworth Hotel.

"That's my informant. He was found dead two days after he mailed me that recording."

She picked up the photo, dismay in her eyes. "He worked at one of my hotels?"

"The Savannah location." It wasn't one of the properties just sold.

"Savannah is a port city," she said.

Yes, Caroline was clever.

While smuggling wasn't restricted to ports, it went without saying that it was one of their defining features.

"So is San Diego," he couldn't resist saying, gesturing to the hotel around them.

Mouth tight, Caroline handed the picture back. "I don't recognize him. How long was this man employed with us?"

"Three months. He was directed to apply there by one of Blackbeard's lieutenants."

There was a long, slow sweep of her thick gold lashes as she absorbed that for a moment. "But he's gone now. The link to my hotel is broken—"

Isaac held up a hand. "Except he asked his supervisor to transfer him to this location just before he died."

Caroline sighed, throwing down her pen. "So, what do you want from me?"

She was going to hate this part. "I need to shadow you to assess threats. I will need to monitor your staff as well. I'll be looking out for anything suspicious."

She didn't appear to enjoy the news that he was handling this personally.

A little pucker appeared between her brows. "And you can leave the Boston FBI for this?"

He nodded. "I've been temporarily assigned to the San Diego office so I can pursue this investigation."

"How temporary? A few days? Weeks?"

He didn't reply.

Her face fell. "*Months?*"

"As long as it takes." After his CI was found dead, his boss, Robert Angel, had given Isaac carte blanche, or at least as close as FBI policy allowed.

Caroline raised her hands, rubbing her face. Miraculously, none of her makeup was mussed.

*She must have practiced that.*

"I realize this is bad timing giving your renovations," he said, gesturing behind him with his thumb.

Caroline leaned back in her chair. If looks could kill, Isaac would have been riddled with holes.

"That is the understatement of the year. This hotel opens to the public in one week. Our reservations have us at seventy-seven percent capacity on day one," she said, tapping her nails on the desk. "And while many of the staff have previous hotel experience, there are at least twenty employees for whom this will be a first. Our spa—one of our main attractions—is behind because the contractor quit halfway through and the new one is scrambling to finish."

She crossed her arms. "And now you want me to do what exactly? Pull people away from their duties so you can interrogate them about criminal activity that may or may not be happening at this hotel?"

Her voice didn't increase in volume, but it had climbed into a much higher pitch. *Shit.* He had to soothe her STAT. Besides, beating the grass to find a snake wasn't going to work in this case.

"I think a subtler approach is in order. I've only identified myself to two people besides yourself—your assistant Janet and Keaton Shepard, your head of security. These are the people closest to you, so they need to be aware of the threat. I also did some vetting before I got here. It helped that Jason remembered them both from back in the day. They have strict orders not to divulge my identity to anyone else."

Isaac tried not to feel offended as her expression of incipient panic grew into outright horror. "You plan on going undercover? *Here?*"

"I'm still debating on how to best handle this. I can go undercover. I've done that sort of work before, although these would be less fraught circumstances. But Keaton gave me another option."

"He told you about the complaints we've been getting about the recent sale?"

Isaac coughed. Keaton had let Isaac listen to some of the messages that had come in. Calling them complaints was downplaying the severity of the vitriol. The small-minded turds were giving him a possible avenue in. But it wasn't the only one.

"Given the recent sale, most will assume we've found a credible threat in the slew." *Oh, she was going to hate this.* He didn't love it either.

"That or we can suggest it's another stalker. Technically, it could be both."

She gave him a brittle smile. "If it's all the same to you I'd rather my personal history wasn't used as part of a cover story."

Wait, had she just agreed to his presence? *Whatever you do, don't point out the fact that she has a choice.*

Isaac cleared his throat. "Understandable. We don't have to decide on anything now. In the meantime, I'm going to have another meeting with Keaton and have a look around, get the lay of the land. Needless to say, your security is my highest priority—if you must go to any isolated parts of the hotel or have a meeting off the premises, please let me know so I can accompany you."

"You can't pretend to be part of security with that gun," she said, pointing to the bulge in his jacket. "Hotels don't have armed security."

"I'm afraid the gun is non-negotiable, but—" he paused as she opened her mouth to object, "I can wear a smaller piece in an ankle holster if it's that important to you."

"It is."

"That's fine." He rose before she could argue, checking his watch. "Your linen appointment is late."

Her cheek twitched. She checked the time on her phone. "Uh, yes...he had to reschedule. He won't be here until eight."

Isaac paused. Caroline's face was the picture of innocence, not even a flicker of those thick lashes betrayed her guilt.

The corner of his mouth turned up. "The meeting was always at eight, wasn't it?"

Primly, Caroline folded her hands on her desk. "Of course not. It was a last-minute change."

He smiled like the predator he was. She was adorable when she lied.

"Sure it was."

# CHAPTER FIVE

*Damn it.* Caroline slumped forward, letting her forehead hit her desk blotter.

*Why me?* What had she done in her past life to deserve this?

Leaning back in her chair, she pulled the bottom drawer open, fishing out her liquid antacid and drinking it directly from the bottle.

Rubbing her chest absently, she took several deep breaths before forcing herself to swallow a second large mouthful of the chalky liquid.

Caroline was too busy to get sidelined by her stress-induced heartburn. Or a frustratingly perceptive FBI agent.

In her defense, her linen man *would* be coming at six during normal operations. Today's later delivery was a one-time thing—she needed to make sure she had enough hands to carry in the new bath towels and dining room tablecloths.

*That reminds me.* Caroline made a note to check with the laundry staff to make sure the dry-cleaning chemicals had come in. She also made a call to remind the laundry room supervisor that only experienced staff should be allowed to man those machines. The last thing they needed was to ruin anyone's clothing during their first week.

Then she called Jason White.

A few minutes later, Caroline received an urgent message from the kitchens about a broken freezer. She was then up and running, putting out fires and marshaling her troops for the hectic week ahead.

Despite what Agent Rivera believed, there was little chance anything illegal was going on here. But she had promised Jason White that she'd give his colleague a chance because he was—quote—"A bit of dick sometimes, but he was rarely wrong about these things."

*Well, there's a first time for everything,* Caroline sniffed.

These were *her* people.

Still…there were some new staff members. It wouldn't hurt to keep an eye on things, maybe get Janet to run a few background checks if anyone stood out.

If anyone were doing anything underhanded, Caroline would sniff them out—preferably before the roughly handsome agent. She ran a tight ship, and she'd be damned if anyone said otherwise.

One week later

Isaac blew out a frustrated breath, his eyes blurring. Reaching for his cup, he corrected his notes listing the various businesses that served the Luxe hotel. It was longer than he thought it would be.

*I may have to ask for another analyst to help me run these down.*

While he was the only agent on the ground, he had the support of the local bureau office. Two junior analysts had been brought on board to go over the background checks Keaton Shepard had done on the Luxe employees. They were cursory jobs at best, but still more thorough than most operations this size conducted.

One of the valet parkers had a few misdemeanors, including a case of drug possession. Two of the maids had shoplifting charges, but they were both over a decade old when the women in question had been in their teens or early twenties. The most serious infraction was the concierge's drunk-driving charge, but Isaac was by no means done checking everyone out since he was expanding the list to include *all* the vendors and *their* staff. However, there had been no red flags so far.

He'd been half-expecting Caroline to gloat or say, 'I told you so,' but each time he spoke, she merely accepted his updates without judgment.

"Please let me know when you'll be done," she requested with flawless politeness before running to check on something going wrong with the elevators in the parking structure.

Well, it had technically been more of a fast walk, but since she'd done it in extremely high heels, he'd been impressed.

*Sure, that was the impressive part.*

Isaac did not want to admit how much time he spent watching the woman walk, but he couldn't seem to help himself. The woman had a world-class set of legs. *And that ass is out of this world.*

*Okay, stop.* There was more to Caroline Wentworth than her scorching hot and capable-of-reducing-grown-men-to-tears body. She didn't take anyone's shit, and she was smart as hell to boot.

From the outside, hotels appeared easy to run. People checked in, and maids made the beds and washed dirty towels. Once they checked out, the sheets were changed and the trash taken out. The most he'd ever asked of a nice hotel was a fresh burger from room service.

But after a few days of watching Caroline get the Luxe ready, he had a new respect for the business. Teams of maids marched into rooms, tearing the protective plastic off brand-new mattresses and replacing them with sheets, fancy comforters, and pillows so fluffy they reminded him of giant marshmallows. Minibars were stocked, and tons of branded tiny shampoos and toiletries were placed in the bathrooms. Every day, the entire ground floor was polished, the upper stories vacuumed. The basement was another world, with half the space devoted to laundry facilities and the rest to water heaters and a large IT-slash-security office.

In addition to that, there were the kitchens that would take care of the all-important room service burgers as well as two restaurants—

one fancy fine-dining place and a more casual eatery with a big wooden deck right on the beach. There was also a bar on the top floor with a huge balcony facing the Pacific.

Across from the bar, on the other side of the building, was a large room open to families with big picture windows overlooking Glorietta bay. It was where tourists would sit at cushioned tables while planning their adventures or decompressing after spending the day sightseeing or frolicking on the beach.

That room was his favorite, mainly because of the snack table and coffee station that was complimentary for the guests and new security staff, who appeared to have the boss lady's ear.

In the end, they had decided the simplest way to explain his presence at the Luxe was for him to start working directly under Keaton as a new hire and to say nothing else. "People will make up their own stories about my abrupt hire," he told Caroline after promising not to wear his service piece strapped under his arm where anyone could see it.

He was quickly proved right. Most staff accurately guessed that he had a background in law enforcement. However, his standoffish demeanor and his appearance—the tattoo in particular—had most concluding that Caroline was doing someone a favor by giving him a job.

A few even whispered he needed work because he got fired for some transgression. Insubordination was a popular theory. Getting canned for taking bribes was another. Of these, he preferred the latter. If any staff were involved in Blackbeard's operation it was best if people thought of him as morally flexible or even mildly corrupt.

Isaac did nothing to feed these ideas. In his experience, it was easier to let people come to their own conclusions. Those who didn't know he was FBI saw a tall, muscular Hispanic man with a full sleeve of ink, and they inevitably came to certain ones about him. Isaac didn't mind. It was that kind of negative perception that fueled his undercover work.

However, being an object of curiosity was making one aspect of his job harder. The Luxe had a generous amount of communal space for the staff, including a nice breakroom full of plush couches. But none of those places were appropriate spaces for him to work. He couldn't even do a basic internet search without someone peeking over his shoulder—not even in the security slash IT center. Caroline had made Keaton move an extra desk in there for him, but he needed his own office.

But it couldn't be just any office.

"Excuse me?" Caroline asked, blinking those too-blue eyes.

"I need to be closer to you," he repeated. "Someplace private."

They were in the high-end restaurant where Caroline supervised the delivery of some new dining chairs.

"Err...why?" she asked, reaching behind her and dropping into one.

"I can't do background checks on the staff *in front* of them," he pointed out.

"Oh," Caroline said, her confusion clearing.

"That and you run all around the hotel, and it's kind of challenge to keep track of you on the cameras."

Her head jerked back, startled. "You watch me on the cameras?" she asked, looking behind her as the moving men spaced the chairs around the tables.

They were on the other end of the room, well out of earshot.

"Caroline, the threat was to your person," he reminded her gently. "I need to keep an eye on you. The cameras are the only way I can do that without actually being with you. Unless you'd rather I accompany you—"

She held up a hand. "No, I don't."

Taking a moment to gather herself, she stared at the distant surf visible through the restaurant windows. "I guess I didn't understand what all of this would mean."

Pulling up a chair, he urged her to take a seat. He chose to stand, resting one hand on the table, the other braced on the back of her seat.

"Since you're not leaving the hotel and are sticking to meetings in public places, I've been giving you the space you need to work. But I haven't forgotten why I'm here," he said before elaborating on the problem he was having doing background checks.

Caroline's cheeks were extra rosy. He took a step back, guessing it was his proximity.

She cleared her throat. "Aside from the security office, the only places capable of accessing the security feeds are the manager's office, which is staffed twenty-four hours, and my office."

"The last would work," he said, brightening. "It's where you go between meet—"

Abruptly, Caroline stood. She gave him a bright, false smile. "I will speak to Keaton about getting one of the storage rooms down the hall from the manager converted into a makeshift office." She checked her watch. "His shift just ended, but I think I can catch him in the parking structure if I go now."

She hurried away before he could stop her. Sighing, he followed after her, intending to ask Keaton if there was a spare room closer to Caroline's office because she wasn't likely to volunteer that information on her own.

By the time he got outside, she was already out of sight.

Isaac picked up his pace, marveling at how fast she could move in Manolos. When the elevator opened on the top floor, the space reserved for employee parking, Caroline was halfway across the lot, raising her hand to hail Keaton Shepard, who was unlocking his sedan.

Keaton's grey head had turned in their direction when Isaac jerked at the squeal of burning rubber.

He watched helplessly as bright headlights illuminated Caroline. She was directly in the path of a big dark van.

Isaac's brain captured everything in freeze-frame fits and starts. One blink showed Caroline frozen in the middle of the lane, her lovely, sun-kissed skin washed out by the fluorescent bulbs. In the next blink, the van was ten feet away.

He shouted a warning, starting to run. But Isaac knew he was too far away. Heart about to explode, he watched the van inch closer and closer, a slow-motion horror show worse than any movie.

It was going to hit her. There was no way to avoid it.

And then Caroline went flying—Keaton had tackled her, pushing her out of the way just in time.

Isaac pulled out his service piece, yanking it out of the strap on his ankle in record time. But it was too late. By the time he'd aimed at the departing van, it had turned the corner. He missed the shot.

Running to the edge, he took out his phone, taking a series of pictures on burst mode as the van sped out of the ground floor of the parking structure.

He should have followed it, but Isaac didn't even try to pursue it. Not only was his rental car not in this structure, but he also had no idea how Caroline was.

He ran toward her, rounding the car that she and Keaton had fallen behind. Isaac had expected some bumps and bruises, so he was shocked to find Caroline on her knees next to an ashen-faced and unconscious Keaton.

She lifted her trembling hands, whimpering when she saw they were covered in blood.

"Please help me," she cried, tears welling in those too-blue eyes.

Swearing under his breath, Isaac knelt, checking for a pulse. His fingers came away coated with blood. A small pool collected under the older man's head. "He's alive."

"I think he hit his head on the bumper," she said, pointing to the car next to them.

"I'll call an ambulance."

Isaac got to his feet and made the call, keeping his piece out in case there was another would-be assassin lurking in the shadows.

# CHAPTER SIX

Isaac dismissed the uniformed police officers at the hospital, promising to give their lieutenant a call about the attempted hit and run.

"Please remember that no one can know about this," he said after implying Keaton was the target. Isaac would tell their supervisor the truth, but he couldn't afford to let news of this leak out. Caroline's busy work schedule meant she wasn't going out at all, but there had been a time when she'd been a tabloid darling. *Especially when she'd been engaged.*

He peeked inside the hospital room, unsurprised she hadn't moved from her spot in the chair next to Keaton Shepard's bed.

"Janet brought you a change of clothes."

She turned to him, her eyes disturbingly blank. "I had her bring them," he continued, pushing the bag of clothes into her hands.

"Janet?" she repeated.

"Yes. I sent her home," he murmured—after swearing the woman to secrecy.

"That's good." Her thick lashes fluttered. "It's late."

Two connected sentences that made sense. It was an improvement. Although he was beginning to wish he hadn't sent her assistant home.

Kneeling over her, he put a hand on her knee. "Caroline, the doctors said he's stable. Do you want to take a break? Maybe wash up," he prodded softly.

He didn't bother asking if she wanted to head back to the hotel. Isaac knew she wasn't budging.

"I can't leave until his wife gets here," she said with a sniff, wiping the tear tracks off her face with her fingers. "He saved my life."

"He was very brave," Isaac replied, moving his hand in a tight circle over her knee. "I didn't realize he was married." Isaac had read Keaton as a confirmed bachelor.

The man worked a bachelor's hours—although Isaac was almost sure he napped in his office to last that long.

"He doesn't rush home," Isaac added when Caroline continued to stare at Keaton's still face.

She opened her purse, fishing out a cloth handkerchief. It was not edged in lace as he expected, but it was monogrammed.

"He's been married for over twenty years. His wife is in Charleston," she explained, dabbing at her eyes. "He started at the original Wentworth hotel. But when Dad died, Keaton offered to come out of retirement to help me set up the Luxe."

"Oh." Isaac was moved and surprised. "That was very generous of him."

Keaton had also proved very heroic—and pretty damn fast for someone his age.

Racking his brain, Isaac tried to remember if he'd criticized Keaton in front of Caroline. He didn't think so, but he was prepared to eat crow regardless.

"Listen, another agent is on his way. They'll keep an eye on him for us while I take you back to the hotel to shower and change. We'll come back when Keaton's wife gets here."

"But—"

"Caroline, honey," he interrupted. "I don't think you should let the woman see your clothes in that condition. It will only scare her worse. You can't do anything for him right now."

"My clothes?" Caroline frowned. Looking down, she jerked, taken aback by the blood staining the cream-colored linen.

"*Oh*," she said in a small voice.

Isaac tugged her to her feet. She stared up at him, dazed and a little lost. "Are you sure the doctor said you were all right?" he asked. "You didn't take a knock to the head yourself?"

"There's no swelling," she assured him.

"Did they take X-rays?" he asked, pushing his fingers into her hair to check for bumps himself.

It said a lot about Caroline's state of mind that she just stood there and let him.

Realizing this was a rare moment of compliance, Isaac wasted no more time. He ushered Caroline to the hotel, managing to keep her out of sight from the staff by using the back entrance that went past the security office instead of going through the lobby.

She showered and changed, then he drove her back to the hospital in time to meet Priscilla, Keaton's wife.

Expecting a basket case, Isaac was caught off guard by the steel backbone wrapped in sugar and perfume that made up Priscilla Shepherd.

Thankfully, Keaton had woken up by then. Relieved to see him talking and aware, Isaac was able to convince an emotionally drained and exhausted Caroline to call it a night.

He walked her to her rooms again, resisting the urge to pick her up as she stumbled like a zombie.

She passed out on the bed fully dressed. He watched her for a few minutes until the spot between his shoulder blades started itching.

*Don't go full voyeur, you damn stalker.*

Shaking his head, he slipped off her heels, then reluctantly left her room.

❧

Caroline woke up with a headache, a grief hangover that somehow managed to feel worse than a real one.

Dragging herself out of bed, she showered, forgetting she had taken one the previous night. Once dressed, she shook a few ibuprofens out of the bottle, clutching them in her hand as she left the bedroom in search of water.

She walked into her sitting room to find a bleary-eyed Agent Rivera sprawled on her couch. Strangling back a scream, she flung the pills at him, not recognizing his face until it was too late.

"Good morning to you, too," he murmured, his voice full of gravel.

He picked up one of the pills from the couch cushion. Thanks to her terrible aim, they hadn't hit him, or so she thought until he fished one out from his crotch.

"Do you want this back?"

Still stunned, she shook her head. Next to him, the throw pillow was crumpled to the left of the balled-up chenille blanket she sometimes used when watching the flatscreen.

"You slept here?" she managed to croak, one hand pressed over her racing heart.

"Yeah." Then he frowned. "Do you not remember me telling you?"

"I guess not. Last night is kind of a blur." Caroline took a deep breath, letting it out loudly. "I was about to call you. Do I have to make a statement to the police about the accident?"

Isaac stood. He was so tall that she felt the need to take a step back, despite being on the other side of the coffee table.

"Caroline, you are aware that it wasn't an accident, right?" he asked, his expression concerned. "Someone was trying to hurt you."

She stared down at her hands, remembering the blood. *Oh, God. Poor Keaton.*

"Of course I realize it wasn't an accident. I misspoke," she said in a low voice. "But I'm not sure they were trying to hurt me. I don't park in that lot. I don't even keep a car in this town because I rarely leave the hotel. When I do, I take a car service. Whoever was driving that van must have been after Shepard."

"Yet, it was *you* that they tried to run down," he pointed out.

"But—"

He held up his hands. "I'm not trying to scare you here."

"You're not?" she asked skeptically.

"Not more than you should be," he corrected with a rueful roll of his shoulders. "And I agree the attempted hit and run was a crime of opportunity. There is a high chance they were lying in wait for Shepard, not you. As you said, you don't park there."

"Thank you," she said, her shoulders drooping in relief.

"Don't thank me yet," he warned. "Because there is a great deal of logic in going after your head of security to try to get to you."

The momentary sense of relaxation dissipated like vapor. "Acknowledged."

Agent Rivera held out his hand. "Come here." He guided her to sit beside him.

The cushion was still warm. Uncomfortable, she sat on the edge of the seat. "I guess you were right about something criminal going on here."

"It does look that way," he said, his face carefully blank.

Considering the man was probably champing at the bit to say, 'I told you so,' she considered this a restrained response.

"I should call the hospital," she said after a moment.

"I already did," Agent Rivera replied. "Keaton is continuing to improve. His most recent scans show the swelling has gone down. Priscilla said he's doing well."

"Oh." She tucked a strand of hair behind her ear. "That's good."

"He's going to be fine, Caroline. But he's going to need some time to recover. I told Priscilla to call you when he's feeling up to it. In the meantime, there's a lot we need to settle here."

Ducking her head, she rubbed her temple. "I know. I have to find a head-of-security replacement. You were right that I shouldn't promote Keaton's subordinates. I don't think they have enough experience. Keaton was just now training them, so it doesn't make any sense to promote from within. I should call Sally Ines, the head of security for the entire chain, to get her input."

He held up a finger. "Before you do that, I have an alternate proposal."

She knew where this was going. Trying not to sigh aloud, she inclined her head. "You want to take over."

He shrugged. "I think it's for the best. I'm already in the department. It's obvious to Tony and Julio that I have more experience than them. They won't be surprised I'm being promoted over their heads."

Caroline collapsed back on the couch cushion. That did make sense. She didn't like it, but she couldn't think of a better alternative, not even bringing Sally in…

Sally Ines was exceptionally good at her job, but this was attempted murder. Someone had tried to kill her yesterday.

*If I die, what will happen to the hotel?* Her next of kin were her aunt, uncle, and their vapid son Cameron, who had never worked a day in his life. Everyone would lose their jobs.

*Who would raise my baby?* Caroline gave herself a shake. She had to stop that. She wasn't even pregnant yet.

"Are you okay?"

She glanced up to find Agent Rivera hovering over her.

*When did he stand?* He looked like he was about to scoop her up and carry her to God-knew-where.

"Are you sure?" he asked. "I think the shock might be doing a rebound."

Caroline swallowed, shaking her head. "I'm fine. I was just thinking—do you believe Tony or Julio could be involved?"

"Not offhand, but I will be taking a closer look at them. But it could be that someone hoped to throw the whole management team into disarray, the security team in particular."

Caroline felt her bile rise.

"That's a worst-case scenario, of course," Agent Rivera said hurriedly.

*Great. Just great.* "And what's the best case?"

For the first time, the man appeared uncertain. "Um, I'll let you know when I think of it."

She closed her eyes, taking a minute to gather her thoughts. "So, what now?" she asked, her voice hoarse. "Do the police come to us or do we go to them?"

"I forgot to say—you don't have to make a statement. I took care of that last night. Also, other than you and Priscilla, only your assistant knows what happened to Keaton. I told her to tell everyone that he tripped over a carelessly dropped tire iron."

"Why?" she asked. "If it wasn't an accident, shouldn't everyone know? Won't I be putting the staff in danger by keeping them in the dark?"

Agent Rivera scrubbed his face with both hands before shrugging. "I'm going to level with you, I don't know the answer to that. Without knowing who is after you, or their real motivation, I *don't* know. But unless you want the staff to panic—"

"I don't," she interrupted.

He nodded. "Then we agree?"

"Yes," she said, feeling sick to her stomach.

"And do you agree that I should keep sleeping here?"

Caroline's eyes widened. "What?"

"I need to be close to you," he said, gesturing to the couch. "I don't think I can get any closer than this."

Confused, she waited for him to make a crack. The silence stretched. Dear God, the man wasn't joking.

"Do you realize what people will think?" Caroline sputtered.

The man's absurdly long lashes fluttered. "No. What will they think?"

"That we...that...*no.* Just no."

Agent Rivera bit back a sigh. "Alternatively, I can put a cot in your office."

He pointed to the connecting door he'd noticed on his first visit. According to the photographs he'd seen of the standard and suite rooms, these had been removed and dry-walled over in the main part of the hotel, but Caroline had kept the pair connecting her bedroom and office. "With those unlocked, I can be in your room in two seconds flat if there's any trouble."

She hesitated. "I don't ever open those doors."

It was stupid, but that was Caroline's homage to maintaining a life-work balance. It was purely a token, but it was all she had.

"Just temporarily," he assured her. "Until we find a better solution."

"Uh…"

"I'm glad you agree. I'll talk to Janet about the cot." Agent Rivera leaned closer, touching her shoulder. "Don't worry. I'll make sure it's done discreetly."

Caroline gave up, collapsing on the couch cushions. "Fine."

# CHAPTER SEVEN

*You do not feel guilty.*

Isaac was doing what was best for Caroline. True, he was taking advantage of a shell-shocked and traumatized woman, steamrolling her into doing what he thought was best. But what were his options here? Sticking close to her was the only choice he had.

*If only I had gotten a shot at the driver.* Picture or bullet. Either would have been fine with him. They had tried to run down a woman he was growing to admire quite a bit. As far as he was concerned the fucker deserved what he was going to get.

Unfortunately, getting Caroline to agree to his 'like glue' arrangement was the only plus in a sea of negatives.

His photo burst from the garage hadn't yielded any clear images. Nearby traffic cameras also failed to catch the driver. Isaac thought he'd caught a lucky break by getting a partial license plate off a grainy ATM camera, but the local cops had found the van abandoned a few miles away. Any hope of tracking it someplace useful was a bust.

To add insult to injury, whoever had cleaned the vehicle had been a pro. There were no prints, no hairs, and no discarded trash with convenient trace DNA he could run. The registration identified it as a stolen vehicle that had been boosted from downtown San Diego a few weeks earlier. The owner had confessed to being a bit of a slob, so the clean-up job had definitely come after it was stolen.

With no smoking gun to pursue, Isaac dived back into his background checks. He also took over Keaton Shepard's office and his duties.

As predicted, neither of the junior security guys so much as batted an eyelash at the announcement. If anything, they appeared relieved he was taking over. Both were too new at the job to expect another outcome. In particular, Tony seemed content to have someone tell him what to do.

Initially, Isaac considered both security guys strong suspects. Who else would know when Keaton left every day?

It turned out that almost everybody did. The maids, the cooks, the room attendants—everyone knew when management left for the day and their nightshift replacements came on.

Everyone also knew that Caroline never left.

"Does that mean you don't want another agent on sight at the hotel?" James Brody, his office counterpart, asked when Isaac mentioned that in a call to the local office a few days later. "I'm sure the Angel would be willing to assign you a junior agent after the attempt on Caroline Wentworth's life. You could get two or three if you included her picture."

Irritated at the suggestion, Isaac pushed aside a stack of background reports. Now that he'd taken over Keaton's office, the issue of hiding was moot. He simply locked the door when he wasn't there. "I could use someone for nights when I'm off duty."

"I thought you were sleeping there?"

"I am. I meant off-duty from the security office. Start the ball rolling on the assignment," he said. "We'll add the agent in as a nighttime security guard."

"I guess that beats being one of the maids."

Isaac sat up, fishing for a fresh pen to take notes. "Actually, that might be better. The maids have carte blanche to enter any of the rooms at will, on the pretense of cleaning."

James whistled. "Whoever gets the assignment is going to hate you."

"Yeah, well, have them infiltrate a white supremacist biker gang when they're Hispanic and see how they like *that*," Isaac muttered.

Laughing, James clicked off after promising to take over some of the third-party vendor background checks. Breathing a little easier, Isaac flipped through the various security feeds until he found what he was looking for.

Caroline was in the reception area, in front of the concierge.

Damn. Even seeing her on a screen was enough to give him a little jolt. It didn't matter that he saw her every morning.

They had a new routine—he'd get up, run out to shower, and then come back before she entered her office, which was at seven sharp every morning.

He was sure she hated finding him there, which was why he was made it a point to be dressed and out of her way, his cot rolled up and discreetly tucked away.

A few days into this routine, the hotel opened for business. The boss gathered the troops in the reception area before opening the doors.

"This is what we've been working for," Caroline said, her hands behind her back as she paced in front of the assembled staff, her shoes tapping on the polished marble.

Narrowing his eyes, he focused on the shoes—not the legs. Isaac had been hassling her to wear practical shoes ever since the incident in the garage. She kept insisting pumps were 'sporty'.

He frowned at the kitten heels. *I told her to wear flats. Those are her compromise?*

Unable to help himself, Isaac kept staring at her legs as she continued her motivational speech. *And I thought shorter heels would make her look less sexy*, Isaac reminded himself. But it seemed nothing could make Caroline less appealing.

*I should paint a wart on her face or something.* Anything to stop fantasizing about what was underneath all those skirt suits.

"We have dozens of hotel reservations representing over a

hundred guests expected today alone," Caroline was saying when he tuned back in. "Everything needs to be running at top efficiency, including the beachside café. Expect walk-ins there and in our fine-dining place. Everyone needs to get the same level of service at both—excellent. We're going to be closely scrutinized all month, but this first week is the most important. We need to be on top of our game—that means *everyone*. But I only hire the best, so I know you can do it. Don't forget to go to Anna or Melvin with any problems," she finished, waving at the daytime and assistant manager, respectively.

She noticed him watching her from the corner of the room. "Discreetly," she added, appearing to emphasize the word just for him.

He waited until the crowd dispersed before giving her a surreptitious salute. Her mouth twitched, but he wasn't sure if she were suppressing a smile or a grimace.

Isaac went out of the main doors, checking the action in front of the hotel. Cars were starting to arrive, families unloading their bags. It should have bugged him. More people meant more problems. But this was what Caroline had been working so hard for, so he was going to support her and hope for the best.

Circling the building, he walked all the way around to the beach, making a mental note to return at sunset. It had been on his to-do list since he got here, but he hadn't managed to make the time yet.

Regardless of the busy work—and he had no idea when he'd be done with all the background checks—this was hands-down the best undercover assignment locale he'd ever been assigned.

The sun barely hit the sand, but the beach café staff were already opening the big umbrellas on the patio tables. Grabbing a latte from the coffee cart on the deck, he headed back to his office.

"You have a delivery," Tony said, indicating a package on Isaac's desk.

"Thanks," he said, closing the door to open it in private.

It was unmarked, but it had a note. *Good luck getting her to wear this.* —*James.* The message had a smiley face with Xs for eyes.

"Brilliant," Isaac groused as his phone rang. He picked it up without checking the caller ID.

"You're less than an hour away now, yet you still don't visit," Sonia, his sister, snapped in his ear. "Mom says you're breaking her heart."

"It's more like two hours," he corrected.

"Not the way you drive," Sonia sniffed.

He smiled, picturing her face as she gave him that set down. *What are big sisters for?*

"I'm glad you called."

"Are you? Because the way Mom tells it, you don't even remember that you have a family anymore."

He took a sip of coffee, savoring the barista's expertise. "I spoke to her two days ago."

"To tell her that you couldn't come for Sunday dinner." His sister laughed. "You know that doesn't count."

"She knows why I can't—this case is taking up a lot of my time. But if I do manage to close it, I can pretty much guarantee the move to the West Coast office will be permanent."

"Like it's made a difference so far," Sonia scoffed. "We still never see you."

"It will," he promised. "I'm going to visit soon. But I need you to answer a question first."

"Shoot."

"How do I get a strong, independent career woman to wear a tracking device?"

"What?"

"It's for my case."

His sister chortled. "Must be some case."

"It is. So, any suggestions?"

"Who is this woman?"

"You know I can't tell you that." Technically, that wasn't true. His was the identity they needed to protect in this case, but there was no need to muddy the waters.

"Is she young enough to understand technology? Cause you could hide it in a piece of jewelry or something instead."

"She's a year or two younger than you."

"*Ah*," Sonia said. "Well, in that case, there's only one solution."

"What?" he prompted when she paused too long. Sonia had always had a flair for the dramatic. Only her husband found it amusing.

"You beg."

"C'mon," he groused.

"It's your only recourse," she said, laughing before saying something in Spanish to someone else.

Isaac frowned. "Who else is there?"

"The kids," she said as if it should be obvious.

He checked his watch. "Shouldn't they be in school?"

"I'm dropping them off now."

Isaac made a rough sound in his throat. "You know I don't like it when you call me from the car. Do you have any idea how many accidents are caused by distracted driving?"

"You only get to lecture me in person, *cabron*, so unless your ass is coming this Sunday, you can shut your trap."

"Don't swear in front of the kids," he scolded.

"*No, mames*," Sonia scoffed. "I'm not the one who got their mouth washed out with soap on the regular."

There was more noise in the background. "Okay, I'm here at the school," Sonia announced. "Say bye to your *pendenjo tio*, girls."

"Bye, tio," the girls chorused from the backseat of the minivan.

His nieces didn't include the swear word in their farewells. As far as he knew, his sister only threatened a mouthful of soap as part of her parenting repertoire, but she was their grandmother's daughter. They were too smart to risk it.

*Definitely true—girls are smarter than boys at that age.* Hell, they were probably smarter at all ages.

"I will ask her nicely," he said, unable to think of anything better than to tell Caroline the truth. It wasn't as if he could trick the woman.

"Who?" his sister asked, apparently pulling into traffic by the sound of the angry honks.

"What did I say about distracted driving?" he scolded, exasperated. "I'll call you later, once I figure out when I'm going to come up."

"Call Mom instead. She's been going on and on about how you don't love her anymore."

He rolled his eyes. "I *just* talked to her."

"To make excuses about not coming to visit. Again, as far as she's concerned, that means nothing."

"Fine," he muttered, getting up and tucking the box from James under his arm. "Are you having a party for the twins next month?"

"Will that finally get you up here?"

"I'll do my best," he said, knowing better than to make any promises in the middle of the case.

"I know you will," his sister said, giving him a rare break. "At least now when you find the time, you won't have to jump on a plane."

"True," he said, promising to call his mother again. "And, as a bonus, I can bill the FBI for the mileage."

"Good. Those f-ers take enough of your time."

His family was not fans of the bureau. They preferred it to the idea of him being a cop or a career soldier, but any job where he might be shot and killed was not going to be on their top-ten list of career choices for him.

If his mom had her way, he'd have been a bus driver. As long as he was union, she was okay with it.

"Kiss the girls for me."

"I will," his sister said before saying goodbye.

Determined to get the tracker issue dealt with, he went in search of Caroline. He found her in the lobby, smiling and waving like she stood on the deck of a cruise ship, departing on a month-long voyage.

Isaac stopped short. He'd seen Caroline smile before, of course. She wasn't stingy about that sort of thing when she talked to the staff. In fact, she praised them quite a bit, enough for him to think she subscribed to the 'you catch more flies with honey' adage in life.

But this was a smile unlike any other he'd ever seen. This was...joy. Pure unadulterated happiness. And then she covered her eyes and pulled them away, mouthing words that were recognizable to anyone who had small children in their life.

She was playing peek-a-boo.

His head drew back. The kid she played it with was across the room in the reception hall, a fat little Asian baby. It was probably a boy. Honestly, until a certain age, Isaac could never tell unless the mom slapped a bow on its head.

*Caroline likes babies. Go figure.*

The aforementioned baby was less than a year old, and it was loving Caroline's antics.

It made sense. Even babies loved beautiful people. According to a documentary on the learning channel that type of shit was hard-wired, but it was still a sweet, tender moment he hadn't expected from the career-driven CEO of a hotel chain.

The mother of the baby was too busy to notice the interplay. Getting her things together, the mom slung her purse on her shoulder and pushed the stroller out of the front doors, heading in the direction of the taxi stand. Caroline turned away with a soft smile that grew strained when a tall man approached her, greeting her effusively.

She hid it well. Only an expert in reading micro-expressions would realize Caroline was not happy to see this guy. But Isaac had the training.

Racking his brain, Isaac tried to bring up a mental image of Jason White's brother-in-law. He'd played poker with Patrick Tyler once or twice, but he had never met Liam Tyler, Caroline's ex, in the flesh.

For a split second, he wondered if this was the guy, but he quickly decided it wasn't. Despite what some people assumed, Caroline wasn't fake. If her ex had shown up at her new hotel, unannounced, Isaac didn't think she would slap on a happy face and be polite.

Giving in to the burning need to know, he pulled out his phone and did an image search for Liam Tyler. Nope. Negative. It wasn't this guy.

But it was too soon for him to lower his hackles. From the cut of the guy's clothes, he was another rich guy trying to mark his territory. The stranger practically salivated over her.

*Any minute now, he's going to lift his leg and pee on her.*

Deciding enough was enough, Isaac walked up to them. "Well, you did an incredible job—enough if you did it without my help," the man said.

Caroline folded her arms. "Well, that's very gracious, especially considering how certain you were that I couldn't do it without you."

Her tone was sweet as sugar, but Isaac could feel the cold chill emanating from them from ten feet away.

Isaac's instant dislike of the stranger increased when he got a closer look. Dark-haired and around his height, the guy was a serious contender—one who wore five-thousand-dollar suits.

"You're more than welcome to say, 'I told you so' all you like...over dinner." The man grinned, an invitation in his tone.

Caroline belatedly noticed Isaac approaching. She gave him a little motion of her hand, silently asking him to wait.

If anything, her expression became more syrupy sweet. "Thanks for the offer, Garret, but I don't think your wife would like that."

"I don't particularly care what she thinks these days," Garrett, the douchebag, declared. "We're separated."

"Oh." Caroline didn't appear to know what to say to this. She finally settled on, "I'm sorry to hear that."

"Don't be. It was for the best," Garrett said more soberly, his eyes going distant with a thousand-yard stare that made Isaac feel a little sorry for him.

*Been there.*

And then Garrett No-last-name blew the tiny bit of goodwill or understanding Isaac might have had for him by pressing the issue.

"So, Caroline, don't you want to join me and show off your new restaurant, the Michelin contender?" he asked. "I'm willing to give it a rave to all my friends."

"You'll do that anyway because it deserves it. Cerise Lions is a wonderful chef," Caroline said with a smile that was a touch too broad. "But I will be busy—it's opening week."

This last was said with a wave in Isaac's direction.

Garrett finally noticed him. The rich man took a step back, his eyes widening a tiny bit as he checked Isaac's muscled form with a top-to-bottom appraisal.

*Yeah, you're not the only one who can loom.* Just to drive that point home, Isaac crossed his arms, a move which made the top part of his tattoo peek out from the shirt cuff.

"This is Mr. Rivera, the hotel's new head of security."

"Hey," Garret said. He didn't offer to shake, his eyeballs glued to Isaac's wrist. Clearly, the man was not a fan of tattoos.

*Good.*

Isaac inclined his head noncommittally.

Garrett turned back to Caroline. "What happened to Keaton?"

They had told the staff that Keaton Shepard had an accident, but Caroline appeared to know this guy. Isaac couldn't chance that she would tell him the truth, so he cut her off at the pass.

"He took early retirement after a small health issue," Isaac edged in smoothly before she could reply.

"Oh." Garret's tone said he did not approve.

*Yay, I have another suspect to run down.* Isaac hoped this one was guilty because he would enjoy slapping a pair of cuffs on this man.

Caroline appeared to read his mind. She stepped in front of him as if to shield Garrett from him. "Yes, it was sad, but Keaton was happy to go home to Priscilla. And Mr. Rivera here is an excellent replacement. He's very experienced."

Garrett gave him a sardonic once-over. "I'll bet." He smirked.

Isaac clenched his jaw to keep from smiling. He turned to Caroline. "I need five minutes boss."

He lifted the box by way of explanation.

"Now works for me. I have to get back to work, Garrett. Please excuse me and enjoy your stay," she said, turning in the direction of her office.

Isaac nodded curtly at the man before following her.

"What about dinner?" Garrett called after them.

"Please enjoy it, compliments of the house," Caroline said, pivoting in a circle with a wave. "I recommend the house special. It's to die for."

# CHAPTER EIGHT

Caroline was steaming mad the entire way to her office.

"What is it with men?" she ranted, throwing up a hand as she dropped into the chair behind her desk. "The minute they think they're free, they start sniffing around like dogs in heat."

"Isn't it only females that go into heat?"

She snapped her head up to glare at Agent Rivera. It must have been effective because he winced before wiping all the softness from his expression.

"So, what's king douchebag's deal?" he drawled, setting the mysterious box on her desk.

Caroline started.

Agent Rivera frowned. "What is it?"

"Nothing."

He cocked his head, giving her a *c'mon* look.

Shifting uncomfortably, she picked up her pen. "You know Ethan Thomas, of course. You work together. Rumor had it that's what he used to call Liam."

The light dawned in his expression. "Liam Tyler... That's your ex, right?"

"Yes," she replied, studiously avoiding his gaze.

"Is Garrett a friend of Liam's?" he asked, a little smile teasing his lips. "Because like usually attracts like."

Unwilling, her lips pulled up at the corners. "I did meet Garrett at a party I attended with Mr. Tyler."

*One that was hosted by Matthias Raske.* But she wasn't about to mention that to him. She didn't want to get into the whole mess that was the end of her engagement. Liam had moved on, embarking on a polyamorous marriage that was reportedly making him incredibly happy.

Well, she was happy, too. And, soon, she would have her own family.

"You don't appear to be a fan," Agent Rivera observed.

She lifted a shoulder. "I have nothing personal against Garrett Chapman, his poor timing aside."

Though she'd been taken aback by his invitation, she didn't fault him for asking her out, not if he were single now.

*It must have happened recently,* she thought. Besides, she had a whole other reason to dislike him.

Agent Rivera crossed his arms. "Try again," he prompted with a smile. "I know there's something there."

Caroline stifled a sigh. She was supposed to tell him these things now, wasn't she? If she didn't, he'd look into the situation for himself and there was no point for him to turn over that stone.

"Fine." She put down the pen to rub her temple. "Garrett is an investor. When the hotel chain was in trouble last year, he came to me with a proposal to buy a percentage of the business. It was a lowball offer. It might have saved the hotel chain, but I would have lost equity and controlling interest."

Agent Rivera rocked back on his heels. "So, he's a shark who thinks you should have fallen all over his offer."

"Garrett took the 'no' gracefully enough," she said, lifting a shoulder. "God knows there were plenty who didn't, given they were dealing with a woman on her own."

"Was that because of the end of your engagement or because your father had passed away?"

Her lashes fluttered in surprise.

Agent Rivera had the grace to look uncomfortable. "Sorry. Janet filled me in on the hotel merger you had to call off. Between her and Jason, I have some idea of what you went through last year."

He stopped short of offering any sympathy or condolences. For some reason, that made her feel better.

"Both," she said simply, leaning back in her chair. "It was a very challenging time."

That was the understatement of the year. In a few short months, Caroline had gone from being one half of the hotel world's premier power couple, the daughter of a man of considerable standing in that same world, to being publicly dumped for another woman *and* a man. And then her father had died...

"But you pulled it off," Rivera said, sitting in one of the chairs in front of her desk. "Without Chapman."

She considered that. "I suppose. But in a way, I do owe him a debt of gratitude—his offer made me face facts. I realized I wasn't going to keep the chain from going bankrupt without taking drastic action."

"*Ah.*" The agent crossed his leg, a casual relaxed move that made her tense inexplicably. "So, Garrett was the catalyst that made you decide to sell three hotels."

She nodded. "It took some maneuvering, but I found a group in Saudi Arabia that wanted to enter the market in the American South."

"And you sold on the condition that everyone at those hotels got to keep their job while leaving you enough money to fix up the rest of the hotels."

Caroline's lips parted. She hadn't known he knew that. Most people conveniently forgot.

Agent Rivera shrugged. "I've been reading the hotel trade journals. The men who wrote those articles don't give you enough credit for how well you steer the ship."

Caroline could feel a something hard and defensive crumple inside her. "They really don't," she admitted.

A moment passed where they just stared at each other. Agent Rivera wasn't giving her the same predatory look Garrett Chapman just had, but it still felt as if the temperature in the room had climbed several degrees.

Caroline cleared her throat. "Anyway, we're not entirely out of the woods yet."

"But the launch is going well," Rivera pointed out. "According to the manager, you've come close to filling the room capacity. Plus, you get a lot of daily business at the spas and restaurants."

He put his leg down and leaned forward. "I should be honest that this last part makes my job quite a bit harder. There are a lot more people coming in and out, and they have unrestricted access to you when you're walking the grounds. I'm starting to think keeping an eye on you through the cameras is not enough."

Caroline pushed her chair back an inch. "But I thought that was the point of adding so many additional devices. You certainly put enough up."

He had been insistent on that point, placing cameras where they weren't strictly necessary. The ones they had were for the security of the guests. The ones Rivera had installed were to track her and keep an eye on the employees. Fortunately for her, the FBI had footed the bill. Otherwise, she never would have agreed. She watched her bottom line diligently.

"Yes," he conceded. "But there were a lot of places we couldn't put cameras, for privacy reasons. Also, they are not wired for sound. Someone could be threatening you with a smile on their face and I'd never know." He stood, then pushed the box toward her. "That's where this comes in."

Caroline scowled at the box as if it were filled with snakes. "What is it?"

He took out a small cylinder that resembled a space-age tampon. "This is an FBI-issue panic button slash tracking device."

She leaned back in her chair. "Oh. I guess that's…prudent."

It wasn't as if the man didn't already track her every move. *In fact, this might be better.*

At least this way, she would know he wasn't spying on her through the camera feeds. She could count the number of times she had stopped dead in her tracks, wondering if he were watching her right at that moment.

*Like that time I had to stop to adjust my pantyhose, and I exposed myself in the hall.* She'd believed herself to be alone, but then she'd spotted one of the new cameras right over her head. She'd had her skirt pulled up to her waist, too.

*God, I hope he hadn't seen that. How embarrassing.*

Agent Rivera's shoulders dropped as if he'd relaxed. "We could have gotten something you wear, but I know from experience the FBI doesn't have the most fashionable jewelry designers," he said with a wry grin. "I thought you'd prefer something discreet and no-nonsense."

"How does it work?"

Agent Rivera pointed to the middle of the device. "All you have to do is press this button. It's firm—you have to hold it down for a solid three seconds. That's to prevent accidental activation. Once it goes off, it sets off an alert on my phone, which I will have charged and on me at all times. It will also go to my smartwatch as a backup."

He handed her the oversized bullet. "You should always have it on you. I suggest slipping it into an accessible pocket, so you might want to consider that when you're picking out your clothes in the morning."

Caroline took the device from his hand. "Thanks," she said in a clipped voice. "How is the search for badness going?"

"It's progressing. Investigative work is a whole lot slower in real life than it is on television or in the movies—it certainly involves a hell of a lot more paperwork."

"So, no progress?"

"I've eliminated a lot of likely suspects. And even more unlikely ones."

In other words, he had nothing.

"All right." She slipped the small device into the pocket of her blazer. "Well, keep me posted."

She couldn't quite keep the dejection out of her tone. Agent Rivera opened his mouth, presumably to comfort her, but the intercom buzzer went off.

"Ms. Wentworth, your two o'clock is here."

*What?* Caroline grabbed her tablet to open her calendar app. *Oh, dear.* She hadn't canceled her meeting with the Lahore Clinic representative, Nurse Lilia.

"Are we done here?" she asked, rising.

One of Agent Rivera's dark eyebrows rose. He checked his tablet. "You do recall you were supposed to give me your schedule, right? There was nothing about a meeting for this time."

*Damn.* Caroline flushed. "That's because I thought I canceled it."

Agent Rivera rose. "Do you want me to send them away?"

Caroline jumped to her feet before smoothing her skirt in a vain attempt to recover her composure. "No need. I have time. I'll take the meeting."

Rivera frowned. "Aren't you supposed to check on the new tanning bed installation in the salon?"

*Hell.* The man did keep a close eye on her comings and goings. "I wasn't intending to test it on myself."

"Oh, I wouldn't." His hand waved up and down to encompass her "Then you'd be all...gold."

He stopped, pressing his lips together as if to stop himself from making another inane remark.

The buzzer sounded again, and he walked backward to the door. "I'll get back to work."

*Double damn.* Caroline hurried after him, trying to intercept Lilia before him. But it was too late. He'd swung the door open.

"Hi," he said, staring down at the nurse for far too long as if he were memorizing her features.

"Hello," Nurse Lilia said, professional and smooth as silk.

"Thanks for the update Mr. Rivera," Caroline said, urging him out with a little push. "Please close the door on your way out."

The look he gave her was blatantly suspicious, but he merely nodded and murmured goodbye. Caroline watched him go with her heart in her mouth.

Was he smirking as he closed the door? He was!

*Son of a nutcracker.* Having Agent Rivera take an interest in her private affairs was the last thing she needed.

# CHAPTER NINE

*I knew she was hiding something.* Caroline had been far too cagey about the woman on day one with Janet, and now she had practically run to shoo him away when she realized who it was on her calendar.

*Something is definitely up there.*

Caroline did not want him to know who that woman was. Isaac rushed into his office, kicking the door shut behind him. He sat at his desk, then pulled up the security feeds of Caroline's reception area on his computer.

Isaac rolled the footage back, capturing a clear image of the woman who'd just walked into Caroline's office. Isaac didn't waste any time starting a facial recognition search.

When he got the results a few hours later, he frowned. Lilia Charles was a nurse. Was Caroline ill?

A few minutes later, he had tracked down the name of the nurse's employer. He stared at the computer screen in open-mouthed surprise.

The Lahore Clinic had one specialty. According to their expensive-looking website, the clinic had been helping couples have babies for over two decades.

*But Caroline is single.*

There had been no one in her life since her break up with Liam Tyler. And Isaac would know. He'd double-checked.

"Oh, damn," he said, the realization hitting him like a brick. *Caroline is going at it alone.*

He sat there, his mind kicking into overdrive as he replayed the scenario of Caroline playing with the baby in the lobby. *All it would take is a dose or two of viable sperm for her to have one of her own.*

That was probably where the clinic came in.

Isaac swore under his breath. *Man, and I thought I got burned by my past relationship.* For Caroline to decide to be a single mother, she must have been scorched.

It might not be true, he reflected. Maybe there was another explanation for the visit from the fertility clinic representative.

*She could be freezing her eggs.*

Yeah, that was it. Career-driven women often did that at her age. It was a sort of insurance plan, in case Prince Charming did a no-show or pulled a vanishing act like Caroline's ex. She was freezing her eggs, saving them for a rainy day.

The inexplicable tension in his shoulders drained away. Sitting up straighter, he began to whistle as he waded through the endless pile of background checks.

❦

"And this is the piece de resistance, the holy grail as it were." Lilia tapped the thick binder she'd placed on her desk with the flat of her hand.

Caroline pulled the binder toward her, a line between her brows. "I thought I signed all the paperwork."

"This isn't another contract," Lilia said as Caroline opened the folder.

The picture of the handsome man on the first page of the binder smiled up. "Oh."

"Yes, this is where the Lahore Clinic puts the competition into the dust. Our exclusive donor list is accessible only to VIP clients like yourself."

Caroline flipped the page, studying the next blandly handsome candidate. "I'm still a little surprised you prefer a hard copy to a website."

Lilia folded her hands in front of her. "This information is far too sensitive and precious to put on the internet."

"Is hacking a real concern here?" Caroline asked.

Lilia waved a hand. "You have no idea how many of our competitors would kill to get their hands on that binder. That is why the contract you signed had such a detailed confidentiality clause. If you were to lose this, you'd be liable for quite a bit of money. So be sure to keep that under lock and key when you're not going through it."

"I'll remember that," Caroline said, flipping through the pages. "I thought that clause was overkill, but I'm starting to understand your need for secrecy."

Man after man smiled up at her from the binder. Concise biographies were printed next to each image.

Some candidates had exceedingly long strings of letters after their names. "These men have very impressive credentials."

"All our donors are college-educated. Most have advanced degrees on top of that. And, as you can see, there is something there for every taste," Lilia added. "We have doctors who rock climb, and lawyers who do yoga. We even have a professional surfer in there and a venture capitalist who climbed Everest."

"Wow." Caroline bent to take a closer look at the man posing with the surfboard on the beach. "Do they also model on the side?"

Several could have. Although none had that smoldering sensuality of her resident FBI agent.

*Nope, non, and niet. Don't even think about going there, Caroline.*

"That particular donor does have an ongoing endorsement deal with a company that makes surfing gear." Lilia's smile was a trifle smug, but Caroline didn't blame her. She had not expected such an impressive array of male specimens.

"Er…how much time do I have to choose?" Caroline asked. "Because, from what you've told me, I assume you want this back as quickly as possible."

Lilia raised a hand. "We understand that this is one of the most important decisions of your life. Some of our clients get back to us in days, and some take six months. But, on average, people take about a month to weigh their options."

Caroline nodded. Surely, she could choose the father of her child in a month. "That seems reasonable. But what if I take too long and someone picks the donor I want?"

"The candidates contracted for exclusive one-time use are marked with a special symbol at the end of their biographies. If one of those donors is claimed in the interim, I will update you with their unique ID number so you can cross them off your list."

Lilia reached down to pick up her bag. "I also brought a few syringes and a bottle of saline solution packaged in the same format as the hormones we recommend in case you want to practice giving yourself injections. In addition to the shots, there will be prenatal vitamins. I have half-a-dozen boxes of those that you can have now, but I can prepare a prescription for you should the process take longer than we expect."

The nurse paused. "Would you like me to demonstrate how to give yourself the shot now?"

Caroline nodded, her throat suddenly thick with unexpected emotion. She paid close attention as Lilia went through the motions of filling the syringe and injecting herself with the saline solution.

*Should I be doing this?* It had been almost a month since someone had tried to run her down in the garage. Caroline hadn't let herself dwell on the incident. She'd been too busy to process it. Aside from a few prodding suggestions that she speak to a counselor, even Agent Rivera had dropped the matter.

The recording Agent Rivera had played for her had been unnerving, the thing with the van downright terrifying. But the quiet since then suggested his other guess was the right one—Keaton had been the target because someone wanted a less qualified person in the security office.

"So that is pretty much it," Lilia said, bringing Caroline back to reality. "Would you like me to leave the hormone vials today? Or would you prefer to wait until you have chosen your donor?"

Caroline hesitated. "I'll take them today," she said eventually.

Lilia nodded and reached into the bag, pulling out a small lunch-box-sized cold bag, pushing it toward her. "Don't worry. As long as you keep them stored in the refrigerator, these will keep until you make your decision "

Caroline took the cooler, thanking Lilia for her visit. The representative left a short while later.

Once she was gone, Caroline put the cold bag in her mini-fridge and spent a few minutes flipping through the folder that held her future.

A few days later

Isaac narrowed his eyes as Caroline closed a folder on her desk, tucking it away into the bottom drawer with exaggerated casualness as if to make it appear she wasn't rushing to hide it from him.

It wasn't the first time he'd seen her with that folder. He'd walked into the office to see her poring over it at least three times in the last week, ever since that fertility clinic nurse had come by.

Isaac tried not to openly scowl, but, given her furtive manner, he could safely bet that folder *wasn't* a very in-depth manual on the egg-freezing process. And that idea bugged him more than he could say. But he didn't know for sure—he wouldn't until he got a look inside those pages.

Spidey sense tingling, he made note of which drawer she put it away in. *The one that locks, of course.*

"I have the latest security report," he said, holding up a tablet.

Caroline blinked. "Of course. Silly me—I sometimes forget that you are pulling double duty."

She shuffled some papers on her desk. "I should add that I'm grateful for all the work you've been doing. You're an excellent head of security."

He could tell that last was difficult for her to say, so he didn't laugh, although it was tempting. "Thanks. If I ever decide to leave the bureau, maybe you'll give me a reference."

"Of course," she said, twisting her hands together while giving him a distant and cool professional smile.

Isaac ran through the current state of security, detailing the improvements he'd made. "A junior agent is joining as a night guard."

"Oh." She sat back deeper in her chair. "Judging from how well you're doing, he's probably overqualified."

"*She* is, actually," He consulted the laptop. "Robbie Rhodes got top marks at Quantico in marksmanship and hand-to-hand combat. I've briefed her on what the job will entail, and she's enthusiastic. Robbie is personable as well. If I didn't need someone from the bureau when I'm not on duty, I'd switch her to days over either of Keaton's men."

Caroline took the tablet he stretched out. There was a digital image of an FBI ID. A well-built black woman gave the camera a direct and challenging stare. "I like her already."

"I thought you would," he said, taking the tablet back. "I had the FBI tech guys rig up two laptops for Robbie and me. They tap into your feeds. That way we don't have to be tied to the security office."

A tiny pucker appeared between her brows. "What if someone else gets ahold of them?"

"They'll be encrypted. I'm also altering the routes the security guys take, randomizing them and patching up holes in the net."

"There are holes?"

He shrugged. "It's more about the guards being visible, but you have to balance that with checking all the sensitive areas regularly. This brings me to the purpose of my visit. We might have a situation brewing."

Her lush pink lips parted. "I thought you said this meeting wasn't about FBI business."

"I'm not sure it is," he confessed. "This could be a run-of-the-mill crime, the kind that happens in hotels."

Tapping his tablet again, he brought up an image from one of the security cameras in the front part of the salon, where the three hair-dressing stations were located. Only one chair was occupied in the picture, by a young woman.

"Her expressionless face is a little off-putting, but I've zoned out in that chair myself," she said.

He knew that—it was where Caroline got her blow-outs. "What am I supposed to be seeing?" she asked.

"This guy." He stood, coming around stand beside her. Pinching and zooming the image on the tablet, he focused on the man to the right of the woman in the chair.

The man he had failed to ID was dressed in a button-down shirt with short sleeves. His arms were crossed, and he was watching the hairstylist with a bored and impatient expression.

Caroline raised one perfect blond brow. He noticed for the first time it was a few shades darker than her hair. Did she darken them? He'd never dated a blonde and his sisters had black hair and eyebrows, but that was something women with light hair did, right?

She noticed his attention was fixed on her forehead. Leaning back, she touched her eyebrow, smoothing it down. "Most men don't want to watch their wife or girlfriend get a haircut, but it's not that out of the ordinary for them to watch anyway."

"Except, I don't think that is what's going on here." Isaac leaned against the desk. "Jessica, the stylist, brought the man to my attention when he came back a second time with another girl. She said he was quiet but aggressive, giving orders on what he wanted to be done to their hair and makeup to make them look different."

Caroline took a deep breath. "This is a human trafficker."

Isaac was surprised. "You've seen this sort of thing before." It wasn't a question.

Caroline nodded, looking tired. "I grew up in this industry. You start to recognize certain patterns and get up close and personal with the underbelly of human society. Not that you get a lot of opportunities to put things right. The best you can do is report what you see. People don't usually resort to violence in the hotel itself."

"Yeah, that would be bad for business. The point of going to a nice place like this is most people wouldn't pick up on what they're actually doing."

"What do you suggest?" she asked, frowning at the man's picture again.

"Since the stylists, masseurs, and manicurists are never on duty alone, I decided they could have a signal between them when they suspect something fishy is going on. We can order a few cell phones and tape help numbers to the back. The stylist can suggest they go to the bathroom and slip the phone into a pocket. If they call, we'll know. If things are really tense, they can send an alert to the security office and one of the guys will head down."

"Will you give them a panic button like mine?"

"I think it would be better to have one permanently installed so they can't forget to bring it with them. It should be someplace they could all touch without looking suspicious—maybe on the table that holds all their supplies or on the power outlet disguised as a fuse."

"Clever," she said approvingly. "That sounds good to me. What will you do if this man comes back?"

He assessed her. "I'll deal with it. *Personally.*"

It wasn't what Rivera said so much as how he said it. The words sent a shiver up her spine. Caroline gave herself a little shake, trying to regain her composure.

Familiarity had bred complacency. There were times when she sometimes forgot the pent-up violence this man represented. Yes, he was on the side of the angels, as her mother would say. But people tended to forget that God created certain angels to be warriors.

"Thank you, Agent Rivera," she said softly. He continued to stare at her with that look he sometimes got with her—inscrutable but intense. Whenever his eyes moved away, it was as if she'd just taken off a weighted blanket. She could breathe again.

He murmured goodbye and she nodded, finally relaxing as he walked away.

"Just one other thing," he said, pausing at the door. "Under the circumstances, it might be time you started calling me Isaac."

"Oh, I hadn't thought of that." She frowned. "Wouldn't Mr. Rivera be more professional?"

"You called Keaton Shephard by his first name," he pointed out. "The manager as well. In fact, you go out of your way to learn everyone's first name. You only call me by last name."

*Was that true?* "I hadn't realized that. Thanks for letting me know…Isaac."

His name tasted like iron in her mouth. *Dear Lord, am I salivating?*

The universe gave her a break. Agent Isaac Rivera excused himself.

When he was gone, she put her forehead on the cool surface of her desk. Why did that man unnerve her so much?

*Because he's so attractive.*

She didn't let herself dwell on it too much, but Isaac Rivera had a smoldering quality that flipped her switches. He stirred things in her she tried to ignore…at least until late at night when she was alone—just her and her vibrator.

Even Liam Tyler, the so-called love of her life and her greatest heartbreak, hadn't affected her this way.

*Get a grip, woman.* She did not have time for a crush. Especially one on a man like Isaac Rivera. She gave herself another little shake, but it did more harm than good because it highlighted how tight her nipples were just *thinking* about him.

Dear Lord, she needed help.

❧

Caroline tucked her blouse in her skirt, debating a belt. *Not today.* She hadn't slept much last night, tossing and turning while trying not to think about Agent Rivera. She didn't think she could bear the added restriction of a belt today.

After casting a hopeful glance at her bedside clock, she groaned. It was still five minutes to seven.

Ever since Agent Rivera—Isaac—had taken up residence in her office, she had given him until seven-thirty in the morning to get up and dressed.

It wasn't easy. She was used to getting in there much earlier since she frequently started her workday at six. Sometimes, it was even earlier, depending on the heaviness of her schedule. But Agent Rivera was not a morning person, a detail she had discovered the first week of his stay next door.

The first time she'd walked in, he'd still been asleep. Isaac had groggily sat up, then promised to be up and out in five minutes. Somehow, he'd managed to do it, too, looking put together and professional in a button-down shirt and hotel blazer.

She hated how men could snap their fingers and do that, while she, as a woman in the public eye, had to worry about her clothes, makeup, hair, and shoes every day—even Sunday.

*There are no days off in the hotel industry.* How many times had her father told her that?

These days, Agent Rivera tried to get out of her office by seven-thirty. It was a sacrifice for him, sleeping in that little cot and then rushing out before he was fully awake.

A flush of guilt crept up her neck. *I wonder if I should tell him the couch folds out into a queen-sized bed?*

Tapping her heel, she checked her watch. *Seven-twenty-seven.* Why did time always slow down to a crawl when she least wanted it to?

Maybe she'd tell Rivera—Isaac—about the bed tomorrow... One more night on the cot wouldn't kill him.

A few minute later, she walked into her office only to find it still occupied.

"Oh," she said, stopping short. "Good morning."

"Morning," Agent Rivera said, his voice rough with sleep—rougher than usual, at least. He sounded as if he had gravel in his throat on a good day.

Reaching behind him to her desk, he picked up a cardboard cup. "Skim-milk cappuccino with two raw sugars."

"Thank you." She accepted the cup, then took a sip. It was perfect. "Did you ask our barista how I take my coffee?"

"No, but I pay attention."

Caroline's lashes fluttered. He must have been watching her closely to figure out how she liked her coffee.

"You're very observant."

The corner of his mouth turned up. "FBI," he said by way of explanation.

Heat prickled across her cheeks as she skirted around him, giving him too wide a berth. Flustered, she sat in her seat, busying herself with arranging the papers on her desk,

"Was there anything you needed to tell me?" He had never lingered in the morning before.

"Nope. Just wanted to give you that."

"Oh." She reached for her pen, but ended up knocking it forward. It rolled off the surface, falling off the edge.

*Damn it.* What was it about this man that made her feel like an awkward teenage girl?

Isaac crouched in front of the desk, his broad muscled shoulders flexing in interesting—and possibly anatomically impossible—ways under the crisp cotton of his blue button-down shirt.

*That is why.*

"Err...thank you," she said when he handed her the pen. Isaac didn't say anything, but the light in his eyes made her feel like hiding. Agent Rivera saw entirely too much.

He inclined his head before leaving to start his day.

She stared at the spot he had just vacated, trying to convince herself that he hadn't noticed her ogling him. Groaning, she took a sip of her perfect coffee.

*Hell's bells.* She had to tell him about the couch now. Grabbing a

Post-it, she made a note, reminding herself to do it the next time she saw him.

# CHAPTER TEN

"Did you see it?" Bethany, one of the concierges, waved the magazine in his face. Stephan, her male counterpart, looked up briefly, rolling his eyes at his bubbly colleague's enthusiasm.

Isaac's smile developed an edge. He looked at Stephan long enough for the other man to redden and drop his eyes.

*That's right, asshole.* Isaac was not about to let anyone rain on the girl's parade. Sure, it was the fourth time someone had shown him the article, but their excitement was cute.

"I did. Read the whole thing," he told Bethany after Stephan had resumed typing.

"But did anyone explain what it means?" She was almost jumping out of her teal blazer.

He pursed his lips, thinking about it. "It's a glowing review, right? They're always welcome."

"But not all reviews are the same." Bethany held up a glossy magazine higher. "At the moment, this is one of the hottest travel magazines. Their reviewer keeps their identity a secret so they can ensure they get unbiased service. They must have been here last week. It's a hotel's worst nightmare, being reviewed right at opening. But it was a rave. He gave us five stars! Or she gave us five stars! They loved the new spa, so it might have been a woman. We had very few men get services during that period."

She added, "That's not all. Melvin, the assistant manager, got a call. *Hotelier Magazine*, the biggest trade publication for hotels, is going to do a profile on us, too. They're sending a photographer to take pictures the day after tomorrow."

"Will they be interviewing Caroline?"

Bethany stared up at him blankly.

"Ms. Wentworth," he elaborated.

"Oh yeah, duh," Bethany said, giving herself a little smack on the head. "You know, I'm not sure they'll be speaking to her. It's mostly about the hotel."

"Of course they'll be talking to her," Stephan interjected flatly. "They'll want a quote from her at the very least. But they'd be stupid not to interview her, too. She's too photogenic for them to skip it."

"That and she single-handedly saved the hotel chain," Bethany pointed out, exasperated with her coworker's lack of enthusiasm.

Stephan shrugged with a sour expression.

Isaac studied the male concierge's averted profile. Technically, nothing Stephan has said or done was wrong or unflattering to Caroline, but the guy was still rubbing Isaac the wrong way.

"I'll be sure to pass on your congratulations," he told Bethany, making sure to soften his words with a smile. He tended to make women nervous if he didn't. "I have a meeting with her now."

"Tell her to wear the blush-pink silk for the interview," Bethany suggested. "Or the coral gabardine. The deep coral—not the pale one. Then again, maybe she could stick to her traditional white. She does photograph amazing in white. Not as good as she does in black, but black wouldn't go with the hotel."

"The hotel is not an accessory," Stephan grumbled, not looking up from his screen.

They both ignored him. "I'll try to remember all that," he promised Bethany. "But I make no guarantees that I'll get all those colors right. Would you rather write it down?"

Bethany's eyes widened. "You mean give Ms. Wentworth fashion advice *in writing*? No thanks."

Chuckling, he headed to Caroline's office. Janet was leaving her desk, a stack of the magazine in her arms."

He held up a hand when she offered him one. "I've been given two copies. Thanks."

Beaming at him, Janet left, presumably to pass out more of the periodical to whatever unfortunate member of the staff hadn't received one yet. He knocked on Caroline's door, entering it without waiting for an answer.

Caroline was dabbing at her eyes with a tissue, her nose and eyes red. She glanced up, pushing back her chair.

"Sorry," he apologized, caught in a frozen half-step a beat too long. "I can come back later."

"No, it's okay," she said hurriedly. "Please, excuse me."

Isaac stepped forward, frowning as she straightened herself up. Like everyone else in the hotel today, she had a copy of the magazine in front of her.

He frowned. "That can't be it."

She stared at him in confusion. "What can't?"

"The article can't be what upset you. It's a *good* review," he stressed, sitting in the chair in front of the desk with his tablet.

Caroline's lips compressed, and she scrubbed her tear-stained cheek with a tissue. "I'm just...relieved."

"Yeah, I get that." It still seemed a bit of a strong reaction. Unless...

"Oh," he said, the uncomfortable realization sitting in his stomach like a brick.

"What?" Caroline sniffed, tissue in hand.

"Nothing," he said a little too quickly.

Caroline threw down the tissue, then crossed her arms. "Please, just spit it out."

For the first time in his adult life, Isaac squirmed in his chair. "I, uh, deduced why you might be feeling a little...emotional."

The last word was wrenched from him like someone was trying to steal his favorite gun.

"*Deduced?*" The balmy San Diego air acquired a distinct chill. "Are you suggesting I have PMS?" Caroline asked in a clipped voice.

"No, of course not," he said.

Her eyes widened, and he sucked in a breath. "However, I know someone who did in-vitro, and the hormones they had to take made them cry a lot, too."

There was a sharp silence.

"What did you say?" she asked.

"I saw that nurse leaving your office—the one from the fertility clinic."

All the color drained from Caroline's face before rushing back. It left bright hectic flags on the top of her cheekbones.

Very deliberately, she placed her hands flat on the desk. "You were *spying* on me?"

Isaac leaned forward. "Caroline, figuring out who she was is part of my job. I told you this going in—you don't get to have secrets. Not right now. Or do I have to remind you that someone is trying to kill you?"

"No, I haven't forgotten. I also know I can't stop living my life because of some amorphous threat—one we haven't conclusively proven is real."

"Not real?" Now Isaac was angry. "You were almost *run* down."

"I know," she snapped. "I was there. I also know you can't rule out the possibility it was Keaton they were after."

"Are we arguing about this *again?*"

"I don't know," she yelled, jumping to her feet. "Wait, yes. *I do.* I am taking a stand. You don't get to sit there all brunette and tattooed, standing judgment on my life. I will get pregnant if I want to—and I will do it without a husband or any sort of man in my life, thank you very much."

*Oh, hell.* This was worse than he thought. *So much for freezing eggs.* Instead, Caroline was freezing out the entire male gender.

Isaac raised a hand. "Woman, listen to yourself. I am not telling you that you can't have a kid. You can have one. You can have ten babies if you like. An even dozen—enough to get yourself one of those TLC reality shows."

Caroline took a shaky breath, narrowing her eyes. "But?"

He threw up his hands. "Why do you want to have one now? You're still young. Not that it matters—I read an article that the female biological clock is bullshit. It's based on centuries-old census data from France. It's completely outdated."

He paused, flicking his hand. "Also, I had no idea you were considering baby via...sperm donor."

The last words came out like they tasted bad, but he couldn't help it. "I thought you were freezing your eggs like women do these days," he finished lamely, rolling his shoulders.

She schooled her features, wiping off all traces of emotion before she dropped back down in her chair. "Well, I'm not."

He snapped his fingers suddenly as a realization hit home. "The binder you keep hiding. It's the list of the possible baby daddies, isn't it?"

Caroline's silence was all the answer he needed. *Brr...* With that hair, she didn't just look like Elsa from *Frozen*. It was the frosty glare that made her a dead ringer.

"What did you want to talk about?" she asked in a crisp tone, pulling a notepad in front of her and jotting something down.

"The new hire for nighttime security. I couldn't swing a second junior agent, so it will have to be a real hire on your part. I've finalized the candidates, and I wanted to know if you wanted to give your two cents or are you comfortable leaving it up to me?"

Caroline's thick gold lashes fluttered. "I'm sure whoever you choose will be fine."

"Okay, great." He stood to leave, but he stopped halfway to the door.

"So, you're not going to wait to meet someone?"

Caroline's hand froze halfway to the paper. It was obvious she was writing gibberish from this angle, but he was not about to point that out.

Isaac knew he should have shut up five minutes ago, but he

couldn't seem to help himself. When it came to Caroline Wentworth, there was a little gremlin pushing buttons inside him. Isaac just went off the rails.

"I know what it's like, you know…being burned by a bad relationship. I've got the scars to prove it." He held up his hand, then pointed to his finger.

Caroline frowned. "What am I looking at?"

He lifted a shoulder. "At where my wedding ring used to be. I'm divorced."

"Oh…" She tucked a stray lock of hair behind her ear. "I didn't realize. My condolences."

"Don't be sorry. I'm not." If he were still married, he'd be flagellating himself for all the lustful thoughts he was having now. "But it doesn't mean I'm against the institution. If the right person comes along, I'd do it again. I haven't quit on the idea."

Caroline dropped the pen to rub her temples. "I don't believe this. I'm getting a lecture on waiting for love from…*you*."

"Why not me?"

She just stared.

Isaac decided to quit while he was behind. Hilariously, disastrously behind.

"I'm going to give the top candidate for night security a call," he said, holding up the tablet displaying the resumes for the applicants. "If he doesn't take the job, my second choice is also qualified."

"That sounds fine," she said, not looking at him as she continued to write nonsense notes.

Isaac left before he could say something else stupid.

# CHAPTER ELEVEN

*Why not me?* Why the hell had he said that? He kept turning the words over in his head, but each time he did, their meaning changed...

"I still don't understand why you're so upset?" Sonia said over the line. "So, some woman you just met is doing artificial insemination. The lesbians in the girl's playgroup went that route. What's the big deal?"

Isaac scowled, adjusting the earpiece. Sonia had been his sounding board growing up. He'd called her on autopilot, expecting her to magically understand his point of view. Now he was irritated with *her* because she didn't get it.

"It's the principal of the thing," he grumbled. "Men are being phased out. What if all career women in the world decided they don't need men anymore and just start having kids on their own?"

"More power to them, I say." Sonia sniffed. "Tell them to storm the halls of Congress while they're at it to secure equal pay and federally mandated paid maternity leave."

He sighed, glad he had closed the door to his office. "You know this isn't about equal rights. That, I support. Hell, I walked in the women's march with you," he pointed out. "This is about something far more basic—procreation and whether you should do it alone. I'm okay with babies being raised by two moms or two dads, or three moms and one dad, plus an aunt or uncle or however polyamorous groups want to define themselves. My point is it takes a whole damn village. But doing it alone because you had a bad breakup…"

"May I remind you that I went ahead and had the girls even though I knew that shithead Armando was going to bail. I was a single mom for a long time, too. Are you saying I was wrong to have the girls?"

"No, of course not." Isaac winced, walking his argument back. "That was different. That was contraception failure. Plus, Armando was there in the beginning. The loser didn't show his true colors until the girls were two, almost three, years old. By the time he finally left, we were all relieved. And now you've married a real man—one who is good dad and loves the girls as if they were his own."

His sister snickered. "My, how your tune has changed. I remember when I first met Tony. You had plenty to say about him then, and none of it was good."

"I had to give him a hard time in the beginning," Isaac explained with a scowl she couldn't see. "It was my job as your brother. I was genetically obligated to."

"A hard time." Something that sounded like a metal soup spoon banged on the counter. "You call having him tailed and hauled out of his car by your FBI buddies a hard time? Until you drove up so you could interrogate him on his past relationships, he thought he was going to be mugged or worse. The man almost peed himself."

"Those were not FBI buddies," Isaac corrected. "That would have been an abuse of power. They were former army buddies. Besides, Tony passed the test, and he wisely chose to be a good sport. We even took him to a bar afterward as a reward."

"Making him miss his own bachelor party," Sonia said dryly.

Isaac scoffed. "He was marrying my big sister. And not only that— Tony was about to become the twins' father. I wasn't about to let him have a bachelor party."

Sonia laughed. "Well, that part, I'm not mad about. But I still think you're getting bent out of shape for nothing. It's not like you are even friends with this woman. You said she's involved in one of your cases.

Or are you feeling sorry for the potential kid? Is the woman a druggie or something?"

"No, it's nothing like that. Caroline may be the most together woman I've ever met. She runs an entire hotel chain. And she loves babies. Every time she sees one, she goes all gooey."

And for a strong, *Steel Magnolia* type of woman, it was something to watch.

"She's going to be a great mom," he muttered grudgingly.

There was the sound of a banging pot as if Sonia had just set one on the stove. She snorted. "Oh my God. I am such an idiot. You *like* this woman. Who is she? More importantly, what does she look like?"

Isaac was tempted to hang up. "My interest in Caroline is strictly professional. I have to protect her as part of this case."

"Too late," Sonia said. "I'm Googling her. Let's see…you told me it was the Wentworth Hotel so let's put in that and the name Caroline… and ooh, I found her!"

*Chingado.* "She's an asset. Nothing more."

Sonia made a *pft* sound. "The hell you say."

"I d—"

"Don't even try it, *hermanito*. I have the woman's picture right here on my phone. She's on the Wentworth website as CEO, looking like Barbie living her best life—and that hotel is the dream house."

There was a pause, then some muttering that told him his sister was on one of her lightning-fast internet deep dives. It was something she and his younger sister Brittany excelled at. The bureau could take lessons from them.

"She wears a lot of blazers, doesn't she? And seriously, how does she get her hair so shiny? Not to mention that skin. This woman has only ever used top-of-the-line moisturizers—Nivea has never touched her face. Nothing used by us common folk. Oh, and here's another of her getting some award sporting a white suit I could only wear in my dreams because kids."

Sonia broke off. "Stop the press. Who is this hunk of yum with her?"

Isaac scowled, adrenaline rushing to his head out of nowhere. "What? Who are you talking about?"

Sonia tsked and groaned. "I hate to break it to you, Isaac, but I'm afraid you are SOL. It says here she has a fiancé, some guy named Liam Tyler. Sorry, but you may as well know now—you aren't going to be able to compete."

His gut unclenched. "Oh, him. No, Tyler is her ex. It must be an old article."

"Oh, well, that's different then. If she's demoralized and on the rebound from this guy, you might have a shot."

Isaac rubbed his temple. His head was starting to ache. "I said I am not interested in this woman, not like that. But you might be right about her being demoralized. Tyler got married last year—to another woman *and* a man. It's a triad or whatever the kids are calling it these days."

Sonia whistled. "You know, I am liking your chances more and more."

He passed a hand through his hair, scrubbing his head roughly. A long beat passed before the words that had been knocking on the inside of his brain, demanding to be let out, finally escaped.

"*Okay,*" he gritted from behind set teeth. "Fine. I might be interested in Caroline."

"Yeah, tell me something I don't know." Laughter echoed in his ear. "For a supposed deductive genius, the family Sherlock Holmes, you're pretty dense sometimes."

Isaac rubbed a hand over his face. "Denying something is true and not being aware of it are two different things."

"So why are you in denial?"

"For all the obvious reasons," Isaac ground out.

"Elaborate, please," Sonia said in a sing-song voice.

He sighed. "Caroline is a prominent player in my big career-making case. Then there's the fact she's on the baby train and is determined to do it alone. Also, there may be the fact she resents my very presence in her life because this case has given me carte blanche to crowd her, follow her every move, and stomp all over her privacy."

Sonia breathed and whistled. "You know, I don't feel sorry for you that often..."

"But?" he asked when there was a long pause.

"That's it. I don't feel sorry for you that often," Sonia said. "And I still don't."

Isaac shook his head. "Why are you my favorite sister?"

"Because I'm the one who tells you the truth," Sonia said. "Also, because Brittany doesn't have time for either of us what with her busy life of clubbing, dating, and clubbing some more."

"That's true," he acknowledged. His supposed wild youth had nothing on Brittany's early college life.

Of course, he'd been able to hide a lot more because he moved out for university. But his younger sister attended a local junior college that didn't have a dormitory. "How does Mom get any sleep at night with Brit out until all hours?"

Sonia laughed. "Whenever she goes out, Mom takes a melatonin pill and hits the sack early. She's out like a light until morning, so, in a way, she has chosen denial as well. I guess it runs in the family."

Isaac grunted a response. "At least Mom is getting some shut-eye. The cot I sleep on in Caroline's office is top of the line as far as those things go, but it's starting to mess up my back. Those are strictly meant for short-term use."

"You *sleep* in her office?" Sonia was incredulous. "No wonder she hates you."

"She doesn't hate me," he protested. "But I'm not her favorite person either. Caroline has been pretty tolerant all things considered. And I can't blame her for my sleeping situation. I insisted—I have to maintain close proximity."

Sonia tsked. "Sucks for you. Just remember—you can look but don't touch. Sounds like the woman is on her own path."

Isaac growled under his breath. "I won't forget."

His sister harrumphed. "Also, weren't you in the army? Didn't you sleep in much worse places than a cot?"

"My back is like six years older now." He sighed. "And I'm not going to try anything with Caroline. I could get fired. Not that she's looked at me twice. Not that way."

At least, he didn't think so. There had been a moment or two in her office when he'd wondered... But that was before he had the brilliant idea to question her reproductive choices.

"I don't know. If you want to make her look, try taking your shirt off. God knows that always worked for you in high school," Sonia sniped. "Do you have any idea how annoying it is for your senior friends to talk about how hot your sophomore brother is? Or how gross it is when they talk about wanting to do him?"

There was a retching sound, but Isaac perked up. "Which friends said that, and was it any of your fellow cheerleaders?"

The dial tone was his only answer.

"Yeah, that's fair," he said aloud, hanging up. Not that he'd been serious.

Saying it aloud to Sonia had made him face facts. For better or worse, Isaac wanted Caroline. No one else had ever gotten under his skin this way. The woman lived rent-free in his head.

Unfortunately, given her involvement in this case, Caroline was the one woman he couldn't have.

# CHAPTER TWELVE

Isaac narrowed his eyes, moving from behind the potted plant to watch the couple arguing in front of the beachfront café.

They appeared to be a married couple, guests of the hotel.

He was too far away to hear what they were saying, mainly because the male was conducting his end of the argument in an angry whisper. The woman wasn't saying much at all. She kept her head down, defeat clear in the line of her slumped shoulders.

The man slashed a hand in the air, and the woman flinched. Exasperated, the man seized the woman's arm, dragging her toward the hotel interior. Her partner pulled her so hard that the woman almost tripped. They went inside to continue the argument—and possibly a beating—behind the privacy of their room's door.

Isaac put his head down, getting ready to follow, when Caroline appeared at his side. She put a hand on his sleeve. "There's nothing you can do," she said in a quiet voice as the couple disappeared into the interior.

Isaac ignored the warning, brushing past her. Caroline followed him, much faster than he would have believed she could in those heels.

"Agent Rivera," she sputtered. Isaac kept going, moving through the busy reception area, before finally spotting the couple at the East wing elevators.

Caroline had kept up with him. "Rivera, please stop."

He narrowed his eyes as the couple stepped into one of the elevator cars.

"*Isaac.*"

She stepped in front of him.

"What is it?" he asked in a low voice.

Caroline swallowed, her eyes wide. But she held her ground. "I'm sorry, but there is nothing you can do. Even if you were to find out which room they are in—"

"It's room five-twenty-four," Isaac said, looking down at her with hooded eyes.

"*Oh.*"

He crossed his arms, resigned to letting the asshole go. "Julio clocked that guy at check-in. He's good at his job."

Caroline's face was grave. "My point is that unless he strikes her in public or she asks for help, our hands are tied."

Isaac shifted his weight back and forth. "Did you see the sunglasses she wore? She's trying to hide a black eye. She tried to hide it with makeup, but you can see it under the bottom edge of the left rim."

"I noticed," she said softly. "It was obvious, even across the room."

He narrowed his eyes. "Doesn't it bother you?"

Her face transformed, a slew of emotions flicking across it like images in a slideshow. "Of course it does. But we are in the hospitality industry—and even if we weren't, it's not like the police can do anything. Not without cause. You, of all people, know that."

Isaac closed his eyes. When he opened them, she was a few inches away. Usually, that kind of proximity to her made his heart race. This time, it calmed him. "I've seen a lot of shitty things in my line of work. A lot of it was worse than this. But it wasn't in my face—not like this. I always got there afterward, busting bad guy's heads, after the appropriate paperwork had been filed."

She didn't laugh at his lame joke. Her gaze pinned him to the spot. "Isaac, I know this is difficult for you. You're a man of action. You're used to being able to ride to the rescue, but this...this is hotel life. People come, people go, the bad as well as the good. Unless things get out of hand, we have to let them live their lives."

He stared down at her, the mesmerizing effect of her blue eyes potent.

"I didn't think this part would be so hard," he said, his tongue thick. "I don't like having to walk away."

"I know," she said, standing close enough that he could feel her body heat. "For what it's worth, sometimes you won't have to. That's why your job exists. We watch and we wait, and, when we can, we help. It's not all about keeping people from stealing towels and bathrobes."

He huffed. "Hey, nice try. But I'm wise to that. I know you just charge them to their credit cards."

Isaac paused, considering his own words. "That reminds me. I should check the credit card transactions. Make sure there's nothing there."

Caroline frowned. "No one is embezzling or overcharging at the Wentworth. Not on my watch."

A slow smile lit his face. He knew he had just been managed by an expert. But he didn't mind. If anything, his admiration had increased by several notches.

"Yeah. I believe that."

# CHAPTER THIRTEEN

Caroline stirred with sluggish movements, too reluctant to let go of the dream. But the buzz of her phone insistently continued, dragging her into consciousness by force.

"What is it?" she yawned into the receiver.

"Sorry, Ms. Wentworth," Walter, one of the night clerks, said. "But we thought you'd want to know that a pipe burst on the third floor."

She sat up abruptly. "Is it in a guest's room? Did we shift them?"

"It was an empty room, and we were able to contain the mess, but the handyman is having trouble shutting the pipe down without shutting the water off for the entire floor."

Caroline looked at the clock. Two AM. "Do it. I'll be right up there to check on the damage."

Swearing internally, she threw on some clothes, grabbing her phone before running out of the room.

&

Isaac popped right up when the static on his walkie-talkie crackled. "Boss, there's a problem in one of the rooms."

"What is it?"

"A broken pipe. It's not a security issue, but you said to keep you in the loop about everything."

"Oh…" Isaac rubbed his eyes. "Did you call a plumber?"

"Maintenance is on it. They're shutting down the water to the whole third floor, but Ms. Wentworth is already there, so you're safe to go back to sleep. It's handled."

"Great." Isaac yawned. "See you in the morning."

Putting the walkie back on the side table, he flopped back down on his cot.

Ten seconds later, he jumped up.

Isaac nearly fell over while yanking on his pants. Swearing aloud, he grabbed the walkie and strapped his service piece to his ankle, just in case.

The water squished under Caroline's Manolos. Kicking herself for wearing her favorite shoes, the first within reach in her closet, she picked her way through the mushy carpet in a vain attempt to avoid the little puddles.

*Thank God they had caught the leak before the water soaked through to the second floor.*

Fortunately, there were no guest rooms below them, just another common area—the billiards and gaming room to be precise.

She found the handyman in the built-in utility closet they used to disguise the pipe junction that routed water to this floor.

"What happened, Sam?" she asked, stooping to take a closer look at the pipe junction that had suddenly fallen apart. "I thought all these pipes passed inspection before the grand opening."

That was less than a month ago.

"I'm not sure what happened," Sam, the grizzled night handyman, said as he tapped the pipe lightly with his wrench. "I checked this entire floor myself. This section was fine. The pipe isn't corroded—it's beaten up. And I can tell you that it didn't look that way when I checked it either."

He straightened, scowling at the mess. Behind him, the night attendants were putting down towels and setting up fans to dry the carpet.

"If I didn't know better, I'd say someone kicked the damn thing until it broke apart. When they couldn't, they took a wrench to it—but the fucker didn't know what he was doing."

Lifting the pipe he'd removed, he pointed to the deep gouges at the top. "They left these tool marks, stripping the threads in the process. I can't just put it back on. I'll have to replace both pieces."

Caroline frowned, disturbed to hear that it was an intentional act of vandalism. "Do you have what we need on hand?"

Sam scratched his head. "I should. If I don't, I can jerry-rig something that should hold until we get the right parts."

She sucked in a breath. "And how long will the water be shut down?"

Sam, an old veteran of the hotel world, patted her on the shoulder. "I'll have it back up in less than an hour. Maybe an hour and a half if I don't have the right size joint, but, either way, I should be done long before the guests get up in the morning."

"Good, thank you," she said before going to speak to the men about getting one of the industrial wet-dry vacuum cleaners brought up to deal with the mess.

Once she was done, it was past three o'clock in the morning. Taking out her phone, she emailed the hotel's events coordinator, pushing their morning meeting back a few hours.

Exhausted, she headed to the main stairs. She was halfway down the second story when she realized it was too dark.

Caroline started to turn, wondering why the running lights built into the stairs were off instead of on night mode. The punch came out of nowhere.

One second, there was the whisper of fabric moving. The next, there was a pain just underneath her right shoulder blade. She flew down the stairs, one of her shoes left behind on the step.

She didn't even have a chance to scream before she slammed into a rock-hard arm.

Agent Rivera was there. He'd caught her, accidentally clotheslining her in the chest in the process.

"What the fuck happened?" he asked, transferring his hold to her upper arms.

Caroline whimpered, rubbing her chest. She had rammed against his arm hard enough to bruise.

"I think I sprained my breasts," she gasped, the words coming out strained because she couldn't take a deep breath.

The world spun and she cried out, but she wasn't falling again. Isaac had picked her up. He was running with her in his arms, taking the left corridor off the stairs. The ceiling moved over her head so fast that he must have been sprinting.

He stopped in front of the utility closet at the start of the hall. Swiping his key card into the electronic lock, he somehow managed to open the door with her in his arms.

He set her down with surprising gentleness. "I'm sorry about this."

Head whirling, she opened her mouth to ask him what he meant—but he was already gone, the door closed behind him, plunging the closet into pitch darkness.

"What the hell?"

Reaching forward with her arms out, she swore as her bare foot contacted the cold stone floor. Her ankle protested painfully. Slipping off her other shoe, she stooped in the darkness, trying to rub the pain away. It didn't feel bad enough to be a sprain, but it was very tender.

Setting her foot down and hopping gingerly, she made her way to the door in the black pit. Caroline found the seam of the doorjamb by feel, but failed to find the doorknob.

Why was there no knob?

A dozen swear words bubbled to her lips. There was no handle—no way to open the door.

"This is a safety hazard," she fumed to the mops.

# CHAPTER FOURTEEN

Isaac ran up to the third floor, looking for the shadowy figure he'd seen at the top of the stairs just after Caroline had hurled toward him.

It was too late. He should have run after the assailant the moment he saw him, but Caroline was out in the open, vulnerable.

She was going to be spitting nails when he finally got back to the storage closet. And heaven forbid he had inadvertently damaged those glorious breasts. That would be a travesty of justice. He'd have to turn in his man-card to make amends.

Isaac pushed that thought out of his mind, focusing on clearing the third floor. The conference room with the leak was still occupied by the staff doing triage under the direction of Stephan, the concierge, and Sam, the night handyman.

Isaac quickly discovered the drawback of doing a room-to-room search in a hotel—he couldn't enter any of the rooms. Not when he was chasing a person he couldn't see because it was too dark. There was also the fact most of the rooms were occupied largely by tourists, many of whom would gleefully tank the hotel's rating if he busted into their rooms in the middle of the night.

Radioing down to Agent Rhodes, he apprised her of the situation, instructing her to look for anything fishy in the security monitors. He also got a list of the empty rooms on the floor, then started going through them one by one, using his security pass to let himself in.

His walkie crackled. "Rivera, we've got movement by the service elevator," Rhodes said.

"Confirmed," Isaac said, running.

But the elevators were empty. "Is the cabin moving?" he asked.

"Negative."

"Can you play the security footage back?"

"I did. Whoever it was stayed just out of sight."

Isaac scowled. "I angled these cameras myself. There are no holes in the coverage."

"There are now."

*Fuck.*

In the distance, a door slammed. It wasn't the gentle swish of the guest room doors. This was a flat metal bang.

"The roof."

"The camera up there isn't on."

Flooded with adrenaline, Isaac double-timed it to the stairs. He burst out onto the roof, gun drawn.

It was empty. The flat stretch of the roof was devoid of human life, and there was no way a person could hide behind one of the protruding exhaust fans. He checked anyway.

"Did they double back down before I got here?" he asked.

"I don't think so," she said after a moment. "I have nothing on the cameras."

"Which doesn't mean much if someone's been fucking with the placement," he groused. Frustrated, he kicked the base of the air vent.

"I'll check them now with Julio," Rhodes offered. She sounded calm on the surface, but he could tell she was as pissed as he was. "He's on duty with me tonight. You can get back to bed."

"I'll do another quick pass of the third floor first." But Isaac changed his mind in the stairwell, remembering Caroline was locked in one of the second-story closets.

*I better let her out before she decides to use one of those sky-high heels to give me a prostate exam.*

His concern turned to outright urgency as he remembered the holes in the security feeds. Given the issue with the cameras and all the connecting hallways in the building, it was possible someone could double back unseen. What if they had seen him stash Caroline in the utility closet?

He'd left her there, alone and defenseless.

Breaking out into a run, he pounded down the stairs, setting what had to be a personal best for a sprint. His heart was beating hard and fast when he finally reached the door. He opened it, acid in his mouth.

It was dark. *Nothing happened*, he told himself. She just couldn't find the light switch.

Then why the hell was she being so quiet?

"It's me," he began.

A dark red heel sped toward him out of the darkness, smacking him in the chin.

"Okay, I deserved that," he admitted, kicking the doorstop down to make sure it didn't lock them inside.

"You deserve more than that, you ass!" Caroline hissed. A small fist hit him in the chest, fairly hard considering the size of the hand that delivered the blow.

The aftereffects of the adrenaline were still making themselves felt. Isaac wanted to crawl out of his skin. He reached out and pulled Caroline toward him, pressing her against his chest before running his hands over her arms, checking her for wounds.

"You're okay, right? No one came—I was worried."

"Not enough to stay with me," she sniffed.

"Someone pushed you, Caroline. I had to look for them."

"And did you find them?"

"No," he said, regret flooding through him. "I'm sorry. I thought there was someone on the roof, but I was wrong. They must have come back some other way—what's good for fire safety is bad for chasing bad guys."

Caroline pulled away. He couldn't see her expression in the dim light of the hallway, but he realized she was hurting when she put her hands to her chest.

"Oh God, sorry." His hands went up reflexively to touch her there, but he stopped himself just in time.

"I, uh, I would feel terrible if I hurt *those.*"

*Smooth, Casanova. Real smooth.*

Ducking her head, Caroline crossed her arms, cupping her chest. "I'm fine, just a little sore."

Isaac winced. "Agent Rhodes is going to check the camera angles on the third floor, so we can go back to bed. I'll walk you back to your suite."

He put his hand on her back, intending to escort her, but she had only taken a few steps when he noticed her limping.

"Hold on." Isaac went to the doorway to pick up the discarded heel. He handed it over before reaching down and swinging her into his arms.

"*Agent Rivera,*" Caroline hissed as he stepped into the hall.

"You shouldn't put weight on that leg," he said. Despite her luscious curves, he found it easy to handle her weight. He could have carried her all over the hotel.

"Is the nurse practitioner the hotel has on-call working tonight?"

"This is not a good idea. Please put me down," Caroline said, squirming in his arms.

Clearly, she had never been dramatically swept off her feet before.

"Not until someone checks out that ankle," he said.

Cringing in his arms, she turned her head to check their surroundings. "What if someone sees?"

"The nurse," he prodded.

"We try not to call her in for staff unless it's an emergency," she said. "Which this isn't. My ankle is just tender—I don't need medical attention. And please take the service elevator at least."

He shifted her weight, bringing that perfectly shaped leg up. "There's no visible bruising. If it still hurts in the morning, I want you to call her."

Caroline groaned, giving up. She rested her head on his chest, going limp.

Isaac relaxed when she did, enjoying the feel of her in his arms.

*Don't get used to it.* And he definitely shouldn't be getting hard at the idea of carrying her over the threshold of her room. That was just begging for trouble.

But he couldn't seem to help himself. He didn't bother to turn on a light once they arrived at her suite. The moonlight from the window was enough to see Caroline's king-sized bed just beyond the sitting room.

She hadn't said a word for the last few minutes. Feeling hot and tense, he put her down, her luscious curves pressed against his chest and groin.

"I think you were right," he muttered, looking down at her flushed face.

Caroline blinked, her blue eyes slightly glazed over. "About what?" she whispered breathlessly.

His hand fisted in her hair. "Carrying you was a bad idea."

# CHAPTER FIFTEEN

Caroline knew she should move. For one, her breasts still ached. Then there was the fact that this man was her subordinate, even if it was in name only.

*Just step away.* One tiny step. However, Caroline couldn't seem to make her feet move.

Apparently, neither could Agent Rivera. His hand reached up to grab her hair. "Carrying you was a bad idea."

Caroline bit her tongue to keep from hissing aloud. The man's body was so hard, muscular, and literally hot. She felt unmoored, almost drugged by his heat.

"Yes…bad," she agreed, her eyes half-mast with desire. "We should stop."

His hands moved down her body, making her skin almost scream with tension. Ever so slowly, his head drifted down until his mouth was hovering over hers. "I'm going to need you to say that a little louder."

She could barely understand him now, her heart was pounding too loud. "Say what?"

"*Stop.*"

Her tongue felt thick in her mouth. She could barely form coherent thoughts, let alone speak them aloud. "I…"

"Caroline?" His voice was like molasses now.

Her heart was pounding so loud that he could probably hear it. "I don't think that's going to happen," she whispered.

"Thank God." He closed the distance. His mouth settled on hers, silky and hot.

Caroline whimpered, lost in the rush of heat and sensation. Her skin stung, aching for his touch.

It had been so long since anyone had even held her. Aside from firm and formal business handshakes, no one had even touched her in over a year, since before her father had died. She had hugged Janet once, on her birthday, but that was it.

As for the last time a man had touched her—Caroline had been kissed by a man in her social circle shortly after the end of her engagement. She hadn't invited it, but she hadn't stopped him either. But that small caress had left her cold.

She told herself it was too soon after her breakup, but that didn't change the fact she hadn't felt any sort of attraction for another man since Liam.

And she hadn't realized how much she missed the feel of a man's hands on her. It felt like she was going to burst, and his hold was the only thing keeping her together.

Fortunately for her Agent Rivera—*Isaac*—complied with her unspoken plea. His hands were everywhere, stroking and caressing her. They were a little rough and calloused as if he'd never had a manicure.

*Why is that exciting?*

But she didn't have time to answer that question because his mouth moved down to her neck. Her thoughts fragmented.

Sucking in a breath, she dug her fingers into his shoulders, her eyes squeezing shut so they wouldn't roll back into her head. Pure unadulterated pleasure enervated her and she sagged in his arms, weakly returning his touches with smaller, more tentative brushes of her own.

"Can I do this?" he asked between kisses, his fingers gently curling around her breast. "Or are you still hurting here?"

Caroline arched, a small whimper escaping, as the heat of his skin permeated her silk blouse.

It wasn't a sound of pain. Isaac clearly knew that, which was why he kept going, stroking and tweaking until she was standing on her tiptoes, her back bowed so she could put as much of herself in his hands as possible.

Isaac groaned aloud. Then he was tearing at the buttons, tugging the shirt open to expose her bare breasts. She'd neglected to put on a bra in her hurry to get to the broken pipe.

His fingers shook a little as he reached out to cup her once again. "Christ, you're gorgeous," he breathed. "The most beautiful thing I've ever seen."

Her nipples beaded against his palm, the buds tightening into almost painful sensitivity.

Isaac cupped the back of her head. "This is the last chance. Tell me to leave or prepare to be on that bed, naked and underneath me, in thirty seconds. Maybe less."

Caroline froze, her lips parting. She was half-naked in his arms, and he was still giving her an out. That had never happened before.

He took her silence for acquiescence. Giving her plenty of time to stop him, he unzipped her skirt. It fell to the floor, pooling around her feet.

Caroline started as his fingers pressed against the soft skin of her stomach. His nails grazed against her ever so lightly before his hands breached the waistband of her panties.

Isaac's fingers caught the elastic, not at her hips as one might have predicted. Instead, one hand slid directly down from her belly button, the other on the other side of her body.

Her breath caught as his index finger deliberately slipped between her ass cheeks. Isaac never took his eyes from hers as he knelt in one molasses-slow movement. Those thick fingers opened her intimately as the panties joined her skirt.

Closing her eyes, Caroline fought to stay upright as he brought his hands together, sliding forward to play with the small, neatly trimmed triangle of hair covering her mound.

The expression on his face was so hungry and determined that she almost took a step back. "You don't have to be scared."

A little shiver coursed down her body. "I'm not," she lied.

He cocked his head to one side. "Really? Because you look a little...concerned."

She jerked her head, the tiniest of shakes.

The corners of his mouth pulled up, the satisfaction in his expression palpable.

The next movement was a blur, the sensation of strong hands catching her up, air moving over her naked skin.

Caroline landed on the bed, her skin so hot that the room felt cold by contrast despite her preference to keep the thermostat firmly at seventy-eight degrees.

The temperature became inconsequential when Isaac kicked off his shoes, climbing over her.

He was still dressed, the cloth abrading her bare skin. His knee moved between her legs, pressing against her bare and now very wet pussy.

The way he looked at her was overwhelming—too intense for her to process.

"I have wanted these in my mouth since day one." His tongue flicked out to lick one tightly furled bud before his lips closed over it.

Her tongue tangled. "That—that would have been wildly inappropriate."

His laugh was rich and decadent, and she couldn't help thinking that listening to it was sinful. Or fattening. Either way, it would come with a price.

But she couldn't think of that now. All she could do was feel and want.

Caroline's hands moved to cup his head, her eyes closing. He turned his attention to the other breast, lathing and sucking until she moaned aloud.

*Too long.* It had been too long since she'd experienced this whole-body thirst. She felt wanton and excited in a way that left her clumsy and barely able to function.

Caroline's senses were on full tilt, each one working overtime to feel and taste. Even Isaac's smell was an aphrodisiac. He didn't wear expensive cologne like some men she knew. He smelled like hot male skin and soap, something with an underlying bite—a hint of euca-lyptus or tea tree oil.

Isaac shifted, her nipple leaving his mouth with a small but audible pop. Sitting up on his haunches, he stripped off his shirt faster than she could blink. His pants took a few seconds longer, but then he was back, his naked body covering hers.

The agent went commando. She had a split second to wonder if that was for sleep or an all-the-time thing when Isaac parted her legs, nudging them wide before taking a hold of her hips to yank her closer.

"Still not scared, right?" he asked.

Her mouth formed a negative, but she wasn't sure if he heard it because no actual noise came out. There was a sound like a chuckle, but she didn't see it. Isaac had moved down her body, his head settling between her legs.

"Fucking exquisite," he breathed as he held her most private place open to his gaze.

Every muscle in her body tensed. It felt as if he were moving in slow motion. Her body was pulsing before his lips touched her. But when they did—*holy shit.*

Panting, she threw her head back on the mattress as Isaac's mouth and tongue moved over her folds. His fingers began to probe as well, penetrating her sheath with sure, determined movements.

Caroline cried out, clamping down around his fingers. "Oh, God," she whimpered, the throbbing building and twisting until she was right on the edge of an ecstasy that she'd forgotten existed.

Then she looked down and saw Isaac was touching her, using the arm with the full-sleeve tattoo. Caroline climaxed on the spot, her vision swamping out as her legs shook with the force of her release.

When her sight returned, it was to see him staring down at her shivering and trembling form. He raised his fingers, licking them slowly.

"I don't believe this—you actually taste better than you look."

Startled, Caroline laughed, but her mirth died when he slapped a string of condoms on the bed beside her.

His hand reached for his cock, pumping it up and down. His eyes were so dark that they looked like coals in the moonlight. "There you go looking scared again…"

"I'm not." But she was a little. The expression 'too much man for you' came to mind.

Isaac slid the condom over his seemingly endless length. Then he moved between her legs.

"See. Not scared," she squeaked with faux bravado.

"Good," he said, pressing his lips to hers for a hot open-mouthed kiss.

Tongue tangling with his, she put her arms around him, whimpering a little as his hard length slid up and down against her slick warmth.

His hands reached out to pin her arms to the mattress. "I'm going to fuck you now."

A squeal escaped, and he smiled. He gathered both her wrists in one hand, using the other to guide his length inside her.

Caroline's lips gaped as his thick shaft forged inside, stretching her sheath in a way her slim vibrator just couldn't.

"You like that, princess?" he asked, his voice hoarse.

She clung to him, her nails digging into his back as he drove all the way home. *"Sugar honey iced tea."*

He laughed. "What?"

"It's an acronym," she panted.

He laughed again and flexed his hips, withdrawing. Isaac held himself up. "It's a tight fit, baby. Are you okay?"

Caroline didn't react right away, her mind a beat too slow. "I, uh, let me see…"

Shifting her weight, she lifted her hips, taking him back in. The feel of him was indescribable. So was his reaction, the way his neck tendons stood out as he held himself over her, savoring the sensation.

"I think that's enough testing the waters," he murmured, thrusting back in once, twice, until he was fucking her at a steady, grinding pace.

Caroline held on helplessly, her breasts bouncing with every thrust. The heat, the feel of his skin covering hers, the way he filled her so tightly, and the silky fast friction—it was all too much for someone deprived of touch for so long.

"More, *more*." Her hands clutched at his back, slipping to cup his rock-hard ass, urging him deeper and harder. Isaac was only too happy to comply. Picking up his pace, he penetrated her with urgent strokes, one hand working her clit with every beat.

Somewhere inside her, a dam broke. Caroline let go of her last vestiges of control, letting herself fall into the raging surf. But she wasn't dashed across the rocks. The powerful surges swept her up in a whirlpool that cycled up and down in an intensity that was governed by his will.

"That's it, *princessa*." Isaac sighed when she cried out, her sheath flexing and fluttering around his length. "Swallow my cock with that pretty pink pussy."

Moving to hold her hips down, he ground against her, his cock rubbing just the right spot. Splintering like a supernova, Caroline buried a scream in Isaac's neck, her hands digging into his broad muscular back.

When her awareness returned, Isaac was prying her hand off his back. Caroline realized she was gripping him too hard, an unconscious effort to merge their two bodies into one. But some of that embarrassment dissipated when Isaac lifted her fingers to his lips, pressing a soft kiss to each one.

Caroline shivered as his dark eyes roamed over her possessively, the aftershocks of pleasure sharp and sweet. And because they were still one, they passed from her body back to his.

Isaac closed his eyes as one of those tremors rocked him. He made a purring sound in his throat—one too deep and dangerous for a domestic cat.

His eyes, those remarkably light, golden glints, seemed catlike too. *Like a panther.* He did make her uneasy that way, too, as if she'd been cornered by a predator. But she couldn't make herself stay away, couldn't resist touching him.

He pumped reflexively, but then checked himself. "Bad idea. I think we've asked enough of this condom."

But he didn't move. Neither did Caroline.

"I guess I'm having a hard time letting go, too," he confessed in that low throaty voice she was beginning to think was just for her.

"I'm sorry." She had probably left bruises on him; she'd dug her fingers into him that hard.

His grin was smug. "Never apologize for wanting to touch me."

Bending his head, he kissed her again, a tongue-and-teeth bumping, curl-your-toes kiss that made her whimper.

"I'll be right back."

Pressing his forehead to hers, he withdrew slowly. Caroline jerked involuntarily as his body left hers. Despite his gentleness, his loss was almost as shocking as their joining.

Uncertain and a little bereft, she pulled the comforter over her body.

Agent Rivera had no such qualms. He stood, naked and unconcerned, by the side of the bed. From the top of his head to the ends of his knees—the lowest part she could see from her vantage point on the bed—he was perfect. Except for the tattoo, he was the embodiment of the Roman god Vulcan.

Caroline had fallen in love with a modern artist's sculpture of Vulcan, bidding more than she should to purchase the piece at auction the year before last. She'd justified the exorbitant price by displaying the statue at the Wentworth Hotel in Savannah. When she sold the hotel, she'd moved it to her family home in Charlotte.

At times, she had regretted not bringing the piece with her to San Diego. But at this moment, she didn't miss it at all. Not with Isaac standing there so very god-like. All he was missing was the hammer.

Agent Rivera paused to pick something off the floor. It was the strip of condoms. There were three left.

Isaac turned, clearly sizing her up for seconds. Never taking his eyes off her, he deliberately separated one of the condoms and handed it to her.

"Why don't you open that up for me, baby, while I take care of this?" he said, gesturing to the prophylactic on his half-hard member.

He disappeared into the bathroom.

Shell-shocked at his bluntness, Caroline looked at the condom in her hand.

*What am I doing?* This was insane. She couldn't have an affair with the FBI agent who was throwing her life into disarray.

Closing her eyes, she let herself spiral for all of one minute. *You could ask him to leave.* If she told Isaac that she'd changed her mind, he would respect her wishes.

Except that was like closing the barn door after the horse was gone, then burning the barn.

She bit her lip, frozen in indecision. Isaac appeared in the threshold.

Heart pounding, Caroline turned the condom package over in her hand. Then she pinched her fingers around the top and tore it open.

# CHAPTER SIXTEEN

Isaac awoke when the first hint of daylight appeared through the window. The shutters were closed, but Caroline hadn't pulled the blackout curtains. She'd been too busy last night.

He hated getting up early, but on this occasion, he was happy to because it meant he could watch Caroline sleep.

Goddamn, she was gorgeous. Sometime in the night, between rounds two and three, she'd gone into the restroom and washed off all her makeup. He knew that stuff was supposed to enhance a woman's features, but he couldn't imagine her face looking better than it did right at this moment, from her thick gold lashes to those lush dusky rose lips.

His sister may have been right about the expensive moisturizer, too. She and Brit had scoffed at one that supposedly contained crushed diamond dust. But that must have been the kind that Caroline used. How else did she get her skin to look like that?

What was the word he was looking for? *Lustrous.*

Caroline had skin like a pearl. And he would know. He had bought his mother a string of pearls for her last birthday, after some determined hints. Isaac hadn't expected to be charmed by such an old-fashioned piece of jewelry, but he'd been damn near mesmerized by the things.

It seemed some things hadn't changed.

The alarm began to buzz. Caroline's face wrinkled, her arms reaching out blindly to the right. It hit him instead of the alarm.

Isaac sat up. "I take it you normally sleep on the left side of the bed."

Caroline's eyes flew open. They widened when they saw him. "H-hi," she stuttered, pulling the sheet up to her neck.

Isaac watched her with lascivious amusement, enjoying the blush he would bet anything went all the way down her body. The layer of Egyptian cotton didn't matter. His excellent memory provided a rather detailed image of what was underneath.

He twisted, picking up the alarm and switching it off, scowling when he saw the time. "It's only six AM, woman. That is far too early. At least sleep in until seven."

Growing very pink, Caroline sat up as well. "You know how the hotel works by now. Everything starts hours before we serve breakfast."

She shifted as if she were about to get up, but Isaac reached over, running a hand down her length over the sheet. "Except you hired excellent managers. They can handle the early morning crowd for a few hours."

"I, uh..." Cringing slightly, Caroline eased away from him, falling back on the mattress. But Isaac wasn't willing to let her go.

He rolled over her, caging her with his arms. "Let me guess," he drawled. "Someone is having second thoughts."

Biting that juicy lip, she stared. "And third ones," she admitted.

He suppressed a grin. It wasn't as if he hadn't been expecting this. "Well, I'm going to be honest with you—I've been thinking about this a lot."

"Is that so?" Her color deepened.

He leaned forward to kiss her again, but she put a restraining hand on his chest. Her color deepened. "Wow, your chest is so—um, never mind. Last night was amazing, but—"

Isaac groaned.

"But this is complicated," she finished in a firmer voice.

He rolled off her. "Isn't that the truth?"

Her brow creased. "Are you going to get fired for this? By the FBI, that is?"

He shrugged, his fingers stroking her cheek. "Well, I'm not going to put this in my weekly report if that's what you mean," he said. Cocking his head, he considered her. "How are your breasts?"

Caroline's pink lips parted in an unholy temptation. "Excuse me?"

"You ran into my arm pretty hard. Then there's the injured ankle."

"I'm fine."

*Hmm.* He'd like to believe that. But Caroline was the type of workaholic who would tell herself there was nothing wrong even when she was hurting. She'd push through the pain, possibly hurting herself worse in the long run.

He was debating the wisdom of telling her that when the phone rang.

"Damn it," he swore as she wriggled out from underneath him.

She practically dived for the phone on the bedside table, one hand clutching the sheet around her naked body.

"Janet?" she asked. "Oh. I see. I'll, um, I'll be right there."

Isaac sighed. The chances of getting her back in bed had just disappeared like fog at noon. Rolling off the mattress, he reached for his pants.

"I'll get out of your hair so you can shower."

She tucked a long lock of golden hair behind her ear.

"Thank you," she murmured. Then she frowned. "Where do *you* shower?"

Isaac pulled his pants up, zipping them closed. "Janet texts me a list of empty rooms every morning. I pick the nearest one, then take my gear and some extra towels in there for a quick wash. Don't worry I clean up after myself. I'm not making extra work for the maids."

"That's very considerate of you," she said before slipping into the bathroom.

Isaac closed his eyes. That had not gone as well as he hoped.

*Yeah, she's going to backpedal faster than he could drive backward.* And after Quantico's defensive driving course, that was pretty damn fast.

It was all right, though. Isaac was up for the challenge.

୧

When Caroline got out of the shower, she was relieved to see Isaac had already left. She dressed and applied her makeup in a hurry before stepping out into the hallway.

She froze in front of her office door, squeezing her eyes shut. *Don't be such a coward.* It had only been earth-shattering sex with an impossibly handsome and sexy man. A forbidden one at that.

Groaning, she let her head hit the door.

"Ow," she muttered. Rubbing her head, she forced herself to go inside.

Isaac wasn't waiting in there. Caroline closed the door behind her, then sagged against it.

*It's going to be fine,* she told herself. So, she'd had a one-night stand. People did that sort of thing all the time. Sure, it was her first one. She was an accomplished, cosmopolitan woman. There was no reason for her to be embarrassed.

But this wasn't typical behavior for her. Caroline could count her lovers on one hand. Well, three fingers to be precise.

*Better make that four now.*

Heat rushed to her cheeks at the mental image of Isaac's tattooed arm coming around her body, his hand gripping her neck lightly as he pulled her back to his front before he thrust inside her. Her memories got fuzzy after that, although the blazing orgasms that followed really stood out.

Stumbling to her desk, she let herself fall into her chair. Belatedly, she noticed the cup of coffee sitting on her leather blotter. It was still hot.

Isaac hadn't entirely skipped their coffee routine that morning. Caroline didn't know why that made her chest ache, but she stared at the coffee cup before she picked it up and poured it down the bathroom sink.

After that, she got to work, making a Herculean effort to get Isaac and the previous night out of her mind. That proved somewhat more difficult when Dr. Torres, the hotel's concierge doctor, came by with his portable X-ray machine.

"Your head of security called us. He said you might have twisted your ankle and possibly cracked a rib during a fall yesterday. He cleared the appointment with Janet."

"He did?" Caroline asked, flushed. "Did he mention I didn't land on the ground? I was fortunate that Mr. Rivera happened along to break my fall."

The doctor grinned. "That doesn't mean you weren't injured. Mr. Rivera happens to be built on a large scale—very fit," he added, lifting his hands to shape an imaginary wall.

Caroline snickered, amused despite herself.

"Hitting him may not be all that different from hitting the floor," Dr. Torres continued. "It's natural for him to be concerned, given that he was the blunt object you hit yourself with. I think it's best to humor him."

"Very well," she grumbled. "Since you brought all the gear out."

Ten minutes later, she had medical confirmation that she did not have a true sprain or any cracked ribs. But Dr. Torres did give her some painkillers for her aches and pains.

Once the doctor had left, Caroline tried to refocus on her work, but it was no use. The coffee cup had been a silent message. Isaac Rivera was willing to give her space, but he would not allow himself to be brushed under the rug.

The image of his bare chest, the sheet pooled around his waist, stayed with her, jumping to the forefront of her brain at the most inconvenient times.

By late afternoon, her jaw was so tight that she was giving herself a tension headache. Caroline groaned, rubbing her temples. She had done something completely out of character, and now there would be consequences—in the form of one sexy and very pushy FBI agent.

A knock at the door signaled the entrance of her assistant. Janet was dressed in the hotel's trademark teal blazer, but she paired it with a cream silk shirt with a big floppy bow. Caroline had a shirt just like it. It wasn't the first distinctive item of clothing Janet had bought after seeing it on her boss, but Caroline didn't mind being imitated, or at least she didn't think she minded. It was the sincerest form of flattery, right?

Janet handed Caroline what should have been her second coffee of the day, along with her missing Manolo. "Agent Rivera asked me to return this to you," she said, about to burst with curiosity.

Reddening, Caroline took the shoe and set it on the floor behind her desk.

Janet sat in the chair in front of the desk. "*So?*" she asked leaning forward with her hands gripped in her lap.

Caroline cleared her throat, deciding that in this case ignorance was the better part of valor. "Thanks. I was missing that. And you should call him Mr. Rivera, even in private. We don't want to slip up in front of the other staff. You and I are the only ones who know he's working here undercover."

"Of course," Janet said, crestfallen. "Uh—would it also be a bad thing if the entire staff was passing around the security footage of Mr. Rivera carrying you down the main staircase at three in the morning, shoeless?"

Caroline slumped over in her chair. "*Yes.* Yes, it would be."

"But it was so romantic—"

Groaning, Caroline let her head fall on her desk's surface. It was becoming a familiar sensation. *I may have to buy a thicker blotter, one with more padding.*

A light touch on her hand made her jerk and sit up. Janet watched her with amused sympathy. "I want this for you so much."

"No," Caroline scolded. "Don't encourage me. This can't happen."

Janet widened her eyes. "That's crazy talk. Have you seen him—well, you've obviously seen him. He's so—"

She broke off and waved her arms around, a futile attempt to capture the overwhelming everything that was Isaac Rivera. Janet bounced on the cushion of the chair. Her tone grew petulant. "Why not?"

"Because," Caroline insisted. "It doesn't matter that Isaac isn't an employee. If the rest of the staff thinks I'm sleeping with a subordinate, I'll lose all standing, particularly with the men. You, of all people, should know that."

A subdued Janet hung her head.

Her assistant had a short-lived relationship with Stephan, one of the concierges, the previous year. Things had ended badly, and although Stephan had wisely never said anything about Janet *at* work, he must have badmouthed her behind closed doors because his buddies had given Janet quite a bit of grief afterward.

Her sensitive assistant had been crushed.

Caroline tipped her head back to stare at the ceiling. "It's hard enough to be a woman and the boss. If people think I'm sleeping with my head of security…"

She slumped back in her chair, regret and longing at war for supremacy.

Janet hummed delicately. "I know this is about perception, but the fact is that's he's *not* your employee. To be honest, given the way he looks at you, everyone already thinks something has been happening for weeks. Watching the super-romantic way he carried you like you were Cinderella only confirmed it in their minds."

Caroline sighed. *It was more like an Officer and a Gentleman.*

And, injured ankle aside, it had been the most romantic thing to happen to her. But she had to cut the memories off there because if she let herself dwell on what happened after—well, she was already feeling faint.

"Nothing can happen between us." *Again,* she tacked on mentally. "Agent Rivera would never risk his career over someone involved in a case, nor would I encourage him to do so. Now, is there anything else?"

Caroline was determined to get her day back on track.

Visibly deflated, Janet consulted her notes. "Just a reminder that the wedding expo is tomorrow. You wanted to handle that personally because Andre Fleming, the jewelry designer, is going to be there."

"I remember," Caroline lied.

*Damn.* She had completely forgotten. Quickly, she tapped on her calendar, double-checking to make sure there were no other surprises.

Her assistant hesitated. "So, you also remember the part where you promised Agent—I mean, Mr. Rivera—that you wouldn't leave the hotel without him?"

"Oh, bloody hell." Caroline couldn't catch a break.

# CHAPTER SEVENTEEN

Isaac had been giving Caroline her space all day, intending on furthering his cause later that night. So, he was surprised when she asked to see him in her office at four.

"Have a seat," she said, gesturing to the chair in front of her desk with a cool and distant nod of her head.

Her perfectly manicured hand curled before flexing. She forced it flat on the desk, but, other than that, there wasn't so much of a twitch of her perfect blonde brows to betray her nervousness.

Well, two could play this game. "Do you need my daily briefing?" he asked, holding up his tablet with the same bland equanimity.

"That depends. Do you have anything of significance to report?"

*Touché.*

"A few things. We had a shoplifter in the gift shop. They were trying to boost the high-end booze you have on display—the one marked with the Caislean name." He frowned. "Why do you sell their booze?"

Annoyance flickered across her expression. "It's a business deci-sion. I don't want to go into it. Was there anything else?"

"We may have had a second sighting of the suspected human trafficker."

Caroline sat up. "And?"

"He made a quick exit with his companion, another Hispanic woman. But we have some good shots of both their faces and the license plate of their vehicle. My colleagues at the bureau are tracking it down as we speak."

Her lips parted. "Then this might be over soon?"

"Well, maybe," he hedged. "We won't know for certain that this involves Blackbeard until we run these guys down and question them."

He paused, feeling guilty for upending her life again. "I also don't need to remind you of how close we are to the Mexican border. We have an alert on the cars with border patrol, but all they have to do is swap the plates or the vehicle itself and they can disappear into another country."

She sighed aloud. "No. I'm aware of all the holes in your investigation."

He raised a brow, but he let her have that one. "Was there anything else?"

Caroline shifted in her seat, looking as if she had just swallowed something sour. "Yes...about last night."

Now they were getting to it. Isaac leaned back in his chair. "Let me guess. It can't happen again."

Caroline's shoulders relaxed, and she laughed. "I don't believe this. We agree."

The fact that she looked so relieved would have been insulting had he not been waiting for this.

"We don't."

Her mirth died away, those lush lips flattening. "I knew you were going to be difficult."

It was his turn to laugh. "Caroline, I don't know about you, but a night like last night doesn't just happen. We don't just like and respect each other—"

Her lashes fluttered. "We like each other?"

"Damn straight we do. A lot." He broke off, cocking his head to the side. "Are you trying to tell me you don't respect me?"

Caroline took a deep breath. "Agent Rivera," she began.

"When you cried out my name last name, it was Isaac," he pointed out.

Her hand flattened on the desk, presumably to stop herself from leaping across it to strangle him.

"I still respect you today. More to the point, I'm...what is the word I'm looking for?" Isaac broke off, rubbing his chin. "*Pride.* I'm proud of myself for sleeping with you."

She looked at him as if he were a lunatic.

He dropped the teasing attitude, looking her dead in the eyes. "It's true. I think there's a lot of men in the world who would be threatened by someone like you—whip-smart, successful, ballsy."

A line appeared between her brows. "I'm ballsy?"

"You took a risk to save this entire hotel chain. I'm privileged to have been here on the ground when your gamble paid off."

Caroline grew very still. "I'm not sure we're out of the woods yet."

He frowned. "You keep saying that, but I think you might be. Or at least you're pretty damn close. As for us...chemistry like ours isn't all that common. I want to see it through."

She opened and closed her mouth several times, seemingly at a loss for words. "I'm sorry. That's simply not going to happen. You see, I have a plan."

Isaac crossed one leg over the other. "A baby-via-frozen-papa plan. Yeah, I remember."

She reddened. "That does not leave this room."

"I would only ever tell the FBI if the clinic ended up being implicated in my case. But, so far, they are clean. I would also never tell any of your employees. That would be a massive breach of your confidence—and your feelings matter to me."

She closed her eyes and shook her head. "If that were true, you'd respect my wishes about ending this now."

Isaac was studying her as if he were going to be tested on all things Caroline Wentworth. "I can respect you without being on board with your procreation plan."

A dozen or so emotions flickered across her face. The roulette wheel landed on anger, and she slapped her hand on the desk. "I will have you know that 'procreation plan,' as you so facetiously call it, was something I considered carefully for over a *year*. I chose the clinic with care from over a dozen highly recommended facilities."

"And through them, you have access to the best sperm money can buy." He pursed his lips. "I wonder how many collective years of university your donors have in that tidy folder you have locked in your bottom drawer?"

The pen Caroline threw hit him square in the forehead.

"Ouch." He rubbed his forehead. "I guess I deserve that."

"Agreed," Caroline said in her best Ice Queen tone.

Isaac wanted to shake the woman, but putting his hands on her was the last thing he should do under these circumstances.

"I don't want to go backward. You're the only woman I've found remotely exciting since my divorce. Well...longer than that. I'm even willing to risk getting fired over you. God knows I've never said that about a woman before."

There was skepticism and doubt in her expression. "Even your wife?"

He took a long moment to answer, but he already knew the answer. "Yes."

Her lips parted. He couldn't decide if she was shocked because she didn't believe him, or because she did. "I—I can't do this. I have a plan," she repeated weakly.

"Yeah. I know," he said softly, making a decision. It was a crazy one, but he knew it was the only card he could play.

She kept watching him. One wrong move and she'd bolt. Isaac stood, taking his wallet out of his back pocket. Opening it, he took his last remaining contraceptive out and showed it to her.

Caroline frowned. "Is that..."

"A condom," he finished for her. "My last one. We used all the others I had left last night."

Hurt and confusion flashed in her eyes. "If you want me to reimburse you—"

"No, of course not," he scoffed.

"Well," she sniffed. "In that case, I can direct you to the gift shop. We sell those there, in addition to high-end alcohol."

Man, she was good at this. He pictured the hordes of men who had confidently gone to bat against the Ice Queen and come away bruised and battered, their tails between their legs. But Isaac was made of sterner stuff.

He held up the condom to the light as if it were a precious jewel. "I'm showing you this condom because it's not just my last one—it's your last, too."

Caroline rubbed her temples, squinting at him as if she were getting a headache. "Isaac, I don't have time for this."

"I have to disagree with you there," he said, trying to break the news gently. "You need to think about this. Because you have a pretty big decision to make."

"And what would that be?" she asked suspiciously.

He set the condom on her desk. "You and I get one more of these. If you choose to share your bed with me *after* we use it, I'm taking you bare."

Her brows puckered adorably. "What did you say?"

"I said if you choose to have sex with me again—and I'm gambling on the fact that you will—you get one more condom. After that, we don't use protection."

He leaned over her desk, bracing himself on the surface with his fingers. "You see, it's not the *baby-having* in your plan that I take issue with. More like the *baby-making*."

She continued to stare, her mouth open in a startled 'O'.

Isaac pushed the condom to the side. "You want a baby. Well, you can have one. *Mine.*"

"I...don't—*what?*"

He'd knocked her off her game, but he needed her to understand—he was playing for keeps.

He flattened his hands on her desk, leaning over until his head was less than a foot from her.

"I am going to fuck you," he said, pitching his voice low, trying to make sure she understood that this was as serious for him as it was for her.

He jerked his thumb at the connecting door she always kept closed. "From here on out, you're going to leave that door open. And every night, I'm going to come through it. Once I'm there, I'm going to strip off everything you're wearing before I kiss or lick every inch of your body. I'm going to do that over and over until you beg me to take you."

She opened her mouth to object, but he kept going, dropping his voice into the lowest register he could speak in and still be intelligible.

"And when I do…I won't be wearing a condom." His eyes roamed over her as if visibly consuming her. "I'm going to bring you to orgasm with nothing between us. And once I've made you scream my name two or three times, I'm going to let go and fill you with my seed. And I'm not going to stop until you're well and truly pregnant."

# CHAPTER EIGHTEEN

"Where are we going?" Isaac asked as Caroline climbed into the passenger seat of his rental car.

She bent her perfectly coiffed head, fussing with her seat belt. Her silence was so pointed it almost cut him. That and her fitted black business suit, which was sharp enough to draw blood.

"You know I need a location," he pointed out, unable to stop his eyes from doing a lingering appraisal. *I could eat her with a spoon...*

"It's not enough to know you have an appointment in an hour," he pressed when she remained silent. "So, you're going to have to start speaking to me again, preferably before I pull out of the parking lot, so I at least know which direction to drive in."

That was technically untrue. Caroline *had* spoken to him today, a crisp 'hello' when he'd brought her coffee this morning. It had been immediately followed by a frosty 'thank you' and 'goodbye'.

He had left without argument, deciding it was best to give her time to think about his offer last night.

*Except it was more like an ultimatum.* Isaac suppressed a wince as Caroline did her best Elsa the Ice Queen impression.

He still had the last condom in his wallet. She had made him take it with him when she'd kicked him out of her office. Still, things weren't hopeless.

*She wouldn't be so mad if she didn't care, right?*

Unless she was so insulted by his offer that she wouldn't forgive him for making it. Either way, he had to try. Or so he kept telling himself. *Go big or go home. Swing for the fences.* Caroline wasn't the only big gambler in their duo. Isaac had just rolled the dice, too, making the bet of his life.

"We're going to the convention center," she said after checking her seat belt twice, avoiding his eyes. "There's a big expo. I have an appointment with a top-name jewelry designer."

He frowned, started the car, and then pulled away from the curb in front of the hotel. "Are you having something made for yourself?"

"No." Caroline kept her eyes on the road. "Andre Fleming was an important contemporary artist. Approximately five years ago, he went dark for about nine months very suddenly and with great secrecy. When he resurfaced, he announced a big show in San Francisco instead of his usual haunts in Soho. He was known for his large, bold canvases, but, this time, there were over a dozen handcrafted jewelry pieces mixed in with the paintings—mostly collars and necklaces."

"I take it they were a hit."

She tucked a hair behind her ear, flicking a glance at him before skittering away. "Yes, they were an instant sensation, enough that he began to devote more and more time to the jewelry side of his business. Today, his output is eighty-percent jewelry, but he hasn't had a major show for two years. I heard from a credible source that he's launching a new collection in the second half of the year, and his new pieces are a throwback to old Hollywood and will prominently feature sapphires. I also heard he was toying with a Casablanca theme for the launch."

"Ah," he said, finally understanding. "The hotel, with all its columns, archways, and ocean views, would be the perfect backdrop."

She nodded.

He gave her outfit a second glance. "So, that's why you're not wearing any jewelry. You want to make Fleming itch to drape some sapphires on you. Anything he puts on you would stand out against the black."

He'd almost swallowed his tongue when he'd seen her across the parking lot. The woman looked like a diamond against all that black.

Caroline turned and frowned. "You spend a lot of time analyzing my clothes and appearance."

Isaac didn't deny it. He lifted a shoulder. "We both know I enjoy looking at you."

"I would appreciate a little more professionalism from you, Agent Rivera."

"Isaac," he corrected. "And I think that's a bridge we already burned. We're currently dancing in the ashes. "

"*Agent Rivera*," she began.

He lifted one hand from the steering wheel momentarily. "Don't worry. I'll behave in front of your business contacts. And I am enjoying the study of your style. Not because of how you look— although the result is sexy as hell. It's more like…appreciation."

"Appreciation?" she echoed.

"Yeah. I'm seeing a master at work."

Caroline snorted delicately, turning her attention to the view out of the window as he took the ramp to the Coronado bridge that connected the island with San Diego proper.

It was difficult not to appreciate the view as they drove over the water, but though he'd crossed this span on numerous occasions before, he found himself tensing.

Suddenly, the curved concrete and steel girder structure seemed too light and insubstantial for the work it did. Tightening his hands on the wheel, he didn't allow himself to turn his head to admire the woman beside him, although he wanted to. But with such a flimsy and busy bridge, he needed to be alert. Caroline's safety was in his hands.

He couldn't help releasing an audible sigh of relief once they were safely across, merging into the regular traffic on the I-5 highway.

"It's true," he continued as if there had been no pause in the conversation. "I've never known a person as on display as you are. From your employees to all the guests of the hotel, and the vultures like Chapman—everyone is constantly watching you. Some, like me, just want to admire. But the rest are waiting to pick every detail of your appearance apart like they're searching for a flaw so they can feel better about their petty little lives."

She twisted her head. "That's unexpectedly deep."

"Not really. Both of my sisters are too pretty for their own good, too." He said it with distaste. "They've gone through some shit."

"But they had you to defend them, I bet," she said, her tone softening a fraction.

"I did what I could." He shrugged. "Tell me more about this meeting."

Caroline was silent for a moment. "Fleming is, in my opinion, due for a resurgence in popularity. His recent marriage to Elliana Walsh, the actress, will ensure that this show is his biggest ever. Every major hotel and conference center would want to host it if they knew. But I know Fleming personally. I bought one of his early pieces for the Wentworth hotel back when he was a starving artist."

She paused, tucking a strand of golden hair behind her ears, her expression pensive. "My father was furious at me for spending so much on what he called a no-name doodler."

"Did he change his tune when Fleming hit it big?"

"No," she said shortly.

*Okay then.* "Was that your last interaction with Fleming?" He glanced over. "Do you think he'll remember you?"

Her lips pursed. "I believe so. I've run into him a few times over the years at events. That and he took the meeting, which is a good sign."

"That he did." She pulled out her tablet and opened the photo app, opening an album of promotional shots of the hotel, getting it ready before she turned it off.

They arrived at the convention center a few minutes later. Isaac flashed his badge to park in some of the restricted spaces closer to the entrance.

Caroline had taken note of that. "See," he pointed out as he held the door open for her. "I can be handy."

"You do realize valet exists, right?"

Isaac was chuckling when they entered the main convention hall. One look and he stopped.

It was wall-to-wall wedding supplies. 'Welcome to the Wedding Expo' a large banner over their heads read.

"Go ahead," Caroline said, a trace smugly. "Let me have it."

Isaac frowned. "What does that mean?"

"I'm sure there's something you want to say for dragging you to wedding nirvana," she said with a sweeping gesture of her well-manicured hand. "As a recent divorcé, you must be crawling out of your skin."

*So that was her game.* Isaac spun on his heel, taking in stall after stall of wedding finery and formal dinner settings.

He put his hand on her back, guiding her out of the center of the path when a cluster of women holding matching blue satin dresses passed them. "I got married in Vegas, so none of this wedding stuff is all that familiar or particularly scary. Also, my divorce was finalized over a year ago and I was separated for more than six months before that."

He inclined his head, a trace of a smile tugging at his lips. "Sorry to disappoint you. I know you'd love to see me breaking out in hives.... As for the insult you seem to be expecting, you're pulchritudinous."

Caroline's mouth dropped open before snapping shut. "That means beautiful."

"I know," he said, his grin intensely flirtatious. "But isn't it a horrible way of saying it?"

That seemed to throw her. Flushed and flustered, Caroline turned away. "There are a few vendors I want to touch base with before the meeting."

"Are we going to have a wedding soon?"

She tripped. Isaac's hand shot out, catching her by the upper arm. "At the hotel," he clarified. "The main ballroom is big enough for that sort of thing."

"Well, it can handle something small and intimate," she said, consulting the conference map she picked up at the door.

"The room capacity is two hundred and fifty. That's small and intimate?"

Caroline turned, brows raised. "In many circles, yes."

Face twitching in amusement, Isaac proceeded to follow Caroline around on her business.

She found vendor number one a few tables away—a florist. At the end of their little convo, the man pressed a miniature rose on her, which she slipped into the buttonhole in her lapel. That was followed by a five-minute meeting with an excitable woman who sold fancy plates and silverware, who was followed by a cake baker. The last two were specialty alcohol distributors.

To his surprise, Isaac was enjoying the expo. He noted several other men going around doing business just like Caroline, but, apparently, there was something about him in particular that made many of the staff at the booths excitable. They kept pressing freebies on him and Caroline.

He was having a grand time eating his third generously sized wedding-cake sample, his pockets stuffed with beautifully wrapped truffles and packets of Jordan almonds, when a woman offered him a glass of prosecco. Assuming it was another alcohol vendor, he slowed Caroline down with a touch to the elbow.

But it was a wedding dress retailer, one with a name his sisters would have recognized.

"You two are such a beautiful couple," the woman enthused, ushering them closer to the booth. "When is the big day?"

"We're not—" Caroline began, dismay all over her face.

"It's in December," Isaac interrupted, throwing an arm around her shoulders. He polished off the drink before handing back the glass. "But I'm afraid she already has her dream dress."

"Oh." The woman looked at Caroline. "How about your bridesmaids? Are they all set?"

"We aren't having any," she said, a deep blush creeping over her fair skin. "Please excuse us, we only have a few minutes to get to our appointment."

She pulled him away. Isaac let himself be led down the main drag a few steps before stepping in front of her and taking her hand to guide her through the jostling crowd.

"You are a lovely couple," the woman called after them in a loud voice. "You're going to have such beautiful babies!"

Caroline's head jerked back fast enough to give herself whiplash. Murmuring soothingly, Isaac pulled her closer so he could massage her neck. He inclined his head until his lip grazed her ear. "Even strangers can see it."

The elbow to the gut was small but very pointed. That and Caroline put her weight behind it.

He gritted his teeth, but the smallest of snorts escaped. "Don't look at me that way." He laughed when she glared. "It's not like I paid her or anything."

Isaac was resolutely ignored until they approached one of the smaller conference rooms branching off the main drag. The space was nearly empty compared to the main hall since it was reserved for Andre Fleming's exclusive use. But instead of blocking it off, Fleming and the conference designers had come up with a novel way of separating him from the common masses.

Fleming's wares were set on a raised dais the size of a boxing ring —one tall enough to make getting up difficult. But instead of crawling under ropes, there were two steps on the side facing the door.

Around the edge were nine free-standing pedestals, three per side. Each was topped with a small glass case displaying a simple item. It was more like a museum showcase than the typical jeweler's display. Fleming wasn't about to let anyone forget that he was an *artiste*.

The man himself was holding court in the middle of the dais, where two curved velvet loveseats faced each other.

Caroline took one look at the couches and froze, the color draining from her face. Sensing danger, Isaac moved fast, blocking her from view.

It took him a few more seconds to recognize the man talking to Fleming.

He spoke without looking over his shoulder, not wanting to call attention to Caroline's presence. "Did you know your ex-fiancé was wooing Andre Fleming as well?"

"No."

Counting a beat, he turned. Caroline's head was down. She pretended to study her tablet screen, but the damn thing wasn't even on.

Isaac grunted. Stepping forward, he backed her against the wall, making sure his bulk was blocking her the whole time. Tellingly, she let him hide her without complaint.

Once he was sure no one had noticed the move, he turned around to study the fool stupid enough to let Caroline Wentworth go.

# CHAPTER NINETEEN

Liam Tyler was around Isaac's height and built along the same lines. But he was more muscular than someone who spent their life behind a desk had any right to be.

Isaac narrowed his eyes, critically assessing the man. *I can still take him*, he sniffed. He put a hand behind him, making sure Caroline was still there. But she hadn't budged from the spot.

Isaac clocked the way Tyler was looking around the room. "When is your appointment?" he asked.

"In five minutes."

*Ah.* Tyler may have been trying to woo Fleming to do his business at one of his hotels, but that wasn't his main reason for being here. The man had come looking for Caroline.

Isaac was suddenly glad he'd brought his gun. Not that he'd use it, of course. But the bulge it made in his jacket was deterrent enough.

"He's getting up."

Isaac turned back to Caroline. Her face was composed…and eerily blank. She had used the time to get ahold of herself. He had to admire the effort. God knew he wouldn't do half as well if his ex-wife strolled through the door.

*That's because your tolerance for drama is gone.* It wasn't because he was brokenhearted like Caroline might be. *Please don't let her be pining for this asshole.*

Whether she pined was a question for another day. He wouldn't read too much into the strain at the corners of her eyes and in the tight set of her lips. Her ex had blindsided her. And Isaac would cheerfully knock Liam Tyler through the wall if it meant wiping the stress from Caroline's features.

"Want me to get rid of him?" he asked.

"Don't be silly. Liam and I are on perfectly cordial terms."

"Right." He checked the man's progress. Liam Tyler shook hands with Fleming.

"The asshole is getting up."

Caroline moved forward as if to meet Tyler halfway.

Isaac pivoted to block her.

"Not before your big meeting," he urged, rubbing her back comfortingly. "If you need to talk to him afterward, I'll find him for you. But, for now, think about your pitch. You need to get in a Casablanca mood."

For a moment, it appeared as if she wanted to argue with him, but Caroline wisely pressed her lips together and nodded. She took a few deep breaths.

When she looked up again, she was ready to do battle.

"All right, the coast is clear." Tyler had left, presumably in search of the woman Isaac had tucked protectively into his side. "Go get him, kid."

She scowled, tapping him lightly with her tablet. "I'm not a child."

"It's a Casablanca joke."

Her scowl deepened. "Is it? That doesn't sound right."

"I was paraphrasing," he said, simultaneously wanting to shake her and throw her over his shoulder so he could find a private room where he could have her all to himself.

"Never mind, go get him. And don't worry about your ex. If he gets anywhere near you, I'll shoot him."

"*No,*" she hissed, poking him in the chest. "Bad FBI agent."

He gave her a devilish grin before patting her on the butt in an unmistakable 'get going' gesture.

She held up a warning finger and shook it. But a smile teased her lips. She marched to Fleming with her head held high.

The jewelry designer's face transformed when he saw her. He beamed, greeting Her Highness with effusive air kisses. Isaac watched covetously as Caroline sat, chatting animatedly as if she didn't have a care in the world. *That's my girl.* She just didn't know it yet.

Fleming said something, looking around and pointing. He was probably telling Caroline that Tyler had been looking for her, but she dismissed that with an airy wave, getting down to business so seamlessly Fleming forgot all about his previous guest.

She was something else, all right. If Isaac hadn't seen her face when she recognized her former fiancé, he would have thought her cold and emotionless. But the hurt and dismay in her eyes had been unmistakable. Yeah—there was a lot of baggage there.

He, of all people, knew how damaging past relationships could be, even when one had fallen out of love with the person in question. Isaac had been burned pretty thoroughly himself. But he'd played the field for a while, had several shallow interim relationships, and now he was ready to move on to the real thing. He'd assumed Caroline had enough time to get to that place, too, but what if he were wrong?

*She went so pale.* Isaac hated seeing her in pain. It made him want to punch something.

But she *had* recovered fast. At this moment, Caroline was doing her hard sell, taking out her tablet to show Fleming the pictures of the hotel. Isaac saw the man nod enthusiastically, gesticulating from across the room. He grinned, a feeling of pride swelling in his chest. But it was mixed with something else—trepidation.

She was the one. He was almost sure of it. But he needed her to be open to the possibility, too.

When it came down to it, he wasn't sure that was going to happen. They were just so different. He was an army grunt turned FBI agent. And Caroline Wentworth was a princess—a damn hardworking one who oversaw an entire kingdom.

*Well, that would make her a queen, wouldn't it?*

Isaac snorted, keeping one eye on his regent. With the other, he carefully noted the other players in the room. Tyler was not one, but there were plenty of people paying attention to Fleming and his beautiful companion.

He made sure to give those men the hairy eyeball. When Caroline stood, he drifted forward to wait at the bottom of the dais.

"I'll have Janet send that contract to you in the morning," she said, doing another round of cheek kisses, this time in parting.

"Sound good," Fleming replied. "And about that other thing—let me know if you change your mind."

"Believe me, if I ever do, you'll be the first to know." Caroline laughed and waved. Giving him a discreet nod, she gave Isaac the 'let's get the hell out of Dodge' signal.

He fell in step behind her, putting his hand on her elbow to guide her to a less populated exit.

"I take it the mention of a contract means you got it?"

"I did."

He tugged, stopping her progress. "Congratulations," he said, unable to resist putting a hand on the nape of her neck. He tilted her head back, looking deep into those too-blue eyes. No sapphire could compare.

"You did great."

Her gold lashes fluttered. "Thank you," she said, a touch breathlessly.

"What did he mean by that last part? What does he want you to change your mind about?"

"Oh..." Caroline turned away. "Nothing."

Isaac snorted, catching her by the waist. "Nice try. What does Fleming want from you?"

She gave him a dismissive shake of her head, surreptitiously trying to put distance between them. "It is nothing of significance. Fleming hasn't forgotten asking me to sit for him when we met, back when I first bought a painting from him."

He raised a black brow. "Sit as in pose for a painting? Isn't he a modern artist? Don't they paint lines and cubes?"

Caroline continued to edge away. "Fleming had a hyper-realistic phase."

"And were you supposed to be nude for this painting?" he asked, his voice going dangerously soft.

She brought her tablet up, waving it airily. "I never asked. Regardless, it's a moot point. He paints so much less these days—it wasn't a serious offer." She turned her head, inspecting their surroundings with exaggerated casualness. "Which way to your car?"

"The hell it wasn't serious," Isaac groused, offering his arm. When she didn't take it, he reached for her hand and placed it deliberately on his forearm. "C'mon. It's this way."

Keeping a hold of her, Isaac pulled Caroline along, heading to a door marked 'Employees only'.

"Are you sure we should be going this way?" she asked when they were suddenly engulfed by silence. All the wedding expo chatter had disappeared the moment they closed the door.

"It'll be fine," he assured her. "I scoped this way out on the map. It passes through some kitchens that should be empty. Most vendors brought their own food and drink. At most, some of the catering companies might need to reheat stuff, but some brought their tabletop ovens."

He glanced back at Caroline. "So, when is Fleming planning his big event?"

"Sooner than I thought. He wants to do it three months from now. Maybe a little less if he has a creative sprint in between now and then. But it shouldn't conflict with any events—he's not planning on using a conference room. He was amenable to my suggestion of converting the outdoor patio and gardens into stages for him. Alternatively, we can use the fine-dining restaurant if the weather is poor. He liked the arches in there."

"Will he be bringing his own security?"

"I think so. He—"

"*Caroline!*"

Caroline startled, her expression one of sickened dismay. She wiped it clean the next second, turning to face Liam Tyler and some blond man with a benign, if slightly brittle, smile.

"Liam," she said, her teeth barely moving. "Fancy meeting you here."

Liam Tyler put his hands on his hips, making his thousand-dollar suit jacket strain at the seams. "Fancy my ass. I've been looking for you everywhere."

Isaac scowled, putting an arm in front of Caroline. "Did this douchebag always talk to you like that? No wonder you broke up with him."

"What?" Liam Tyler's eyes were bloodshot. He stared at Isaac as if he hadn't even noticed him.

"Technically, that's not what happened," the blond man offered, his air an annoying combination of chagrin and resigned amusement. He immediately joined Tyler on Isaac's shit list.

"No, and you know that," Caroline hissed, digging an elbow in Isaac's side.

He narrowed his eyes at the two men, lingering on Tyler with skepticism. "Yeah, seeing him in person and seeing you, I now have my doubts about the official story," he murmured in a quiet aside that was perfectly audible to the two men.

The blond man snorted, hiding his mouth with his hand.

"Who is this person, Caroline?" Tyler asked, glaring at Isaac like he was a piece of shit he needed to scrape off his shoe. However, he then changed his mind, slashing a hand in the air. "Never mind, it's not important. Look, I've heard some things that suggest you might be in danger."

"Let me guess. Your brother-in-law filled you in?" Caroline said crisply.

"My sister overheard enough of a conversation of his to put two-and-two together," Liam said. He rolled his shoulders as if they were tense. "After she told me you might be in danger, I didn't let up on him —Jason cracked yesterday. We flew out as soon as we could, but your assistant wouldn't tell us where you were. Then we got an alert that

Fleming was going to be at this expo. I remember that pervert was always trying to get you to pose naked for him, but he's big in the jewelry world now so we decided to try here before going to your hotel."

"Is that so?" Caroline rubbed her temple, a sure sign she was getting a stress headache.

Isaac gave both men a dark stare. "Coercing a federal agent is against the law. And if you don't mind my saying that it's fairly stupid to confess to a crime in front of yet another federal agent."

He opened his coat, flashing the badge strapped to his belt.

The other man put a restraining hand on Tyler's arm. "Liam, I think we're meeting the FBI agent assigned to Caroline's case. Another FBI man who is no doubt armed—try not to piss this one off, too."

The man must have been referring to Ethan Thomas, who hated Liam with the passion of ten fiery suns, or at least he used to.

The blond nodded at Isaac in a conciliatory fashion. He stuck out a hand in Isaac's direction. "Matthias Raske."

*Ah, the new husband.* They must have left Peyton, the wife, at home. Isaac gave the blond man a speaking glance. Matthias nodded as if this made sense before slowly putting the hand down.

Liam ran a hand through his hair, messing up what was likely a two-hundred-dollar haircut. "Caroline, I think you should come back with us to Boston until whatever mess you've gotten into blows over."

"Whatever mess *I* got into—" Caroline was incensed.

"She's not going anywhere with you," Isaac snapped at the same time.

Liam moved forward aggressively, reaching for her. "Caroline, this isn't a joke. You need to be protected."

Isaac gently but firmly pushed her behind him. "Go ahead and touch her. I *dare* you."

Tyler stepped back, throwing up his hands. "Caroline, you need to come back with us."

"The hell she does," Isaac shot back before enlightenment struck.

He passed a hand over his face. "Wait—are you sure you're not trying to make your little trio a foursome? Cause, I can tell you now, Caroline is never going to leave with you."

The woman in question, tired of being ignored, jerked on his sleeve, *hard*. "Isaac, don't speak for me."

Liam's expression turned smug until Caroline rounded on him. "And you—where the hell do you get off coming here and making demands? I have my own life, one that you no longer have a say in."

Tyler stared at her as if he'd never seen her before. "That's not it. I'm here because you're in danger."

Caroline drew herself to her full height "That is being dealt with. As you can see, Agent Rivera is on top of this."

Raske held up a finger, looking as if he was going to make a smart-aleck comment, but one glare from Isaac and he wisely shut his mouth.

Tyler gaped like a fish, his mouth opening and closing. "But—"

Raske sighed. "Liam, she said no. You can't force her."

"You should listen to your better half," Isaac said with a glower. "Or should I say better third?"

Surprise flashed in Tyler's eyes. He turned to Caroline in confusion. "You told him?"

There was so much angst in this room that Isaac was going to choke on it.

"No, she didn't," Isaac snapped. "I'm from the Boston office. We know all about you there. And Caroline's had a long day. So, if you are done making her feel like shit, we're going to leave now."

"*Isaac,*" Caroline warned. But her tone was more tired than angry.

He looked down at her, resisting the urge to touch her—but only just. "Can you give me a moment with these two?" he asked quietly.

Raske was whispering something in Liam's ear as well.

"I don't think that's a good idea," Caroline said, enunciating from behind set teeth.

Isaac pointed to the door at the end of the hall, one with a head-sized window in it. "I can see you on the other side of that. I only need a minute. I promise."

Holding up her hands in surrender, Caroline walked away.

Isaac waited until she was on the other side of the door to turn around, the hands on his hips moving wider, enough to flash the gun holstered to his side.

Raske's head drew back, but Liam just crossed his arms and gave him a dirty look. "If you get her killed, I will personally make your life miserable."

Isaac huffed. "Ethan Thomas was right about you. You *are* an asshole."

"Listen here—"

"*Shut up*," Isaac said. "Because I'm not done."

Liam's jaw looked tense enough to crack at the joint, but he closed his mouth.

Isaac narrowed his eyes. "I know you thought you'd come here, riding to the rescue, but did you spare a thought for what would happen afterward? Caroline would be trapped with the lot of you— totally dependent on her ex and the man and woman he left her for."

Silence.

"You didn't think about that at all, did you?" His lips pulled back in a grimace. "I bet all you thought about is how *you* feel knowing she's in a bind, not about how she wants to handle this situation."

Liam opened his mouth, but Matthias nudged him hard enough to make him step sideways to keep his balance.

Isaac decided it was long past time someone straightened Liam Tyler out.

"Let me lay this out for you once and for all. Caroline is not your business. Not anymore. You gave up the right to interfere in her affairs when you broke off your engagement, so get the fuck out of her life. Because you aren't the hero here—in Caroline's story, you are the villains."

Liam flinched, blinking in stunned surprise. Raske cleared his throat, staring at the ceiling.

Done with their bullshit, Isaac turned on his heel and walked away, taking Caroline out of their reach.

# CHAPTER TWENTY

When Caroline fell apart, she shut down. She was still walking, but Isaac could see her withdrawing, a layer of invisible ice accumulating on her skin.

Isaac managed to get her in the car, but once there, she sat, listless, staring straight ahead. She didn't move, not even when he fastened her seat belt.

Making a snap decision, Isaac made a call. "Hey Harry, it's Isaac Rivera. Can you set up one of your specials for thirty minutes from now? Thanks—I'll send you the pics."

Caroline lifted her head, the confusion in her eyes making her look drowsy. "What is it? Are you planning something?"

"It's a surprise."

"Oh, Isaac, I don't feel like going anywhere. Can't we head back to the hotel?"

"You'll enjoy this. I promise."

Caroline groaned, slumping in the seat.

"That's the spirit," he enthused, turning on the car. Thirty minutes later, he was pulling into the parking lot of Humboldt's Range.

"Where are we?" Caroline asked as he ushered her past the nondescript front counter. Her expression didn't clear when they reached the back, where partitions separated the firing lanes.

He waved to Harry in the control booth. "Thanks, Harry," he called out loud, enough to be heard through the bulletproof glass. Harry clocked Caroline, giving him a thumbs-up before holding up his fingers. Three, Four, and Five.

Isaac nodded and turned back around, holding his arms wide. "Welcome to my favorite shooting range. Well, my favorite in San Diego County."

The look Caroline gave him could have curdled milk. "Isaac, what are we doing here?"

"We're getting the special, of course." Taking her hand, he guided her to lane three. "Harry calls it's the ex-girlfriend special. In your case, it's the ex-boyfriend special."

When he pushed a button, one of those mobile targets moved forward. But the outline of the man had Liam Tyler's picture pasted over it.

"Harry has a big printer in the back to make these up," he explained as Caroline stared at the black-and-white picture in bemused silence. "I'll be right back."

He returned shortly with a box of bullets and a small-caliber gun.

"This is a 22. It has small bullets, guaranteed to have little-to-no recoil—the kickback you see on TV."

Caroline took the gun as if he'd offered her a live snake. "I'm supposed to shoot this?"

"At the picture." He gestured to the target. "Trust me, you'll feel loads better afterward."

She passed a hand over her face, the gun hanging limply at her side. "I appreciate that some people might find this therapeutic, but I don't think I'm one."

"*Okay*," Isaac said, studying her with narrowed eyes. "So…you don't want to shoot Liam Tyler in the face? Can't say I agree with that, but to each his own. But how about this one?"

Taking the weapon, he tugged her to the next lane. A picture of Peyton Carson, now Peyton Tyler-Raske, was taped over the target.

Caroline groaned, but made no move to take the gun back from him.

"Not that one either, huh?" Isaac sighed. "I have to say, you're a very evolved person. If someone had slapped my ex-wife's picture on one of these during my divorce, I would have put two between her eyes—purely in a figurative sense of course."

"Of course," she echoed weakly.

"All right," he said, gesturing to the last lane, the one that featured Matthias Raske. "Last chance to be as un-evolved and petty as the rest of us."

Caroline opened her hand, shaking it up and down.

He frowned. "What's wrong?"

"Give me the damn gun."

"*Oh.*" Blinking, Isaac set the bullets on the shelf built into the partition, realizing she had gone pale when she spotted Raske, not Tyler. "Sorry."

He loaded the gun. For the next five minutes, he proceeded to give Caroline a crash course in marksmanship. Once she was geared up and safe, he put the gun in her hands, pointing it at the target.

"If I didn't know better, I'd say this whole thing is an elaborate excuse for you to put your hands on me," Caroline said when he adjusted her stance for the third time.

His grin was flirtatious. "We can kill two birds with one stone." He put his hands on her hips, lingering. "And, to be honest, seeing you hold a gun while wearing that outfit, in those heels, makes me want to strip every inch of fabric off you and take you to the supply closet."

"*Isaac.*"

"I would take it back, but that would make me a colossal liar."

Caroline laughed, and he stepped away. She hit Raske's face on the first try—right in the kisser. Isaac whistled. "Nice shot."

The next one was better. It hit the nose. She kept going until the target resembled Swiss cheese.

Finally, all the bullets in the gun were spent.

Isaac took the gun from her. "Did that help, or shall I have Harry print up another copy?"

Caroline bit her lip, but she smiled. Almost. "I think I'm done, thank you."

"Really? You don't want to take a crack at Liam's picture?" he asked hopefully.

"No, I'm good."

Unable to resist, he stroked down her back, urging her a little closer. "Then would you mind if I shot at it? Because I'm feeling an extraordinarily strong yen to do so after today."

Caroline moved forward until she was pressed against him, her face buried in his chest. It was muffled, but he heard something that sounded like 'thank you'.

His hand slipped up to cradle the back of her head, holding her close. "You're welcome," he said.

Isaac could have held her like that forever, but Caroline's stomach growled. He checked his watch. They'd blown past the normal dinner hour, but if he were right, there was great food close by.

Exerting a little pressure, he tilted her head up until she met his eyes. "Do you like tacos?"

# CHAPTER TWENTY-ONE

Caroline sat at the picnic table, trying not to drool as Isaac put the tray down. It was late, the area around them quiet and dark, but the parking lot where the taco truck had parked was busy. Chili pepper lights and strings of bright white stars were strung over picnic tables. Judging by how full each was, the food was excellent.

Isaac pointed to the five rows of tacos on the tray.

"So, these are standard carne asada tacos. And these three are Adobado. These are cheese. And this last row is my favorite—*Lengua* —I'm not going to tell you what that is until after you try it."

"I know that means beef tongue," she said, reaching for one of the empty paper plates. She loaded an assortment, one of everything.

"I thought you said you've never had street tacos," he protested, referring to an earlier conversation they'd had in the car.

"I've eaten at some of the finest restaurants in Mexico City, Puerto Vallarta, and L.A.," she informed him primly. "Many of those did their own twist on the taco. I've just never actually eaten any in the street."

Isaac's mouth curled up in that sexy way that made her lower bits clench. He offered her a choice of oversized Styrofoam cups, one filled with a rice milk drink, Horchata, and Jamaica, which was made from hibiscus flowers.

"So…" he began after she'd polished off most of her tacos. "What did Raske do to break you and Liam up?"

She sighed, sipping her drink. But there was no reason not to tell him. At this point, Isaac probably knew more about the end of her engagement than any other living soul. Even her girlfriends back home hadn't heard the nitty-gritty details. A few had called, wanting to dissect the breakdown with her. While she'd appreciated their offers, the hurt was too fresh for her to confide over the phone— particularly to friends who were happily married, most with children.

"Liam and I were broken up at the time Matthias came into our lives," she began. "We did that a lot—break up, get back together, break up again… But we didn't let it get in the way of our business. We did a lot of networking together."

"How civilized," Isaac observed.

"I thought so at the time," she said, staring off into space. "I guess part of me was still expecting to get back together. Liam had made some overtures that indicated he was headed in that direction. I had the brilliant idea of introducing him to Matthias, whom I was trying to woo as an investor. They hit it off, which I thought was great…up until the point where I found them in bed together."

"Wow." Isaac's nose wrinkled. "I am all for gay rights, but that is pretty messed up. Especially if you weren't expecting it—Tyler had never let on he liked men before that?"

Jason must have told him that.

She shook her head. "No. I was blindsided. I don't care about Liam anymore—not like that. I'm not heartbroken. I'm not even that angry. Not most of the time, anyway."

"But you're pissed at Matthias," he said softly, searching her face. "And rightly so. He's the one who wrecked your happily ever after."

Caroline leaned on her elbow, thinking it over. "I realize now I was never going to have that with Liam. I could never be what he wanted me to be—"

"Namely a man," Isaac interjected.

"No." She laughed. "I mean flexible. His needs are far more compli- cated than I am comfortable."

"Because he's bisexual."

She nodded. "The woman he married is his childhood friend."

"*Blech.*"

Caroline laughed. "Some people find that romantic."

His lips twisted sardonically. "I married my childhood sweetheart. Trust me, it's not *that* romantic." He leaned forward. "And just because you don't want to be in a polyamorous bisexual pod, or whatever they call it, doesn't mean *you* are lacking anything. Most people wouldn't want that kind of relationship. God knows I wouldn't, not even if it were two women. Not even if they looked like you."

He broke off, staring into space. "Actually, let me walk that back... If you cloned yourself—"

Caroline, who had been fiddling with the paper cover of the straw she hadn't used, twisting one of the ends, chose that moment to blow the wrapper in his face.

Isaac burst into laughter. "Nice shot."

"Thank you."

Still chuckling, he paused to inhale a taco. He did it so fast that she was concerned about him choking. "My point is that we are all wired differently," he said, wiping his mouth with a paper towel. "You want one man. I want one woman. It doesn't mean we're not evolved or some shit like that."

Caroline waited to see if he were about to add that they wanted each other. He didn't, but she heard it anyway.

"Can I ask you something?" he asked after polishing off the rest of the taco tray.

She picked at the last few crumbs on her plate. "Yes."

He cocked his head. "You got engaged to Tyler after the incident with him and Raske. Why?"

"It's complicated." Caroline bit her straw, chewing on it a bit while organizing her thoughts. "A lot of it has to do with my father. He never had a son, and he made no secret of the fact he would have preferred one. He just couldn't wrap his head around leaving his hotel chain to a daughter. That was why he was so elated when I started seeing Liam. By that point, he was a big name in the hotel industry.

My father was relieved that there would be a man holding the reins when he was gone."

Isaac scoffed. "No offense, but your dad sounds like an ass."

"No, he was just…very set in his ways—very old-school Southern. The kind of man who didn't let his wife work and never intended for his daughter to follow in his footsteps. I was supposed to follow in my mother's footsteps, doing charity work, throwing parties, etcetera—all of which I still do by the way. But I always thought Father would come around about me running the hotel someday. In the end, he didn't have a choice."

He raised a brow. "I wonder why he didn't keep trying for a son if he thought it was that important."

Caroline shrugged. "I suppose he didn't have the heart to remarry after Mom passed. Anyway, when Liam suggested a platonic marriage—"

Isaac chose the wrong moment to take a sip. His *horchata* went down the wrong pipe. Eyes watering, he started coughing.

"Sorry," he said, wiping his mouth after he recovered. "Did, um, did Tyler think the two of you were going to be celibate?"

"Not exactly," she said. "He had it all planned out. His idea was that we'd be partners in the business and in any future children we had, but, in private, we'd go our separate ways. It was going to be very modern and Parisian."

His neck flexed as he grimaced. "And this sounded good to you?"

"He was such a huge part of my life and my business. And to be honest, I was scared of trying to do it alone." She shrugged. "So, I agreed."

Isaac reached for her hand. She tried to pull it back because her fingers were a little greasy, but he smiled and held on, playing with her fingertips. "How big a hit did the business take when things fell apart?"

Dear Lord, how could she even quantify that? "Big."

"Are you sure you don't want me to shoot him?"

"Quite sure," she said, rolling her eyes. "Besides, we still do business with the Tylers. The Wentworth and the Caislean chains have a reciprocal rewards system, where guests can earn points toward discounts and services. Since we're the smaller chain, it's to our benefit to maintain that. It brings in more business and adds prestige."

Isaac appeared disgruntled. "Damn. So, I really can't kick Tyler's ass to the curb?"

"I'm afraid not," she said, extracting her fingers and wiping them with a paper towel. "What about you? Am I ever going to hear the story on your divorce?"

He frowned. "If that's what you want, I'm game. However, I should warn you that it's a lot less interesting."

She picked up the Jamaica, taking a long pull from the straw. "Did you meet your wife in high school?"

"I did." He gave her a sardonic smile. "She was the prom queen."

Caroline giggled. "And were you her prom king?"

Isaac snorted. "Hell no." He held out his arm. Pulling up his sleeve, he showed off the edge of his tattoo. "I was the high school bad boy. Or, at least, I told myself I was."

His self-deprecation was charming. "Oh, I see. It was a case of opposites attract."

"With a romantic back story and everything," he confided. "See, she was dating the football team's running back. He was the school's biggest star. But the guy was full of himself and he didn't treat her well, so guess who came riding to her rescue?"

She had thought it impossible for him to be more attractive, but she'd been wrong. "The bad boy makes good."

"Something like that," he admitted with a sour expression. "But the drama that brought us together—it turned into a pattern. Things in her life would go wrong, and I would step in and straighten them out."

"That sounds...exhausting."

Isaac acknowledged that with a nod. "Honestly, I didn't recognize the pattern right away. Not until after I had been in the army and was finally working as a field agent for the bureau. I had so much going on. It was more responsibility than I had ever had in my life. I didn't understand why she wouldn't cut it out, why she was making my life so much harder than it had to be."

"Sounds rough." At least Liam had never intentionally sabotaged her.

"We started fighting more, little arguments that got bigger and bigger. Neither would let anything go." Isaac wiped his own hands, then tossed the napkin down on the tray. "I started putting in insane amounts of overtime because the apartment had become a war zone."

"So, you got divorced."

"Not right away. I wanted to try counseling. We went for a while, but then she stopped going. I guess I didn't put up much of a fuss about that. I had seen the writing on the wall. That was when she had the bright idea to fix things in one fell swoop by having a baby. I said no."

Caroline startled, sitting back on the bench. "Wait—she wanted to have a baby and you didn't?"

He reached out and took her hand. "Caroline, my ex-wife didn't want kids. Honestly, I don't think she likes them all that much. She was never interested in them before that. Not even my nieces. She was just after a quick fix."

The adrenaline spike started to fade. "I'm a little confused. After what you said the other day—what you offered—how can you be certain you want a baby now? What if—"

Isaac held up a hand to interrupt. "Caroline, I'm an uncle three times over," he said. "All my cousins have kids. I've been around children of all ages, at every stage of their development. I know I like them and want my own. And I would make a damn good father."

Well, that was decisive. "Oh," she said in a small voice. "Okay."

Isaac rose, holding out his hand. "I think that's enough strolling down memory lane for one night. Let's head back to the Luxe."

Caroline hesitated, but every part of her body wanted skin contact. *Holding hands will have to do.*

Twinning her fingers in his, she let him lead the way.

# CHAPTER TWENTY-TWO

Caroline let go of Isaac's hand when they arrived back at the Wentworth. She wanted to keep holding on, but she couldn't allow herself that freedom. Someone would see. And neither could afford to let that happen.

Today's events—seeing Liam and rehashing their old relationship with Isaac—had hollowed her out. She felt emotionally bruised but also lighter and free, like a deflated balloon that was about to bounce off a cliff.

However, she didn't have time to dwell on her feelings. Delfina, the night manager, spotted her and waved her over to make a report. She was with Stephan at the concierge desk.

"One other thing," Delfina said after giving Caroline a concise run-down. "The chef had a slight meltdown when the sous-chef didn't show up."

Caroline frowned, checking over the occupancy report on the manager's tablet. "What happened?"

"Food poisoning."

Her head snapped up. *"What?"*

Delfina held up a hand. "Don't worry, he didn't eat what made him sick here."

Relieved, Caroline's shoulders sagged and she blew out a breath. "Good. Did you get her some extra help?"

Ever since the hotel review had come out in the trade journal, local papers had been mentioning the hotel more and more. The reservations for their fine-dining restaurant had gone through the roof. Cerise Lions, the chef, liked to complain about it, but she secretly thrived on the stress.

"We had some trouble there," Delfina said cautiously. "It turns out the sous-chef had eaten out with some of the other kitchen staff. When we tried our one remaining alternate, we couldn't get through to her because she was ill as well. We ended up having to call in one of the grill cooks from the café."

*Oh God.* "What did Cerise do?" Caroline asked, waiting for the shoe to drop.

"The grill cook did a good job," Delfina said, patting her on the arm. "She ended up loving him and intends to poach him from the café—with your approval, of course."

"She can have him," Caroline decided, glad that disaster was averted. She was also pleased that her star chef was easy to appease. That had not always been the case. "Start looking for someone for the café."

"Will do, boss."

"I'm sorry to interrupt," Stephan said, his eyes fixed over her shoulder. "Did you need something, Mr. Rivera?"

Caroline glanced back. *Well, he is extremely hard to ignore.*

"I'm just waiting to walk Ms. Wentworth to her door."

"All right..." Stephan said slowly before turning back to his computer.

"Is everything all right with you, Stephan?" she asked. "No fires to report?"

"Not a one." He smiled a touch too broadly. "The guests kept the crazy requests down to a minimum today."

"That's always good news." Her mind already on tomorrow's tasks, she bade them goodnight.

Isaac fell in step behind her. They made it to her hallway without incident. However, it still felt as if there were dozens of eyes on them.

He must have sensed her reticence because he saw her to her door without trying to convince her to invite him in. "Good night, Caroline," he murmured before disappearing into her office.

Surprised and a little disappointed he hadn't tried to kiss her, Caroline entered her suite with a grunt. Heavy-hearted, she kicked off her heels, washing up and collapsing on the bed without enthusiasm.

She twisted to stare at the connecting door.

There was no reason in the world to open it. So much had happened today. Also, judging from his cursory goodbye, Isaac wasn't expecting her to invite him over tonight.

*It's actually kind of him*, she told herself. He was giving her space to figure things out. But why did that make her chest ache?

Why was this room so cold? The temperature on the alarm and weather station device she kept on her bedside table read seventy-eight degrees like always, but Caroline still felt chilled. The only time she felt warm these days was when Agent Rivera was around. It was as if she'd become addicted to his heat. Not that she had to touch him. Just being in the same room was enough to raise her temperature several degrees.

Groaning aloud, she flopped back on the bed, a flush enveloping her. *Or you can just think about him.* That worked, too.

*Open the door. For once in your life, stop overanalyzing everything and take what was being offered.* What was the worst that could happen? Aside from possibly getting her heart broken into smithereens all over again?

A person couldn't survive that twice.

Rolling on her stomach, she buried her face in the comforter, inhaling the clean crisp scent of the fabric softener.

*Ocean breeze.* She'd chosen it herself. She'd selected every item of furniture, decor, and cleaning supplies for the hotel because that was what she did.

Caroline was a planner. Sure, she was more detail-oriented than was good for her, but that was who she was. It was something she had come to terms with long ago.

However, this quality left her with two choices. She could set aside her carefully crafted plan for the future—possibly permanently. Or she could throw all reason out the window and open the connecting door.

Caroline rolled over and sat up. Her body flashed hot and cold, but she didn't let herself think as she flipped the deadbolt on her side. If she knocked loud enough, he would open up on the other side, right?

But she didn't have to knock. The second she swung the door open on her side, Isaac stepped through.

"Thank God." He caught her up in his arms.

Caroline yelped as his hands cupped her ass, picking her up off the floor. He buried his face against her neck, guiding her legs around his waist.

"I was beginning to think you were never going to open up," he said between kisses.

His mouth covered hers, taking possession.

Caroline sagged in his arms, all sense obliterated. His tongue invaded, licking the inside of her mouth, stroking and encouraging as his hands squeezed her cheeks, making her squirm against the bulge in his pants.

When he broke off and set her on the bed, she was panting.

Helpless, her eyes consumed him as he unbuttoned his shirt, pulling it off to reveal an expanse of bronze muscle so chiseled and defined it should have been in a museum. "This is insane," she whispered.

"Yeah, it is," Isaac said, stripping off his pants in a hurry.

Caroline was nonplussed. "I didn't think you were going to agree with me."

"I have been on the edge of insanity since I met you. I'm only glad I'm not in Crazy Town by myself."

"But—"

Fishing something out of his pocket, he came over her, pressing her down into the bed. He pressed his lips to the flutter of pulse at the base of her neck, licking it in a slow circle. "Crazy is what works for us," he said, the words muffled against her skin.

His mouth covered hers again, a searing caress that melted her bones until she was a limp pool of melted wax.

"*Isaac,*" she whimpered.

He held up his fingers, showing her what he'd taken out of his pocket. It was the last condom.

"Wait." Caroline pushed on his shoulders, urging him to roll until they had reversed positions. He didn't complain when she sat on his six-pack.

Her breath was short, her vision narrowing on the condom. Acting on impulse, she plucked the foil packet from his fingers. It felt like the small square was the only thing she could see.

*Think about what you're doing.*

Isaac stroked her hips, his hand coming to rest on the nape of her neck. "Babe, calm down. I bought more protection—and not at the gift shop either. You can have more time."

"Shush," Caroline squeaked, covering his mouth with her free hand. "I'm making a life-changing decision here."

Isaac's lips pressed shut under her finger. She half-expected him to make a joke, but his eyes were serious, his glorious body still beneath her. He just held her, his thumb stroking the sensitive skin at the base of her neck.

A shudder passed through her.

He opened his lips, shifting them enough so he could talk. "Whatever you decide, I'm here for it."

"I know." Her heart was racing so fast that it was threatening to burst out of her chest.

Winding up like a pitcher, Caroline threw the condom across the room. It hit the connecting door, then slid down to the carpet with a small scuffing sound.

Frozen, she stared at it as if she'd just hurled a priceless Baccarat against the wall.

Isaac touched her cheek. He wore the expression of a man talking a jumper off a ledge. "Do you want to go get it?" he asked slowly.

Tongue suddenly too thick for her mouth, Caroline managed the tiniest shake of her head.

"That's...that's good then," he said, bringing them together until his forehead touched hers. He pressed his lips to her cheek, grazing her jawline.

His touch was tender and sweet. It helped slow her racing heart, filling her body with hot molasses. Panic receding, Caroline began to kiss and stroke him back.

Isaac's hands skimmed over the silk of her nightgown and beyond, lingering on the satiny skin of her thighs and the insides of her arms.

Determined to be an equal participant, Caroline began to nibble at Isaac's neck, making him groan aloud.

"Naked," he urged, tugging at her nightgown. "I need you naked."

Lifting her arms, she let him peel off the slip. Then he pressed her back on the mattress. "Your skin is softer than the silk," he said, laughing softly. "I'm not even joking."

She wanted to reply, but she was too breathless—he had moved down her body to suckle her breasts. Isaac lavished his attention on them, his roughly calloused hands continuing to touch, sweeping over her every curve until she was squirming, pushing her hips against him reflexively.

The sound Isaac made in his throat made her insides cliché. "I want to taste you."

She clutched at him, digging her fingers into his waistband to try to pull his boxers down. "After, *please*. I need you inside me now."

Isaac made a rough sound in his throat. Tearing at his boxers, he pushed them down. His hot, steely length landed in her hands. She pumped him twice, and he swore aloud. "Guide me in, baby."

Shivering Caroline did just that. Isaac hissed, the tip of him dipping into her heat. He took hold of her hands, carrying her back down to the mattress as he slid home.

The sensation of him, so thick and hard sliding into her, filling her up was almost too much to bear.

"Holy shit," he whispered. "The feel of you..."

"I know," she gasped, her arms tightening around his chest. "I *know*."

She hadn't expected to be able to tell the difference, but having his naked length inside her was hotter, more intense than she could have imagined.

His mouth took hers again, but his tenderness was gone, blown away by the force of the fire between them. Caroline didn't care—she was just as rough, just as hungry as he was. They grappled, each trying to ravish the other. But it was greed that gave and fed the flames.

Caroline stroked every inch of his skin that she could reach, worshiping hard planes and contours that were already starting to grow familiar.

Isaac swore. "I'm sorry. I can't last," he panted, riding her with hard and fast strokes.

Caroline tightened her legs, moving them higher on his waist to give his hips more room. "I'm so close," she managed to say in between ragged gasps. "Do it just like this. Take me like this always."

"*Fuck.*" His face was pulled back so tight that she couldn't tell whether he was feeling pain or pleasure. "I don't deserve you."

Caroline laughed, tears in her eyes as she fell off the edge, pushed over by his ruthless thrusts. Her entire body bowed, spasming and trembling as she clamped down on his hard shaft.

His hand fisted in her hair, rhythm breaking as the last vestiges of his willpower burned away. Pinning her to the mattress, he pistoned a little slower, grinding his hips against her as his orgasm overtook him and his cock throbbed, his hot seed jetting in strong spurts.

She held on to his shoulders tightly, expecting the last ripples of ecstasy to dwindle and die away only to be hit by another tremor, like an aftershock in an earthquake that was almost as strong as the quake.

When Caroline finally managed to unclench her hands, Isaac had collapsed on top of her. But she didn't mind. The pressure of his body on hers was the most luscious weight.

Surreptitiously rubbing her cheek against the smooth skin of his chest, Caroline held Isaac until he rolled over, taking her with him. He stayed inside her, running his hands down her back until she tugged his arm up so she could trace the lines of his tattoo with her fingers.

Sated and lax, they held each other, both unwilling as the other to stop touching, fondling and brushing every bit of each other they could reach. At least until a sudden thought occurred.

Her head snapped up. "The sheets."

Startled, Isaac's head pressed back into the pillow. "What?"

Caroline sat up and looked around the bed in dismay. "I don't make the bed. The maids change the sheets. They're going to know we're sleeping together."

Isaac pressed his lips together, but a small huff escaped.

She narrowed her eyes. "You think this is funny, don't you?"

The cords on his neck grew more prominent. "No. It's you—your movement. It's…stimulating."

"Oh." Caroline looked down at his rapidly stiffening length. "Already?"

He propped himself against the headboard. One hand snuck up to squeeze her breast, the other cupped her face. His thumb grazed her lower lip.

"Look at how beautiful you are, flushed and fucked by me. How could I *not* get hard again? Christ, every time I see you, it's like I'm fourteen again. Now that I know what it's like to have that tight and pretty pink pussy wrapped around me bare, I can pretty much guarantee I'm going to be a permanent walking hard-on." He pressed a kiss to her neck. "Every time you pass me in the hall, that's the deal. Just a warning."

Caroline bit back a giggle. The blunt speech should have been a turn-off. However, coming from such a controlled and roughly masculine man, in that deep drawl, just made her shudder with renewed hunger.

She rubbed her forehead against him like a cat, unable to stop herself. "Warning noted."

"Good." He stroked a long line down her hip, palming her cheek possessively. "And don't worry about the sheets. I'll take care of it."

Craning his neck forward, he nipped her lower lip before sucking it into his mouth and licking the bite. "But since the sheets will need to be changed, let's make the most of these—because I'm not done with you yet. Not by a long shot."

# CHAPTER TWENTY-THREE

A few days later, Isaac kept trying to read a report from the bureau on his phone, but he couldn't focus on it. He was too busy watching Caroline with the guy from *Hotelier Magazine*.

*She's fine*, he told himself. This was her victory lap. And this journalist wasn't one of the pricks who'd excoriated her in the press when she sold some of her hotels. Isaac had checked him out before letting Janet schedule the meeting.

No one saw the boss without getting cleared by him. Her assistant understood that. Every time Caroline had to meet someone new, Janet sent him their name and business affiliation. Which was how he knew this particular man was one of Caroline's biggest fans. In fact, he had always written a little too enthusiastically about her…

And as long as his enthusiasm was restricted to the written word, Isaac wouldn't have to toss the smitten man in the pool, an impulse he was actively curbing at the moment.

Walking a discreet twenty paces behind, he followed as Caroline gave the guy the grand tour—starting with the lobby and adjoining seaside bar and café. Isaac switched over to the camera feeds when she took the man to the kitchens and the spa, but, somehow, she knew he'd been watching the whole time.

"Why didn't you just tackle him?" she hissed, a fake smile plastered on her face as she cornered him near the café after the reporter had left.

"Tackle who?" he asked blandly, wishing Caroline weren't so adorable when she was mad. It made it so much harder to look contrite.

When she continued to glare, he withdrew his peace offering from the counter behind him—a perfectly prepared skim-milk cappuccino with two raw sugars.

He'd asked the barista to prepare it when Caroline began her goodbyes with the magazine man. After the way he skulked after the pair, Isaac had known she'd come looking for him.

"You know full well who I mean," she said from behind set teeth. "You can't lurk in the background being menacing just because I am talking to another man—one you knew was here to interview me, I might add."

"I look menacing?" he asked, fluttering his lashes, a picture of innocence.

"You know you do."

"What did I do that was menacing?"

"You—you stand there all muscular and intimidating." She gestured at his biceps in exasperation. "Do I have to remind you that we are in the service industry? Try smiling occasionally."

"Like this?" he asked, giving her his most lascivious grin.

"*No.* Not like that." Caroline blushed, twisting around to see if anyone were watching them.

"I did give you space to complete your tour, didn't I? Even after he asked if he could take extra pictures of you by the pool…" The man hadn't been stupid enough to suggest she change into a bathing suit, but only because he valued his life.

Caroline rubbed her temples. "That was for the feature. He suggested the first pictures he took of me behind my desk would be too staid, and he had a point."

"He had plenty of candids of you from the tour." Isaac scowled. "He was snapping your picture every other minute. I'm surprised your vision isn't compromised by all the flash photos."

Caroline gripped the tablet in her hands as if she were fighting the urge to hit him with it. "You know he didn't use the flash. And can I ask why you even felt the need to follow us around, as if Roy hadn't been pre-vetted? Isn't that why you run everyone who meets with me through a gauntlet of security checks?"

She had him there. He took a sip of his coffee, then licked some cappuccino foam off his upper lip. "No comment."

Caroline's eyes strayed to his mouth and stayed there, obviously derailing her train of thought. "You can't start treating me different because I'm—because we—because you're going to be…"

She kept tripping over the sentence, her color heightening. Isaac took pity on her…after a fashion. "I believe the term you're looking for is 'your baby daddy'."

It was unfortunate that she'd chosen that moment to take a sip of her coffee. Hacking and coughing, Caroline spit cappuccino all over her cream-colored blazer.

Three of the lobby staff, including the concierge, came out of the woodwork, cleaning cloths or towels in hand.

Caroline accepted a napkin from Stephan. "Coughed at the wrong time. Thank you." Red-faced, she dabbed at her blouse.

"Good thing you already had your photoshoot, boss," Stephan pointed out.

"Yes, that is lucky." Caroline thanked the staff, excusing herself. "I should go change."

Isaac started to follow her when Stephan cocked his head. "Are you going to help her change?" he asked with a leer.

Isaac's blistering glance wiped the smirk off the man's face. Ignoring the comment, Isaac nodded at the guest waiting at the concierge desk. "You have a customer waiting."

Isaac hurried to catch up to Caroline, grateful she hadn't caught that. He was already in hot water.

Once she reached her office, she saw Janet and turned to hide the coffee stain, making a beeline for her office so he could follow her inside.

Isaac paused, a feeling of satisfaction washing over him when she walked through the connecting bedroom door.

Leaning on the doorjamb, he watched her strip off her stained blazer and shirt with barely concealed lust. "Isn't having the connecting door unlocked so much more convenient?"

"That door was closed for a reason. I was trying to maintain a work-life balance," she informed him, tugging off her blazer and throwing it at his head.

Isaac pulled it off, giving her a wicked once-over as she stripped off the pink blouse. "So, it was purely symbolic?"

Caroline huffed, her eyes going from her blouse to the door. "We've only been whatever we are for a few days now, and already it feels like the ground is turning to quicksand beneath me."

"Aww, poor Caroline." Isaac tugged her into his arms. "A woman with the body of a goddess now has someone worshiping her every night, and she's having trouble coping."

"You're terrible." Stern-faced, she pushed him away, but he could tell her heart wasn't in it.

Her lips parted when he backed away, taking her bra with him.

"How did you do that?" she asked, covering her creamy breasts with her hands.

"What?" he asked innocently. "It had coffee on it. You have to take it off, or you'll be all sticky."

He started toward her, but he must have been broadcasting his bad intentions a little too clearly because Caroline ran to the other side of the bed. She wagged a finger. "Don't you dare."

"Why not?" He laughed, kicking off his shoes and crawling over the bed. He stopped in the middle, then started to unbutton his shirt. "Magazine boy was your last meeting for the day."

"I still have things to do..." Caroline's voice trailed off as he stripped off his shirt. Her eyes skittered over his chest, fixing on his arm. Yeah, the tattoo really did it for her...

"You have to clean up first. I'll help," he said generously.

Isaac hopped on the other side of the bed, walking forward,

prowling toward her. Catching her breath, she backed up until she was pressed against the wall.

Caging her with his arms, he stared at her lips until they parted, her head tilted up in expectation of a kiss.

Laughing, he buried his face between her breasts instead.

"*Isaac*," she gasped, trying to push him away with a giggle.

Picking her up, he tumbled her on the bed. "I promised to clean you up. I just neglected to mention I was going to use my tongue."

True to his word, he held her giggling, squirming body while licking her up and down. Caroline laughed so hard that she started wheezing. Giving her a little time to recover, he lay on his side, stroking her body until she caught her breath.

"Hey, I have an idea. Are you busy on Saturday?"

Caroline lifted a shoulder. "Always. I run a hotel. Several, actually."

He gave her a 'yeah, yeah' hand motion. "Well, do you think you can get away *this* Saturday?"

Her fingers reached for his arm, tracing his ink. "Like for a date?"

He pursed his lips. "Sort of. We'd be driving up to Irvine, outside of L.A. And we'll have to leave by eleven to get there in time."

Her brows puckered. "So, not a date?"

He kissed the line between her eyes. "Just a break."

"Will I enjoy it?"

"Uh…" He gave that some serious thought. "To be honest, I'm not sure. But it's important to me."

The line reappeared between her brows. "Can I ask you a serious question?"

"Yeah?"

"Will there be more guns?"

He guffawed. "No…but you might be wishing you had one at some point."

Now she was confused. "To use on who?"

"Me, of course. Who else?"

"Who else indeed?" Caroline shut her eyes. But they flew open when she felt his mouth traveling south.

"What are you doing?" she gasped.

He looked up from between her thighs. "I thought that was obvious." He tsked. "Now I know for sure Tyler was a shit boyfriend."

"It wasn't—" Caroline bit her lip, fighting back a ladylike snicker.

Isaac nudged her knee with head. "None of that. In this bed, you hold back on nothing. What were you going to say?"

She hesitated but then groaned and let it out. "That part of my relationship with Liam isn't something I want to talk about..."

"But..." he prompted.

"But our sex life was probably better for him."

"Tell me something I don't know," Isaac said, the corner of his mouth turning up.

"I mean that it wasn't his fault. Not all of it. I had a hard time relaxing with him. I was stressed out all the time."

Isaac abandoned his position between her knees. What possible reason could this golden goddess have to be stressed? "Why? Was he an asshole?"

"No." Caroline searched for the right words. She picked at her coverlet. "It wasn't him. It was me with him. I'd had a boyfriend by then, but he was my first serious relationship. And I was younger— not by a gross amount, but enough that I felt insecure."

Isaac grunted. There was a hell of a lot he wanted to say to that, but now was not the time.

"He's the kind of man people defer to," she continued. "People flock to him. They either want his business or his connections—or they just want him. But I was the one on his arm."

*Ah.* That must have been nerve-wracking. "All eyes were on you," he said, filling in the blanks. There had no doubt been a lot of catty bitches waiting in the wings, ready to tear her down. Remembering the countdown clock, he hoped she hadn't read the gossip rags or blogs at the time. *Never read the comments.* A rule to live by.

"Even in private, it was hard to relax," she said with a sigh, staring at the ceiling.

"Not even during..."

"I was always worried about how I looked—my makeup, my hair," she confessed. "It's so stupid in retrospect."

Isaac scooted his way up the bed, wrapping his arms around her so he could kiss the back of her neck. "In case you haven't noticed, I like you just the way you are—makeup or no makeup. As long as you're willing to get sweaty with me, I couldn't care less if you've got on lipstick or foundation."

She pinched his side. "Looking perfect is an idea I've outgrown, although I still have to keep up appearances during working hours."

He thought of the amount of effort she put into her appearance. It was part of her job. She was the face of an entire hotel chain, but now he realized part of the effort would always be fueled by insecurity and old wounds.

Men had it so much easier.

Well, even he had his scars. "No one gets out of a relationship entirely unscathed. I have a list of shit that might set me off after my divorce—remind me to write it down for you sometime."

She turned to face him, brushing her lips against his collarbone. Used to being the instigator, he stilled, half-afraid that if he appeared to enjoy it too much, she would stop.

"Isaac, will you please take these off?" Caroline asked, pushing at the waistband of his pants.

The politely voiced request nearly undid him. "For future reference, this is something you never have to ask," he said before pressing his mouth against the soft skin near her ear. "Consider this me consenting to anything and everything you ever want to do to me."

She laughed as he wiggled out of his pants and boxers at warp speed. He stripped her with rough but efficient moves.

Then she took hold of his dick, and things got serious fast.

Her hold was tentative, uncertain. Holding his breath as she stroked him experimentally, he stayed still, up until she inched her body close enough to press her lips to the tip of his cock.

Isaac fisted a hand in her hair as she opened her mouth to lick the underside of the flared head, her tongue playing with the rim, keeping her big blue eyes on him the entire time. Already hard before she touched him, he swelled impossibly more until he was threatening to spill over in her hands.

Unable to take any more sensual torture, Isaac grabbed her wrist. "I shouldn't be this close to coming, but you are too fucking sexy. Give me a minute."

A wicked glint in her eye, Caroline ran her teeth over her plush lower lip before leaning forward to take the whole head of his cock into her mouth.

Isaac gritted his teeth. "You are a bad girl," he wheezed.

Giggling around her mouthful, she sucked him hard before letting go of him with a pop. The last shred of his willpower broke, and he gathered her in his arms. "I'm going to get you back for that with a pussy-eating session that's going to make you scream, but it has to be after. I need to be inside you *now*." Pressing his lips to her ear, he said, "Only this time, you're going to be riding me."

She squeaked as he gripped her, pulling her over his lap. When Caroline's silky buttocks came to rest on his thighs, he groaned, putting his knees up to rock her against his aching length.

Sucking her nipple in his mouth, palming her ass cheeks, he savored the satiny feel of her. Caroline took his mouth, her tongue licking and teasing as she shifted to take him inside. Hissing, he gripped her tight as his dick was enveloped by her snug wet sheath.

"Hell, yes." Neck still corded with the effort not to take over, he urged her to start riding him. He had to fight from swearing as her gorgeous tits began to bounce in time with her pulsing sheath. It was better than every X-rated fantasy he'd ever had of her—and he'd had a lot.

"That's it, baby," he purred. "I love feeling you so slick and tight around me. Now fuck me however you want—slow and tight or hard and fast."

He broke off, closing his eyes as she threw her hips back, taking him whole and squeezing him hard every time she came down. "All right," he said his voice hoarse. "Fast and tight works, too. *Christ.* I can feel all of you, like hot silk. It's too damn good…"

Using his hold in her hair to bring them close, he pressed his forehead to hers, his free hand tight on her ass. She bounced up and down, little noises escaping her that made him want more, but louder.

He was starting to burn, the blistering pleasure at his dick traveling up his spine. "Fucking beautiful," he ground out between soul-stealing French kisses.

She was starting to get that that expression again, the slightly scared one that told him she didn't quite believe what she was doing.

Wrapping his arms around her, he pressed her down harder, throwing his hips up at her in deep, hard lunges. He waited until she began to shudder, her little whimpers growing more urgent and higher in pitch, before he buried his hands in her hair.

"That's it," he panted, his vision starting to fuzz as he worked his length in and out of her, his willpower nearly exhausted. "Fucking come all over my cock *now*," he said, roughly pulling her against his hips.

Her rhythm broke and Caroline cried out, tightening and flexing around him. The taste and feel of her in his mouth combined with the viselike grip of her sheath—it was all too much. Isaac pressed Caroline close, pinning her as he ground their bodies together, flooding her with his seed with a wrenching gasp.

Moaning, Caroline collapsed against him, little shivers racking her body. She mumbled something against his chest.

Helping her out, he picked up her head. "You still need to breathe, my *princessa*."

"Don't call me princess." She poked him, panting between words.

His chest moving up and down, too out of breath to chuckle. He stroked her cheek, holding her close. "Right now, you can ask me for anything. I'd call you Galactic High Emperor if that's what you wanted."

Her lips parted as she searched for a polite response. "Thank you, but, uh, I think I'll pass."

"Then how does My Queen sound?"

Caroline raised her head, her swollen lips and flushed cheeks making him hot again. "Now that works for me."

§

Isaac was a little nervous as he drove Caroline up the I-5 Saturday morning. Even though they slept together every night now, it was still difficult to find time to be alone. Caroline worked so hard for such long hours that he kept the sex to two rounds max, because he didn't want to rob her of too much sleep. That kind of restraint was hard for him, though, given that all he wanted to do whenever he saw her was fuck her against the nearest wall.

Even now, he was tempted to pull the car over and find some secluded place where he could have his way with her. Then he'd hold her while she told him about her day.

He was a bit surprised that he enjoyed discussing all of that with her—working at the hotel had given him an insider's perspective on the hotel business. Isaac liked finding solutions to problems, and he knew people. Whenever personality conflicts arose among the staff, he could usually dissect the problem just as well as Caroline.

"Let me handle some of these people," he'd told her the other day when it seemed like everyone and their mother had wanted five minutes with her. "It's only a matter of time before they take over everything Luxe, right?" he'd pointed out. "It's better if they get used to flying without a net."

"Yes, but not all my appointments and phone conferences are about *this* hotel. There are a few others that require my attention, too."

She had stopped what she was doing, going over some figures her assistant Janet had just given her, her expression naked in its anxiety. "Once the Luxe is ready to run without direct supervision, I should resume visiting the others. I used to divide at least half the year among them equally."

She'd looked so worried that he couldn't help going to touch her. He went around the desk, pulling her into his arms. "You'll let me know when that is so I can book airfare."

"What about—"

"You are my priority, in my case and currently in my life."

Those crystal blue eyes searched his. "What happens when you have to go back to Boston?"

"You don't have any hotels in Boston?"

"*Isaac*. You—"

"Let me worry about tomorrow," he said, stroking her soft hair, the shade like gold that had been heated until it glowed white-hot. "I have some things in the works that need to be wrapped up before I can answer your questions . Otherwise, I'd be guessing or making shit up."

Caroline hadn't liked that dodge any more than he'd enjoyed making it. But she'd accepted that he couldn't say anything yet.

As for the hotel, he hadn't succeeded in taking half the load, as intended, but he did manage to talk her into delegating more of those matters to the managers, both day and night.

Caroline spent the last hour of the drive on her phone, her fingers flying as she texted back answers to her loyal subjects.

"Are you ever going to tell me where we're going?" she asked for the fifth time after finally setting her phone aside.

"I could, but we'll be there in another minute or so," he said, pulling off the highway at the familiar exit.

"Who lives here? A friend from the bureau?" Caroline asked as he squeezed into a narrow space in front of the neat two-story house. A bunch of pink and purple balloons had been tied to the front door light fixture. " And why all the cloak and dagger? Is it someone in witness protection? "

"Oh, no. This is going to be full of people way scarier than that," he teased. "You're about to meet my family."

# CHAPTER TWENTY-FOUR

*"What?"* Caroline had intended to shriek, but her voice came out in a hoarse squeak instead.

Placatingly, Isaac held up his hands. "It's going to be all right."

"Why didn't you warn me?" she cried, running her palms over her simple summer dress. "I'm not dressed to meet your family."

"You look amazing."

"No, I don't." She clutched at her skirt, a full A-line that fell well below the knees. "This dress is too low cut."

He laughed. "Only a wimple would cover you more, and that would be weird in this heat. What you're wearing is more than fine— my younger sister will be wearing way less, unfortunately. Trust me on that. You're perfect."

Caroline shot him a look appropriate for negotiations with a deranged clown. "I had no idea your family was even on this coast. Why didn't you tell me?"

He reached out and touched her cheek. "I didn't want you to freak out. But this isn't a big deal. It will be mayhem, but that is par for the course at my family's gatherings. I told you at some point that I have twin nieces. Well, today is their fifth birthday."

Isaac pointed at the house. "My older sister Sonia lives here with her husband of three years. The twins she had with another guy. If the bio-dad decides to show his face, there will be fireworks because he's an immature prick. My sister Brittany will be here with her latest boyfriend—a guy with enough piercings to set off unplugged metal detectors. I haven't met him in person yet, but if he's anything like the last one, there will be at least one public spat when he doesn't read her mind or says something stupid. This doesn't include the soap-opera-quality drama that will be provided by my aunts, uncles, and cousins."

He stroked a hand over the skin of her cheek and neck. "You might be an object of curiosity for a few minutes, but it won't last."

She felt as if she were going to be sick. "Who else will be here? Your mother and father?"

"Just my mother. My dad took off ages ago. He's not in the picture."

"Oh." Caroline winced. "You never mentioned that. All you've ever said is that you have a big extended family."

He took her hand. "Sorry, I haven't gone into that much detail. I would have eventually, but this party came up so fast and I'm finally within driving distance. As for my dad—he's kind of a deadbeat. I don't think about him much at all."

Her lips parted, and she gestured to encompass him with her free hand. "So, *this* came from an all-female household?"

Isaac grinned. "I was surrounded."

She gave him a tiny smile, but her heart was beating too fast for true levity. "We don't even have any gifts."

"Sure we do." He gestured back with his thumb. "It's in the trunk. And it has both of our names on it."

"What is it?" she asked, getting out of the car.

"Something *My Little Pony*." He shrugged, exiting and coming around to her side. "It was on their wish list."

"I guess that works." Caroline stared at the house, feeling as if it were going to spew the creatures from *Alien* at any minute. "But you should have told me about this. I have several darling children's boutiques bookmarked on my computer. I could have bought them something special."

He threw an arm around her. "And have you bought any baby clothes yet?"

"No," she said primly. "That would be premature."

He was about to ask something else when the door flew open and an attractive Hispanic woman in her mid-twenties stepped out, her hands on her hips. "Are you going to stand out here until the twins turn six instead?" she called from the front stoop.

"We'll be right there," Isaac called back with a wave. "I'm just going to get the gift."

The woman snapped a hand towel in their direction. "And bring that poor woman you doubtless tricked into coming today inside."

Startled, Caroline jerked her eyes up to Isaac's face as the woman —presumably Sonia—had stepped back inside. "Did you tell her?"

"Nah." He wrinkled his nose, fishing the gift out of the trunk. "She just knows me."

"You have nothing to worry about," he assured Caroline, tucking the present wrapped in festive unicorn wrapping paper under his arm. He put his free hand on the small of her back, propelling her toward the door. "They won't start dissecting everything about you until after we leave."

"Great," Caroline muttered.

It was strange. Caroline had grown up in the hotel industry. She'd had every rule about hospitality drummed into her before she could spell her own name. She had mingled with British and Saudi royalty and second-generation crime lords. She'd negotiated big-ticket deals at dinner and cocktail parties.

A children's birthday party should have been no problem, but judging from the way her heart was racing, her body was having a hard time believing that.

# CHAPTER TWENTY-FIVE

It had probably been a bad idea to spring his entire family on Caroline without preparing her. It was an even worse one to bring her to the lion's den when he hadn't seen any of his relatives in person for over six months.

As soon as they cleared the front hall, they were swarmed. Two aunts and a slew of cousins—most under four feet tall—broke over them like a tidal wave of hugs and sticky kisses.

Caroline shuffled to the side in self-protection, looking more awkward and uncomfortable than he'd ever seen her.

"Who are you?" one of the shrimps asked her when his assembled relatives let him come up for air.

"This is Caroline," he said, raising his voice so everyone inside the house could hear him. "She's my friend. I tricked her into coming here today, so everybody needs to be extra nice."

Caroline shot him an exasperated glare as she very formally offered his six-year-old cousin her hand to shake. "Hi, it's nice to meet you."

The shrimp found that hilarious. "Hello!" she chirped, twisting behind her to shout to the others. "Everyone, come shake hands."

A line of giggling small people dutifully formed behind her.

Caroline smiled down at them, her expression equal parts charmed and bemused. "It's the novelty," Isaac apologized.

In his family, children under five were nearly smothered with affectionate kisses on a routine basis. Handshaking was what grownups did, and, even then, it was usually on television—his people were huggers.

Once they ran the Lilliputian gauntlet, he ushered Caroline to the central point in the house, a spacious living room with screened French doors. His nieces left these perpetually open to the backyard. Directly across from the doors was a large passthrough window that opened onto the kitchen. Excited by the pretty newcomer, the kids followed her like she was the pied piper.

Delia, his six-year-old cousin, took his hand, tugging. He crouched so she could whisper in his ear. "No, she's not a princess," he corrected gently, grinning up at Caroline. "At least she's not *that* princess, but I'm sure that one will be here soon to paint your face."

His mother appeared at the kitchen door, shooing the girls outside with a few words.

Grinning at her stern expression, Isaac bodily picked her up and swung her around. *"Hola, mamá."*

His mother fussed until he put her down.

*"Hola,* he says, after months and months of nothing from you and now, suddenly, it's *hola."*

If she'd had a *chancla,* she would have hit him with it.

"I call you every week," he protested, giving her a loud, smacking kiss on the cheek.

"Not every week," Mirna Rivera groused, giving Caroline a once-over as she stood across the room being monopolized by his younger sister.

"Let me introduce you to my guest," he said, dragging Caroline forward. *"Mamá,* this is Caroline, Caroline, this is my mother, Mirna."

"It's a pleasure to meet you," Caroline said, her smile a little too wide and bright.

"Welcome," his mother said, bemused. She introduced Sonia and

Brittney, nudging his sisters forward pointedly. Taking the hint, Brit offered to give Caroline a quick tour of the ground floor.

"And who is this woman?" his mother asked, lowering her voice and switching to Spanish as Caroline was led away, being too well-mannered to shoot him a dirty look for allowing his relatives to separate them right off the bat.

"My new girlfriend," he said with a boyish grin. "Just don't tell my boss."

"*Una huera?*" his mother scoffed. "Are you serious? And why can't your boss know?"

"I'll get into that. But trust me, you're going to love her."

His mother rolled her eyes. "First a Dominican and now a white woman. How hard is it to find a nice Mexican girl? Can she at least cook?"

"I have no idea," Isaac confessed. "Caroline is too busy to cook for herself or anyone else—she runs a hotel."

"And you think she'll love her why?" Sonia said, waving the spatula streaked with pink icing a little too close for comfort.

He snatched the kitchen tool out of her hand, licking one side.

"*Hey,*" Sonia protested.

"It's self-defense." He grinned. "My shirt was in danger. As for why Mom will love Caroline, let me answer that with another question. Did Gabby bring her new baby?"

Sonia frowned. "Why would she leave her at home?" she asked, pointing out the cousin in question through the sliding glass doors. The young mother was juggling the four-month-old girl while simultaneously trying to feed her three-year-old son.

He grinned. "Let me demonstrate."

Isaac grabbed a soft drink, then went to rescue Caroline from Brittney. They went to greet everyone outside, including his brother-in-law at the grill. The round of kissing and hugging was repeated for the relatives who had missed it at the entrance, giving the general impression that it had been ten years since he'd seen them and not just last Christmas.

Somewhere in the melee, he plucked his newest baby cousin out of her mother's arms on the pretense of helping. Then he ushered Caroline back inside.

"Can you hold this for me?" he asked her.

She held out her hand, clearly expecting the soft drink in his left hand. She got a baby instead.

"*Oh.*" Caroline's face was a mix of awe and surprise. She cradled the baby, rocking instinctively. "I can hold it?" she asked as if she hadn't been wistfully eyeing the baby the moment she saw it.

"You can hold her," he said, booping the baby's nose, making the little one gurgle. "Her name is Teresa, and she loves to be held."

Isaac took her elbow, guiding Caroline to the couch and urging her down so she could focus on the baby. "I think there are at least two other babies expected at this shindig. Enjoy."

Caroline shot him a glare, but it was clear her heart wasn't in it. She was in her happy place. Cooing, she went back to stroking fat cheeks and trying not to look too obvious as she leaned in to smell the baby's hair.

He went back to the kitchen where his mother was putting candles on the cake, watching the whole interaction through the pass-through window. His aunt joined her, and they started gossiping in voices too low for him to hear.

Allowing them to talk about Caroline, he joined Sonia at the refrigerator. "Beer me, sis."

"Did you bring that woman here to discourage her baby-making plans?" his sister whispered. "Because I'm not sure you can get Teresa to cry on command unless you pinch her, and I don't condone that sort of thing."

Chuckling, he shook his head. "On the contrary, my plans are far more nefarious."

"What does that mean?"

Isaac avoided looking directly into her disapproving eyes. "Let's just say I've gotten on board with Caroline's plan."

His sister frowned. Her face transformed as the light dawned. "Holy *shit*. You mean literally."

She punched him in the arm. "I don't believe this. You wouldn't even talk about having kids with your ex."

"That was different." His expression tightened. "You know that was just her way of slapping a band-aid on our problems. But Caroline wants a baby more than anything. She loves them, and I…I want to give her what she wants."

Isaac turned to look at the woman who'd turned his life upside down and inside out without even trying. She was talking to the baby earnestly as if they were having a serious conversation—a gorgeous woman and a baby. They were so adorable that it made his heart hurt as if the sight was forcibly rewriting its rhythm, reworking it for a new purpose.

"She's the one," he murmured. He didn't even question it anymore. Somewhere along the line, Caroline had become a rock-solid certainty. He just needed to convince her of that.

Their baby was only the first step.

"How convenient," Sonia snorted after processing. "A rich, gorgeous blonde falls into your lap while you are investigating your career-making case. Your ridiculously charmed life holds."

She smacked him on the arm for emphasis, getting pink icing on his shirt. "That or you made a deal with the devil. You didn't run into any dogs with glowing red eyes on a dirt road in the middle of the night, did you?"

Isaac snickered. He had been obsessed with that old wife's tale as a boy.

Sonia looked him up and down and sighed. "Are you sure you known what you're doing?"

"Yes, I do." Isaac craned his neck for a better look. "And even if I didn't, it seems I jumped off this cliff some time ago."

He caught her concerned expression, then smiled reassuringly. "What do you need help with?" he asked, redirecting her focus.

Her expression resigned, his sister gestured in the direction of the five-gallon orange drink dispenser filled with *Jamaica*. "Start by putting that outside on the food table. And when you're done with that, the twins wanted to rearrange their room—again—and Tony could use some help moving the beds."

Pulling her in, he gave her a hard hug. "I missed you, *cabrona*."

His sister sighed, leaning into him. "Me too, *cabron*," she said before pushing him toward the drink dispenser.

He hoisted the plastic cooler up on a shoulder and saluted. "Out of the way, *pollitos,* unless you want me to step on you with my big feet!" he called out, scattering the children who'd gathered at the threshold.

Screaming with delight, the rugrats scattered as he stomped and growled like a monster, clearing the path so he could leave the kitchen.

Five hours later, he was putting an exhausted but happy Caroline back in the car.

Her dress was stained and she was a bit sticky, but she'd been adopted by his nieces. Caroline had been given the grandest of honors by being shown the inner sanctum—their bedroom. Not only that, but she'd held two of his infant cousins for most of the afternoon, giving the babies' respective mothers a much-needed break.

To say that she had been a hit was an understatement. True, his family wasn't the type to say as much out loud, but Brittany and Sonia had friended Caroline on Facebook and that was almost as good.

She buckled her seat belt before collapsing in the seat. "Isn't Teresa the sweetest baby? She's so well behaved."

"You mean sleepy and quiet," he observed with a smile. "I sometimes wonder what my cousin Gabby puts in that baby formula."

Caroline tsked. "Teresa was perfectly alert. Her interaction and engagement seemed right on par for a baby her age."

Bemused, he turned to study her. Caroline lifted a shoulder. "I've been reading baby books."

"Ah. That's a good idea," he said, turning on the car and getting on the road. "You should let me borrow some."

She gave him one of those I'm-worried-about-the-future looks, but she didn't have the energy for that conversation, so she remained quiet.

"Will you freak out if we don't go back tonight?" he asked impulsively. "We could look for a place to stay near here—not a hotel. Maybe an Airbnb?"

Her expression told him how bad he'd miscalculated.

"An Airbnb?" Caroline cried. "Do you have any idea what those are doing to the hotel industry?"

Isaac tried not to laugh. His failure to hide his amusement earned him an earful. "You are beautiful when you're riled," he said when she was done cursing him out as genteelly as possible.

"Riled?" she scoffed. "Sometimes, you talk like a sailor while other times you sound like you're from the fifties."

"I watched a lot of old movies growing up. And don't worry, I'm taking you back to the Luxe. You'll probably turn into a pumpkin if I don't."

Caroline replied with something that was likely very snarky in return, but it was too mangled by a huge yawn to decipher.

"Settle back, princess," he soothed. "You can nap the whole way back if you want."

"I'll be fine, too, if you want to split the driving," Caroline offered, sitting up.

"Don't worry about it." He lifted the can of soda his sister had pressed on him at the door. "I'll be good for the whole trip once I drink this."

"I insist on splitting driving duties."

He hummed noncommittally. Five minutes later, Caroline was asleep. Isaac didn't wake her until they pulled into the Luxe's VIP lot.

The small parking area was reserved for guests staying in the luxury suites. It required passing a parking barrier arm, but Isaac had finagled a permanent parking pass from Janet. He hadn't wanted to park in the structure, not when he was Caroline's escort out in the world.

Caroline was still half asleep, but the cool night air roused her long enough for conversation. "It was nice meeting your family. Thank you for parading all those cute babies in front of me. I have a much better idea of what I'll be getting into now that I've decided to leap feet-first into your gene pool without so much as a by your leave."

"Picked up on that, did you?"

"You weren't exactly subtle handing me baby after baby."

"I don't do subtle." Isaac grinned, throwing an arm around her. "Oh, and by the way, you have *all* my leave. Seriously, it's one hundred percent yours."

Caroline stopped in the middle of the parking lot. Her lips compressed as she bit back the scathing response that he knew she wanted to make.

Heedless of the cameras trained in their direction, he leaned over to kiss her on the forehead. "You've already made your bed, Caroline. You just have to lie in it—a task I intend to make as pleasurable as possible."

He took her hand, tugging her toward the entrance closest to her rooms. "And speaking of bed..."

# CHAPTER TWENTY-SIX

Caroline tried to get out of bed. Tsking, Isaac pushed her back down. It wasn't difficult for him. She was as weak as a geriatric penguin.

"I have to get up," she protested, pressing a tissue to her sore red nose. Only actual clowns had brighter ones.

"You can't." Smoothing a hand over her hair, he made a clucking sound in his throat. "You have the flu, *mi cielo.*"

He tucked the summer-weight down comforter more securely around her. "Sorry, you picked it up from one of the kids at the party. A slew went down like a row of pint-sized dominoes, taking most of their parents with them. So that's something about kids we have to look forward to."

"Is baby Teresa sick?" she asked, concern pinching her lush mouth at the corners.

"No, and neither are her mom or brother, so they are probably in the clear," he said, touched by her concern.

"I still need to speak to Janet," she insisted, turning her head as if expecting to see her assistant standing in a random corner of the room.

"Not in person, you don't. I'll get your phone and your computer, but you have to promise not to spend more than ten minutes at a time trying to work. You should try to sleep as much as possible. If you can't, at least shut your brain off by watching some mindless TV."

He set the remote beside her, then poured water from the electric kettle into the mug with the powdered flu treatment. "This is the over-the-counter stuff," he said, stirring it before handing it over. "But I'm going to get one of those concierge docs over here to give you a shot or some prescription pills because I know you'll be trying to get out of this bed too soon."

It was telling that she was too weak to argue with him.

He stroked her forehead and frowned. "You're too hot—literally this time. But you're not burning up, so it must be a mild fever. I'd kiss you anyway, but I think you'll be more upset if I pull a Typhoid Mary and spread those germs to your staff."

Her bleary eyes squinted. "Is that why you're wearing a mask?"

He'd picked the thing up in the hotel infirmary after Caroline's restless night.

"Yeah, baby," he said, trying to convey everything he felt for her in his eyes. She didn't react, proving that without the rest of the face, the whole 'windows-to-the-soul' stuff was a bunch of crap.

Smiling under the mask, he retrieved the computer and her cell phone from the charger. For good measure, he added the latest issue of *Hotelier Magazine* that Janet had left for her on her desk to the stack.

By the time he came back to check on her at lunch, she had read it cover to cover and was worked up enough to sit upright in bed when he came in. Unfortunately, she was far too dizzy for that.

Caroline shifted to the right, falling over the pillow with a dramatic groan. "What is this?" she asked, pushing the periodical at him with a weak shove.

"Your article." Frowning, Isaac put his hand on her forehead. "How feverish are you? Because you feel the same to me."

"I don't mean the article. I mean this *in* the article," she said, flipping the page and pointing.

Isaac glanced at the glossy image depicting one of the hotel rooms.

"It's a glamour shot of one of the ocean-view suites. It looks great," he added absently, setting down a tray bearing a steaming bowl of chicken soup and warm fresh bread from the kitchen.

"No. This is not supposed to be here." She took a pen from the bedside table, then drew a messy circle over the table in the photograph.

He squinted at the image, wondering what he was missing. "The vase is bothering you? Should it have been on another table?"

"Not that, *this*." She pointed to the other object in the off-center circle, a little knock-off museum piece that resembled the fragment of a frieze. The rough square was propped up on a little pedestal just off to the side.

Isaac frowned. "Those, or pieces like it, have been in most of the rooms I've checked. What's wrong with them?"

Caroline gave him a disgruntled scowl. "My decorator had the poor taste to suggest this be an Atlantean-themed hotel. I shut that very terrible idea down in a hurry, but it looks like she snuck some of her pseudo-artifacts into the rooms without approval."

"Can you get me a Post-it or something?" she asked, fishing around the bed. "I need to make a note to call her about this."

He studied the picture before setting it aside to make room for the tray. "It doesn't look bad."

Her head fell back on the pillow in exhausted outrage. "That piece does not go with the room aesthetic—not at all."

Picking up the magazine, he used it to fan the hot soup. "She was probably trying to add a little color to the room. Something offbeat."

"There isn't supposed to be anything offbeat or quirky. Every object in that room has been carefully selected to function in harmonious equilibrium."

Caroline was adorable in her indignation.

"You chose everything?" How long had that taken?

"*Yes*. And I told that woman in no uncertain terms—no ocean fossils and no fake relics."

He chuckled. "All right, my control freak. I understand."

"It's not funny," she said, waving the pen threateningly. "No doubt she added those to the decorating bill."

"Ah, well that's a horse of a different color," he said, helping her adjust so the tray legs didn't dig into her side. "I'll make the note and leave it on your desk. You can take care of it once you're back on your feet. In the meantime, finish that soup and go back to sleep."

Giving up, Caroline picked up the spoon. "Is everything going all right out there?"

"Everything is fine," he assured her. "Anna and her minions have everything in hand. You hired good people, and they are doing their jobs."

He sat on the bed. "Maybe this can be a trial run for delegating more."

"I delegate," she mumbled indignantly around the spoon in her mouth.

"You'll have to do more of it eventually," he said with a significant glance at her flat midriff.

Caroline bit the spoon, then set it down. "I am aware of that. I just want to make sure everything is running smoothly before I get pregnant."

Her expression shuttered, growing guarded. "And I think that's a little, I don't know...hypocritical coming from someone who can't even say what coast they're going to be living on after they wrap up this case."

*Ah.*

He reached under the cover and ran his hand up her leg, wondering at how smooth it felt given that he'd never seen her shave. "I've been thinking about that. It was always my intention to ask for a transfer to L.A. so I can be closer to my family, but San Diego is close enough should you decide to make this your home base, at least for the next few years."

"That might be doable," she said slowly.

"Good. Because I put in for the transfer. The paperwork is done."

"*Oh.*" Caroline took a moment to digest that. "But, er, what if making this a home base is not enough? You already know that I will have to spend a big chunk of the year traveling, regardless of where I call home."

"I do."

She lowered her flushed face. "Isaac…"

Reaching out, he took her hand to forestall future conversation. "We'll worry about the details later. But I don't want you to be concerned. We're going to make this work because as I told my sister —you're the one, Caroline."

Fumbling with the tray, Caroline clutched the spoon, holding it up to her cheek. "You told her that?" she asked hoarsely.

Isaac hadn't intended to have this conversation when she was feverish, but maybe it was better. *At least she doesn't have the strength to run away.* "Yeah, I did."

"Oh."

He waited, but she just continued to stare at him, pressing the spoon to her flushed cheek. Deciding she needed time to process, he stood. "I should get back. I promised Anna that I'd walk her through the setup and security precautions I've drafted for the Fleming jewelry exhibit."

Caroline dipped the spoon back in the soup, surreptitiously wiping her cheek as he started to prepare another hot flu drink. "That sounds great."

After stirring it, he set the mug next to the soup on the tray. "The doctor mentioned that he stopped by. I asked him if you could still have this on top of what he gave you. He said it was fine."

"Thank you," she said, looking up at him from beneath her thick lashes.

"Sleep some more," he suggested. "You can afford it. Everyone is doing their jobs, and we haven't burned down the hotel yet."

Caroline groaned. "Bite your tongue."

Grinning, he paused at the door. "I'd rather bite yours."

She threw a pillow at him, but given her weakened condition, the missile fell short by a good five yards.

"Aww," he murmured, executing a kickflip he'd perfected in soccer to get the pillow back on the bed. "Better luck next time, My Queen."

Scowling, Caroline flipped him off, a gesture she wouldn't have used even a month ago.

*Aww, I'm rubbing off on her.* Perversely delighted, he went off to meet Agent Rhodes.

# CHAPTER TWENTY-SEVEN

"So, are you going to quit to be with your girl?"

Isaac looked up from the report to see the junior agent, Robbie Rhodes, studying him over one of the café's excellent cappuccinos. The drink was sweetened with Mexican *piloncillo*, an unrefined sugar typically bought as a solid cone.

Isaac didn't pretend not to understand. Robbie Rhodes was a trained FBI agent, and Isaac hadn't exactly been the soul of discretion these last few days. "It may come to that."

It was strange, but saying the words aloud wasn't the kick in the gut he had expected.

For most of his life, Isaac had worked toward one goal—to become a kick-ass FBI agent who put the bad guys away. Well, he'd done that for years, but, lately, it had started to appear that for each one he put away, two more sprang up to take their place.

Deep down, he still knew his work had value, but it wasn't the same as before. He used to get pumped when he closed a case, but whatever satisfaction he received lately was increasingly more and more short-lived.

There was also the fact that a transfer to the West Coast wasn't going to fix his geography problem with Caroline, and she knew it.

Robbie was good at reading people. The idea of leaving the bureau was something that had been buzzing in Isaac's head for the last few weeks. He hadn't wanted to say anything about it to Caroline yet because he wasn't sure. It was a big step.

Putting away the security plans, he sipped his own coffee. "*Damn*. It tastes so much better with the *piloncillo* than regular sugar."

"I like them this way, too," Robbie said. "It's going to be hard going back to the swill they serve at the bureau field office after this."

Isaac leaned back in the chair. "How many people know about Caroline and me? Among the staff, that is?"

"I think there are a couple of maids and a busboy who haven't heard yet." Robbie pretended to check her watch. "But it's still early. By tomorrow, I imagine the gossip will have complete penetration."

He narrowed his eyes at her choice of words, but let it pass. "Word of our relationship won't make it to FBI ears from you, will it?"

Robbie's head pulled back. She replied with an arch of her finely tweezed brows.

"Thanks," he said.

"I wouldn't mess up your game." Robbie shrugged. "And Caroline seems pretty okay for a white woman... Although I'm kind of surprised she went for you, what with all your scruffiness and tattoos. But she's a good boss."

He laughed. Coming from Agent Rhodes, that was high praise indeed. "Yeah, she's a keeper. As for the tattoo—she loves it."

The corner of Robbie's mouth turned up in genuine amusement. "Oh, so it's like that?"

His laughter was the only answer, but her next words killed it.

Robbie held up her phone. "I just got Brody's report on those men who came from the salon. They *are* cartel, but they've gone to ground. We might have an in, however, to their operation over in Tijuana."

Scowling, he took out his own FBI-issued phone and opened the PDF he'd only glanced at.

"Brody said the Mexican authorities are actively investigating this group. The higher-ups are floating the idea of having someone go undercover." Robbie leaned forward. "You may as well know—it's being mentioned that your name is being considered for the op, given your experience and ability to fit in."

"There are other Hispanic agents." Isaac scowled at the screen. "I won't leave Caroline on her own, not while this threat hangs over her."

She winced "But what if this is the source of the trouble?"

He grunted. "There's no evidence of that."

Robbie shot him a look. "We won't know that until one talks. The quickest way that would happen is to get someone on the inside, and you're best-versed in the case. Another agent can protect Caroline. It could all be over in a few months. You can always quit after the threat is neutralized."

His shoulders tightened. "I *can't* leave her."

Agent Rhodes narrowed her eyes. "What aren't you telling me?"

He considered confiding in her, but they weren't there yet. Isaac finally settled on 'something private' and she let it go.

Caroline had been dozing when her cell phone rang with a very distinctive ringtone.

Startled into full consciousness, she stared at the device, dismayed to see her ex's name on the screen. After half a dozen chimes, she sighed and picked it up. "Hello, Liam."

"What's wrong?" her ex said sharply. "You sound weird. Have you been crying?"

She wanted to shake her head, but she was too exhausted. "No. I have the flu. What do you want?"

He ignored her question. "How long have you been sick?"

"Not long."

There was the sound of rustling in the background as if he were standing up and pacing while he spoke. Which he probably was—it was a habit of Liam's.

"Have you consulted a doctor?" More rustling. "Because I can have one over there within the hour."

A corner of her mouth lifted. "That's very generous, but Isaac took care of it."

There was a long silence. "So, you *are* sleeping with him."

It wasn't a question.

Caroline groaned. *Why did I answer the phone?* She turned on her side, letting her aching head rest on the pillow. "What do you want, Liam?"

"To apologize."

Caroline would have sat upright had she possessed even a scintilla of energy. "Has hell frozen over?" Liam never apologized for anything.

He sighed heavily across the line. "I am sorry I went down there. I didn't intend for it to come off the way it did—as if I have a right to run your life. I know I don't. But I still care about you, and I was worried."

The irony was she knew he was telling the truth. Liam did care about her, after a fashion. But even though their relationship had once been intimate, the way he saw her changed after they stopped sleeping together.

"I'm not your little sister."

"I know that," he growled.

"Then act like it."

Liam made a rough sound in his throat. "Fine. Maybe there is an element of brotherly concern to our relationship now. But I worry about all my close friends as if they were family."

Another thing that was probably true.

"Are you sure you're safe with him?"

Caroline wanted to reach through the line and smack some sense into the man, but Liam was just being Liam. "Yes," she sighed. "I am. Not that you'll actually believe me."

Liam huffed. "I spoke to Jason about him. And Ethan Thomas. They only had good things to say about Isaac Rivera as an agent. But both reserved judgment on him as a romantic partner. He's divorced. They don't know what broke up the marriage."

"Well, I do know what ended it, and he's not a philanderer or anything like that. He's an exceedingly kind man who treats me as his equal in every way."

There was another grunt. "Ouch."

"Admit it. You never saw me as an equal partner in our relationship."

"Maybe I didn't," Liam admitted. "You were younger. Five years didn't seem like a big gap at first, but back then, I didn't think about things like that. It ended up mattering more than I thought."

Caroline almost laughed. "You are a hell of a lot more in touch with your feelings now, so I guess we've both matured. Perhaps it's to be expected given the nature of your marriage. Having both a husband and a wife means having to talk things out a lot more than you're comfortable with, I bet."

Liam's deep laugh made the line buzz. "You've got that right. Our arguments, which are thankfully few, age me years at a time."

A tightly wound coil that had been present in her chest for more years than she could count was suddenly not there anymore. "It's worth it," she confided.

Liam paused for a moment. "You make him take care of you, Caroline," he said, suddenly serious.

"I will, and he is."

"And tell him he was right."

"About what?" she asked.

"Never mind," Liam grumbled. "But if this thing he's investigating gets dangerous, don't take any chances. Come to one of our properties, and we'll take care of you. Promise me."

Caroline gave up, settling deeper into the pillows. "I promise, Liam," she said in a muffled voice.

He snorted. "Thank you for lying to spare my feelings."

"I'm just placating you until you finally hang up so I can sleep."

Liam laughed softly. "All right. I get the picture. Get some rest."

"Goodbye."

"Bye." He clicked off.

Drained, Caroline just let the phone fall out of her hand. She was asleep within minutes.

# CHAPTER TWENTY-EIGHT

Thanks to Isaac's excellent care, Caroline recovered from her flu in record time. It wasn't as quick as she would have liked, of course, but nothing short of not contracting it at all would have satisfied her.

Once she was out of bed, she hit the ground running, trying to make up for lost time…only to find that everything was running smoothly and on schedule.

"We did have our moments," Anna, the manager, confessed when Caroline met her at the reception desk late that first morning after her recovery. "Particularly when we found out someone had accidentally double-booked the large meeting room. The parties involved were rather angry. But with Mr. Rivera's help, we got everything straightened out very quickly—he's much more diplomatic than I would have expected."

Anna peeked at Caroline from under her lashes, suspiciously coy. "He's a handy man to have around. Multi-talented."

Caroline could feel herself redden. She cleared her throat. "Yes, he is."

She checked the latest occupancy figures, ignoring the speculation in the eyes of the assembled staff. Judging from the knowing looks being exchanged, it was a futile effort.

*You won't be able to hide your relationship once you are pregnant and begin to show.* She was going to have to speak to Isaac about this. What would they do if the FBI found out? Would they reassign him?

Ignoring the incipient panic, Caroline put her pen down, remembering her note about the decorator. "Anna, can you confirm that the decorator credited back whatever she charged for those artifacts?"

Stephan looked up from the computer terminal a few slots down. "What's this?"

"The fake museum pieces in the room," she said for his benefit and Melvin's, who had just joined them. "Gillian, from the design company, added them despite my explicit refusal. They have to go."

"Oh?" Stephan cocked his head and shrugged. "People seemed to like them."

"Well, I don't like them—they don't go with the rest of the decor," she sniffed, turning back to the manager.

The concierge stepped closer. "Do you want me to round the pieces up? We could sell them in the gift shop."

Caroline shook her head. "That's a good idea, but it's done."

"Weren't you listening? We've returned the pieces to the decorator." Anna nudged him before turning back. "I checked the accounts this morning. They haven't been credited back so I left a message. But it's likely they only received the box today at the earliest. They probably have to inventory the lot before processing the refund."

Stephan leaned against the corner, propping his head on his arm. "Well, should they refuse to credit it back, we can pick up the boxes and sell them in the gift shop."

"If that designer wants to keep our business, they'll credit back the money they charged. Also, I'm not going to give them a choice." Anna wagged a finger. "Trust me. You give these creative types an inch and they'll take your shorts."

Caroline laughed at the mixed metaphor, bidding them goodbye before checking in with the kitchens. The chef showed her appreciation at having Caroline back with a special lunch, served right there in the kitchen. Cerise knew she liked to watch them prep for the evening rush.

After polishing off her meal, a lobster patty *en croute* served with fresh vegetables, Cerise handed her a large to-go box.

"What is this?" Caroline asked, peering inside to see a massive cheeseburger and a side of fries.

A playful light sparked in Cerise's eyes. "I was hoping you'd do me a tiny favor and drop that by the security office for Mr. Rivera."

The chef's expression grew more serious. "We owe him our thanks. One of our waitresses was being harassed by her ex. Mr. Rivera caught him on the premises, and he had words with him. I don't think we will be hearing from him again."

Caroline cleared her throat, trying not to blush. "He's very intimidating when he wants to be."

Cerise pulled down a pot from the overhead rack. A little smile played on her lips. "More importantly, he knows when to be kind like he was to the little girl we found wandering the garden. She'd been separated from her parents, and she was inconsolable. He calmed her down right away, then they went on a quest to find her parents, complete with a fake sword he found in the gift shop. She drew his picture. I believe you can find it in the security office."

Caroline's heart swelled. "Yes, he's great with children," she said, aware her voice had grown husky with emotion. "Isaac—Mr. Rivera— mentioned having nieces when he interviewed."

The twinkle returned. "Good with kids. What a useful skill in a man who works in security…"

Biting her lip, Caroline nodded, deciding a strategic retreat was in order. She didn't find Isaac in the security office, so she texted him and left the burger on his desk. On her way, she spotted the children's drawings taped to the side of the filing cabinet.

There were six. Putting her finger on the one with 'Tio Isssax' written at the top in crayon, Caroline decided it was time she demonstrated her appreciation for Isaac as well. She ran right to her office and ordered him something special from one of her favorite boutiques, paying extra for overnight shipping.

However, when she gave him his "appreciation gift" the next day, she didn't get the reaction she expected.

"You don't like it," she cried, crestfallen when he frowned down at the luxury watch nestled in a satin-lined box.

He was leaning against the front of her desk, looking impossibly handsome in a blazer and charcoal pants. She admired the way the cloth stretched across his arms and chest.

Caroline gestured at his wrist. "I thought all men liked watches. And you wear one...this one is a Piaget," she added in a small voice.

Giving her an inscrutable glance, he came around the desk and pulled her up. "Come here." He guided her to the couch, pulling her down on his lap before holding up the box.

The crystal face winked in the light. Isaac kissed her cheek, wrapping his arm tightly around her "This is hands down the most beautiful watch I've ever seen. But you said it's in appreciation—for what exactly?"

Caroline cuddled against his chest, playing with the buttons on his shirt front. "I wanted to thank you for all the things you've been doing at the hotel, especially how you handled things when I was sick."

"Oh." He cocked his head at her, but he appeared confused and a little unhappy.

She ran her teeth over her upper lip. "Are you upset because it's too expensive?"

He cocked his head, considering that. "No, I don't mind that you have more money than me—I don't. It's more that you felt the need to get me an expensive gift when you went down for the count."

Caroline fussed with his collar. "It's just a little thank you."

Smiling, Isaac put one of his big hands on the back of her neck. "I know and I'm going to keep it because it's the first gift you've ever given me, but I don't want you to feel obligated because I'm pulling my weight."

"I don't understand." She was confused and a little hurt, as if his reaction to the watch was a rejection. "I'm not supposed to show my appreciation of your efforts?"

"Of course you can." He rubbed his face. "I'm explaining this badly. I love my gift and love that you were thinking of me—seriously, it's a gorgeous watch. Almost as beautiful as you."

Isaac set the box on the couch. "But all I did was pick up the slack when you got sick like a partner should. I don't need a special gift afterward."

"What if it had been a more economical watch?"

Isaac played with her hair, rolling a lock of it around one of his fingers. "I don't want to start out with you believing you're in my debt because I take care of you or vice versa. I've been in a relationship where we kept score. Trust me, you don't want to go down that road."

He broke off, pressing a quick kiss next to her ear. "Unless, of course, you'd like to thank me some other way…"

Ticklish, Caroline squirmed. "So, sex is an acceptable way of showing gratitude?"

He laughed. "Okay, no. I take that back. I definitely don't want that aspect of our life to become transactional."

Leaning over, he kissed her slow and sweet. "Thank you again, but let's save the gifts for special occasions like birthdays and anniversaries."

Relaxing, Caroline leaned into his embrace, remembering how her relationship with Liam had devolved into a gift arms race. And not as thank you's either. They bought each other presents as a way to make amends for letting each other down. The number of gifts they exchanged could probably fill one of the Luxe's suites and spill over into the adjoining room.

Caroline was starting to realize Isaac simply didn't work like other men. Just when she thought she'd figured out how he ticked, he would pull the rug out from under her. But everything she learned chipped away at her walls a bit more.

"Liam called," she shared, deciding to trust his response.

Isaac's expression darkened, his arms tightening around her. "What did he say?"

Tracing the border of ink at his wrist, she lifted her head to meet his eyes. "He apologized for assuming he knew best, and he had a message for you."

"What was it?"

"That you were right." Caroline studied him. "What did he mean by that?"

Isaac smirked. "It's nothing."

She tugged on his tie. "Tell me."

He brushed his lips against her hairline. "It means Liam Tyler made a wise decision—he decided to get the hell out of my way."

# CHAPTER TWENTY-NINE

Caroline pushed her chair back from her desk, taking deep breaths to slow her racing heart.

Lilia, the Lahore fertility clinic rep, had just sent one of her *'just checking in'* emails. Caroline had stared at the brief one-line message for almost five minutes before impulsively dashing off a reply.

*I am no longer in the same place I was, and I have decided not to proceed with my plans at the moment. I would like to return your folder of candidates at the earliest opportunity.*

Gripping the edge of her desk, she pulled herself forward, pressing send with a decisive push of her finger.

For some reason, that only made her heart race faster. Where the hell had this anxiety come from? She was short of breath and starting to sweat.

*I don't get it.* The panic attack should have come when she decided to have Isaac's baby instead of a donor's.

*Wait. You did have one then, too.* She snorted aloud. *Well, at least I'm consistent.*

A few minutes later, Lilia replied. It was a smooth and professional response that said whatever decision Caroline had made was fine. The Lahore clinic was happy to work with whatever timeline she chose.

The email also gently reminded her that under no uncertain terms was it acceptable for her to hold onto the donor information folder if she wasn't actively choosing one to inseminate her. Unless she changed her mind about delaying, Lilia would pick it up on her next trip down to San Diego.

Caroline rose, making her way to the sidebar to pour herself a drink. The scotch was for her business acquaintances, but she kept a bottle of French walnut wine in the mini-fridge for moments like this.

Filling a cordial glass to the brim, she took it back to her desk and opened the bottom drawer to retrieve the donor folder.

Sipping her drink, she flipped through the pages, wondering how many babies these men had collectively been responsible for bringing into the world.

The more she drank, the more relaxed she felt, so Caroline decided a second drink couldn't hurt. A cordial glass only held a couple of ounces anyway.

She was licking the inside of the glass, balancing her beige Manolo's on her toes, when Isaac came into the room, breezing in without knocking. Startled, her shoe hit the floor as she jerked straight.

"Hi!" she said brightly, setting the glass on the shelf behind her, a little embarrassed to have been caught drinking in the middle of the day.

Isaac grinned back, but his smile faltered and fell away. "What are you doing with that?" he asked, pointing.

Caroline looked down at the folder. "Oh, I was just putting this away."

Face hardening to a granite-like consistency, Isaac nodded. "Are you sure you want to do that?"

Warning bells began to sound in the back of her brain. "Yes," she said carefully. "I just emailed the clinic to let them know I'd be returning it."

Isaac gave her a tight, mirthless grin. He gestured at the empty glass behind her. "So, you decided to pour yourself a drink and give it a proper send-off?"

"Not exactly," she said, trying to toe her shoe back on. Instead, she ended up pushing it farther away. "What's wrong?"

"Nothing." Isaac shoved his hands in his pockets. "I get it. You wanted to take a last look at what you're giving up—all those genius-level PhDs and doctors whose baby you won't be having."

Caroline's stomach sank. "*No*," she protested. "That's not it at all."

"Really?" The hurt in his expression was unmistakable now. "Because that's sure as hell what it looks like."

"I assure you that is not what is going on."

Isaac took a deep breath. "So, you—a woman who never has more than one glass of wine at dinner—are day-drinking because you're celebrating not having to pay up the nose for some rando's sperm...or could it because you need to reconcile yourself to the fact that you'll be having *my* kid instead of some fancy Ivy League douchebag?"

Stung, Caroline blinked a few times. "That's not fair, and it's completely untrue."

She could feel his anger from across the desk. It beat at her like a wash of heat from an oven door. "Then what is going on?" he asked.

Caroline slammed the folder shut. "I already explained. I just emailed the clinic to inform them I'm returning their highly confidential donor folder."

He snorted, then muttered something under his breath.

Flushing, she kicked off her other shoe and stood, aggressively bracing herself over the desk blotter. "I will have you know that I planned my pregnancy for over a year. I researched and agonized and then researched some more. And now I've changed everything because of you. Excuse me for taking a minute to process. But this is a huge step for me, and I'm allowed to have feelings about it."

Isaac's lips firmed as he walked around to her side of the desk. "I never said you didn't have a right to your feelings, but what the hell am I supposed to think when I come in here and it looks like you're in Goddamned mourning!"

"It's not, that's no—" Caroline was so incensed that she couldn't form complete sentences anymore. Clamping her teeth together, she uttered an incoherent growl. Impulsively, she reared back and kicked Isaac in the shin.

To her everlasting rage, he started laughing. Truly incensed, she kicked him again.

Amusement dancing in his eyes, Isaac held up a finger. "Caroline..." he began in a warning tone.

Biting back a frustrated scream, she kicked him a third time.

"All right. That's it." Isaac reached out and pulled her closer, covering her mouth with his.

Still angry, she pushed him away, but that just made him redouble his efforts. His mouth slanted over hers more aggressively, demanding entry...

"I'm still mad at you!" At least that was what she tried to say. But her words were muffled against his mouth.

He withdrew a fraction of an inch. "I know, baby. I know."

His mouth softened, sipping and coaxing instead of demanding. Her justified anger evaporated, transmuting into a haze of longing and painful need.

Whimpering despite herself, Caroline parted her lips for his invading tongue. Isaac's taste exploded inside her mouth as his hand cupped her ass, roughly pulling her against him.

Knees melting, Caroline collapsed against his chest. Minutes went by in a delirium of pleasure. But when he raised his head and laughed, Caroline blinked, startled to realize she was trying to climb him like a tree.

"You know what?" he asked softly, rubbing a lock of her hair between his fingers. "I think you were on the right track—we should give the donors a proper send-off."

She shook her head, trying to clear the hormonal haze. "What?"

Isaac put his hands on her shoulders to spin her around. He guided her down until she was bent over with her hands flat on the desk, echoing her earlier posture.

"You were on to something," he drawled, opening the folder and flipping to a random page. "I think we should say goodbye to them."

He moved closer, his heat almost burning her back. Confused, she tried to twist far enough behind her to meet his eyes but, like his hands, Isaac's attention was occupied.

Murmuring softly spoken Spanish words, he pushed up her skirt. Her underwear went the other way, dropping to her ankles before he lifted her feet one after the other so he could toss her panties away.

"Now, now," he murmured, taking her hands and placing them back flat on the desk when she inadvertently lifted them. "I didn't say you could move these."

His chest pressed her down, urging her to bend over the desk with his weight. One of his hands slipped between her legs, stroking up her thigh before his fingers shifted higher, tracing over her already wet folds.

Shuddering Caroline strained backward, silently asking for more contact. Isaac obliged, pushing inside her with one and then two fingers.

Closing her eyes, she leaned against the desk and moaned, throwing her hips back harder to deepen his penetration.

Isaac's arms came around her, his free hand coming around to grasp her lightly by the neck. Her vision blurred, the ink on his arm swimming slightly as the dominant hold made her shudder. Her pulse turned ragged, the sense that she was at the mercy of a predator sharpening the edge of her desire to an almost unbearable intensity.

"Something tells me a few fingers isn't enough for you," he purred as he continued to tease and torment. "You need to be fucked with my cock, don't you, baby?"

Long past the point of shame, if there was one where Isaac was concerned, Caroline sucked in much-needed air, nodding as much as his grip allowed.

The hand around her neck tightened a touch. "I want you to say it. Ask nicely."

She took a shaky breath. "I want you to fuck me," she whispered.

Isaac's mouth moved over her neck, licking the soft skin. His teeth grazed a sublimely sensitive spot at the base before biting down gently. "I don't think I heard you."

"Please, please," she begged, her ass cheeks rubbing up and down over the cock that was like an iron brand, hot and hard.

He pressed his face against her cheek, licking a line from her ear down her neck. "Never say I don't listen to you."

His hand covered her bare pussy, stroking her clit with sure, deft moves. Something inside her rattled until she was almost vibrating, an animal impatient for its mate to penetrate her silky depths.

Little sparks of electricity coalesced into bigger and bigger bolts of lightning that shot straight from her core to the top of her spine. Throwing her head back against his shoulder, Caroline bit back a cry as the silky blunt head of his cock pressed against her. *Finally. Oh, thank you.*

Isaac's hand shifted up to cover her mouth. "There now," he whispered. "Scream as loud as you want."

Moaning behind his palm, she pushed back, widening her stance, then lifting and twisting to ease his entry.

Isaac hissed as she enveloped his cock. "Goddamn, you have the sweetest pussy on Earth," he groaned, thrusting deep before withdrawing until just the head of him rested inside. Her body clenched on him instinctively.

"See how your pussy fights to keep me inside?" he murmured. "It's because it knows where I belong, even if your mind disagrees."

Risking his displeasure, she took a palm off the desk to pull his hand down. "I don't disagree. I don't."

There was a plaintive note in her voice that made him pause. He held her tight against him, his chest hitching. But that moment of hesitation was over in a minute. He started to pump, fast but with purpose. His thick shaft opened her up, maneuvering with a little flourish at the start and end of his thrusts as if he were trying to write his initial deep inside.

Suddenly, he broke off and laughed. "Did you just say, 'dot the *i*'? What the hell does the mean?"

"Never mind," she panted, reaching back with her hands to grab his hips. *"Don't stop."*

Pushing her chin in his hand, he turned her just enough to kiss her cheek, then the ticklish spot next to her ear. "I won't. I *can't.*"

Folding his arms around her, he resumed thrusting, his hard, forceful drives making her turn back around to brace herself against the desk.

"Shit, shit, shit," she cried as the telltale spasms began.

"Open your eyes, baby. Take a look."

Caroline obeyed, belatedly realizing she had closed them. Isaac had pulled the Lahore clinic donor folder forward. "Say goodbye to Dr. Westin Chambers," he said, bucking two times in quick succession.

"Who?" she squeaked, her body no longer in her control.

He slapped the photo of the smiling blond man facing her. "This jackass, who, might I add, has a receding hairline—that's not going to be a problem with me."

He withdrew and thrust again, as deep as he could go. His breath was short, but he still reached out and turned the folder to a new page. "And this jackhole, with the skinny chin and all the capital letters after his name. Say goodbye to him, too."

Reaching with one hand, he squeezed her breast, making her see sparks behind her eyes. He turned the page again, his thrusts deep and relentless. "This fuckstick, too, with the stupidly expensive rug masquerading as hair. Wish him a bon voyage."

Torn between laughter and a little concern, she leaned forward. "I don't want anyone but you."

He knew that, right?

It seemed he didn't because his hand fisted in her hair and he pushed her over, driving into her, going harder and faster until all she could hear was the sound of his flesh meeting hers.

Whimpering helplessly, she tightened so hard she broke, a convulsive orgasm sweeping through her like a wall of flames overtaking her weak, prone body. They burned her up and she collapsed, unable to see anything.

But she could feel. Isaac's heat was at her back, his thick cock throbbing and jerking inside her.

"*Fuck,*" he swore, grinding against her ass as his seed flooded her with scalding heat.

Isaac collapsed on top of her. A few minutes passed as they caught their breath.

"Did...you say...goodbye?" he panted.

Caroline came to awareness slowly. Her cheek was pressed against the open page lying on her desk. She forced her slack muscles to work, making her lips move. "I can't...see yet. Get back to me later."

His heat began to retreat, peeling off her back. "Don't leave me," she gasped, a jolt of adrenaline hitting her at the thought.

He stopped. "Never, baby."

Isaac wrapped his arms around her chest, backing into her leather chair with her in his lap, his softening length buried inside her.

Sighing, she rested her head against his chest, little quivers racking her body every few seconds.

"It's true," she admitted after a minute, flattening her palm over his ink. "I don't want anybody but you."

"I know." He stroked down her side, all the way to her thighs, where he lingered. "I do. But I saw the folder and got upset." He was quiet for a moment, his fingers stroking the underside of her breast almost absently.

"Why do you still even have that thing?" His tone was schooled, very casual, but Caroline knew it cost him something to ask.

"They have to pick it up in person," she explained. "It's in the contract I signed."

He huffed. "If they want it back, we can FedEx it to them."

Twisting her head, she stared up. "If it gets lost, I'm legally liable. I would have to pay a fine."

"*Oh.*" His lips compressed, but his body relaxed underneath her. "I bet they stick it to you. How much is the fee? A couple of grand?"

"It's closer to a hundred thousand. Two if they can prove financial loss down the line."

Isaac jerked. His arms tightened. *"Holy shit.* I had no idea sperm was that expensive."

She lifted a shoulder, a corner of her mouth turning up. "It's the premium list. They have cheaper options, but they could be used by more than one person. I was worried about my future child getting into a star-crossed romance with a half-sibling. I saw that on a medical drama once."

His silent laughter shook her belly. "So, it's like high-end versus custom cars?"

She reached up to stroke his head. "Something like that. I'm sorry I kicked you."

"It didn't hurt. You're barefoot so it was like tiny baby kicks. Come at me with those heels on, then you might have to worry if I'm in pain."

Caroline frowned, belatedly registering that his closely cropped hair was wet. One of the things she had learned in the last few weeks was that Isaac liked to shower in the morning—a freezing cold one that he insisted was tepid. It was the reason she had stopped showering with him.

Twisting to press the side of her nose against his chest, she took a deep sniff. "Is that chlorine I smell? Did you go swimming at lunch?"

"Not exactly."

She pulled away to take a better look at his face. "What happened?"

"Some kid fell in the pool." He lifted a shoulder. "I fished him out."

Her lashes fluttered. "What? Are they okay?"

"Yeah. He's fine. Just a little shook up." Isaac rubbed his nose. "The kid's little sister got tired of him razzing her, and she pushed him in. He swallowed water and panicked, going under. But he's fine. He coughed it all up."

Caroline put her hands on her face. "I knew we should've put a lifeguard on duty."

"Anna said the pool was too small."

"It is."

"And there are a ton of signs posted—no one swims without adult supervision, yadda, yadda, yadda."

"I know, but parents overestimate their children sometimes and they leave them alone—"

"Babe, the parents were there. Arguing."

"Oh."

He nuzzled her neck. "Yeah, people can be douchebags. But I will teach our kids to swim from the get-go. You don't have to worry about that."

The repeat phrasing was warning enough. He was mostly over it, but Isaac was still hurting, unsure of her.

"I'm not worried about our baby—not with you as the father." Reaching back, she buried her hand in his hair. "These other kids were lucky you were there today."

He held her for a long moment. "Can I ask you something? Why were you drinking?"

"Oh, there's this walnut wine from France. It's my favorite aperitif."

Isaac poked her. "Nice try. But I asked *why* you were drinking, not what."

Caroline scratched her chin. "I was just…processing."

"Regretting the fact that you decided to make a baby with a tatted guy with only a master's in criminology?"

"No." She squeezed his forearm, drawing his arm around her tighter. "I told you it's not that, and I meant it."

"But…" he prompted.

"I am afraid of getting hurt. I don't want to fall in love. Not ever again."

Isaac burst out laughing.

"*Hey.*" She smacked him in the arm. "It's not funny."

He clamped his jaw shut and nodded, but a little snort escaped.

Her lips parted. "You think I love you already."

She slapped at him again—not hard, but enough to make her point.

Reaching out, he took hold of her wrists, his arms a steel band over her flailing arms. "Caroline, think about it. You're letting me put my baby in you—of course you're in love with me."

She could not believe what she was hearing. "You are so arrogant," she bit out, her jaw tight.

"Maybe," he admitted with a grin. "But I'm not wrong."

Still peeved, she struggled in his arms. "Hey," he said, soothing her with a hand to the side of her face. "If it helps, I am madly, deeply, and very unwisely in love with you. "

Startled, she met his gaze. "You are?" she asked, her voice trembling despite herself.

He pressed a kiss to her forehead, holding her close. "I am," he said seriously before his humor returned. "Did you think I would try to impregnate just anyone?"

Giving up, Caroline turned her head back around to relieve the crick developing in her neck. She collapsed against him, stroking the lines of his tattoo with her fingers. "I do love you," she whispered eventually.

She half expected the earth to open up and swallow her up, but it stayed mercifully still despite the admission she'd clawed tooth and nail to keep from making. But her FBI agent had seen through her prevarication. He probably always would. *How annoying.*

Isaac squeezed tighter, rocking her from side to side. "I know you do. But it's good to hear it aloud."

She scowled suddenly. "Why is loving me unwise?"

Another soft kiss was pressed to his favorite spot next to her ear. "Because you are way out of my league, and everyone knows it."

She made a *pft* sound as she laid her head back on his chest. "Anyone who says that doesn't know you."

# CHAPTER THIRTY

Isaac hung up the phone in his office, letting the tension in his shoulders go.

*It's done.* He'd just gotten off the phone with his supervisor in Boston. His transfer had been approved. Robert Angel had been pissed at him, although he'd hidden it well. Even when dealing with a hand he didn't like, the Angel didn't lose sight of the brass ring—Robert was gunning for FBI directorship. Consequently, he didn't burn bridges, although the Angel had made it clear he'd been hoping Isaac would change his mind.

*Wait until he hears I am leaving the bureau altogether.*

Isaac was fairly certain that was going to happen in the next year or so. At the rate they were going, Caroline was going to get pregnant any day now. His mind flashed to this morning when he'd fucked his woman in the shower, pinning her against the tile wall after she successfully negotiated a seven-degree increase in the water temperature.

He'd felt like a boiled lobster, but it had been worth it to have Caroline first thing in the morning.

Isaac knew that the second the stick showed two pink lines, he'd be unable to work the same insane hours his job demanded. The only reason it was working now was that protecting Caroline and investigating the hotel was part of his case. But once he moved on to another one, things would start to break down. And he wasn't about to let that happen with Caroline.

*And I sure as hell won't be going undercover anywhere else.* That was already off the table.

Then Caroline texted, asking him to bring the Lahore clinic folder back to her office.

Why the hell did she want it back? It had only been yesterday that she'd asked him to store it in his office safe.

Isaac had taken it as an unspoken gesture of her commitment. Her asking for it back was a kick in the gut.

His phone buzzed again.

*The clinic nurse is here to pick it up.*

Isaac leaned back in his chair, breathing deeply. *Ah.* Well, that made sense. The fertility clinic was a business after all. Caroline had probably freaked them out by backtracking. They would be worried the big fish they had hooked was going to wriggle away.

Well, she was. Caroline was his fish now. *And she'd no doubt be thrilled to know you think of her in such romantic terms...*

Slipping his phone in his pocket, he went to the safe and retrieved the folder.

The clinic lady waiting in Caroline's office was just as he remembered her, only her outfit was mustard yellow today. Caroline was in yellow, too, but a lighter, brighter, shade.

Nodding at the rep, he handed her the folder. She frowned, dismay clear on her face. "I'm sorry, but why do you have this?"

Pivoting, she faced Caroline, who was sitting behind her desk. "The contract you signed was clear; this wasn't supposed to leave your possession."

Caroline leaned back in her chair, folding her hands in front of her. "I can assure you confidentiality was not breached. I had Mr. Rivera lock this in the hotel's safe in the security office after I decided I wouldn't be using it. I don't have a strongbox in this office."

She was very reassuring, however, the rep was just winding up. "I hate to be a stickler, but according to the conditions of the contract—"

"Let me clear this up, Caroline," Isaac interrupted, stepping forward to get the woman's attention. "I can assure you that I didn't take the million-dollar jizz list and photocopy it. I am in charge of security here. I secured it. Nothing more."

"I see." He could tell the woman didn't like it, but she quit arguing.

"Well, that's fine then," she said, plastering a smile on her face and turning back around. She put the folder in her briefcase as Isaac took up position to the left of Caroline's desk. "And just know that when you decide the time is right to continue, you can have this back at any time."

Crossing his arms, he leaned against the wall. "She won't be needing it. She's got her own source now."

"*Isaac,*" Caroline chided, a telltale blush splashing across her face. "Please excuse him, Lilia."

Confusion flickered across the woman's face before it cleared with a startled smile. "Oh, I guess I do see now."

Formerly dismissed, Isaac found himself being given a surprisingly thorough appraisal. Lilia was now checking him out like he was a stud horse, lingering on the width of his shoulders, his legs, and his tattoo with something that looked like amused approval.

"You went another way than I thought you would," she murmured to Caroline before clearing her throat. "But, of course, it goes without saying that the Lahore clinic can adapt to any changes you make to your conception plan."

Pulling her chair sideways to face both, Lilia now included him in her spiel. "Since that appears to include you, let me formally offer our services to you as well."

His head drew back. "I'm not clear on how that would work, but I'm just going to say thank you and hard pass."

Caroline made a strangled sound, but he didn't seem to notice.

Lilia's lips twitched. "I was referring to our genetic counseling services."

She gestured to Caroline, but she kept her eyes on him. "As you know, Ms. Wentworth underwent extensive genetic and fertility screenings to make sure her baby would get the best start possible. As her new partner in this endeavor and because she's a premium client, we can extend those same services to you. We also have fertility tests for men should you not conceive right away—not that I think you'll have any issues in that area. You appear extremely...*virile*."

Caroline had chosen the wrong time to take a sip from her water bottle. She choked on it but recovered. Isaac moved as if to go to her, but she held up a hand to stop him. "I'm fine," she said, wiping her mouth with a cloth handkerchief she'd materialized out of nowhere.

After a pause, Lilia continued her pitch, her gaze direct. "Anyway, I'm sure you're just as concerned as she is that your future child be healthy and happy."

*Damn.* Isaac had to give the woman props—she was good.

"I've met Isaac's extended family," Caroline chimed in. "They all seem very healthy."

"Wouldn't you want to be sure?" Lilia asked, pitching her tone into a perfect semblance of deferential concern. "It's why you tested yourself. You wanted peace of mind."

Isaac held up a hand. "Aside from a little Type II diabetes in our old age, my family doesn't have any obvious health problems. But if it's included in what Caroline already paid, I'm fine getting twenty-three-and-me'd."

He turned to his woman. "I don't mind," he told her in a tone best reserved for the bedroom.

The clinic woman beamed at him in approval and with a little smugness. "Of course it would be covered. And then there's our sperm storage service, something we highly recommend our couples take advantage of. You are a couple, right? Because if you're not, we're always looking for new donors—"

Isaac snorted, shaking his head. "That's, um, that's flattering but no thanks. Caroline has exclusive rights to my stuff."

"No problem." Lilia leaned forward. "But I wouldn't be so quick to decide on the storage option. Banked sperm is like life insurance. I don't mean to sound morbid, but I've had many clients who were so happy they did it. One nice banker in Miami now has a second child thanks to his forward planning, even after testicular cancer."

*Wow.* Talk about a hard sell.

Caroline looked uncomfortable, but he fought a grin. "We'll discuss it and get back to you."

Lilia smiled, apparently deciding she had done the best she could. Standing, she opened her bag, retrieving a swab stored in a clear plastic wrapper. "Why don't I take a DNA sample today and we can get started on that genetic profile without delay?"

She motioned as if to do it for him, but Isaac plucked it out of her hand, opening the package to do it himself.

"Don't worry," he told Lilia. "I have some experience taking DNA."

He opened the flip cap at the end of the swab, then proceeded to rub it over his inner cheek in a brisk, efficient movement. Closing it, he gave it back.

Lilia raised her brows. "A man of many talents."

She left soon after.

The minute the door closed behind her, Caroline groaned, letting her forehead hit her desk blotter with a muted thump.

"Hey, hey," he said, coming around the desk. He pulled her into his arms before sitting back down with her in his lap. "We'll have none of that. Don't bruise that beautiful skin."

Caroline put her hand on his chest. "I'm sorry you had to go through that. I'm so embarrassed."

"Why?" Isaac stroked her hair, bemused. "That wasn't so bad."

She bit her lip, her expression chagrined. "I didn't expect her to pressure you that way."

Stroking up her leg, he nuzzled the downy spot next to her ear. It was like a baby's peach fuzz. "I wasn't lying when I said I didn't mind. Lots of couples get genetic counseling before they have a baby. It's just a precaution. I don't expect any surprises, but it would be good to know for sure."

She returned his caress, choosing to kiss his neck instead of his ear. "You were rather good with that swab. I guess you've taken lots of DNA samples on the job from criminals."

His smile dimmed. "Actually, I think I've taken most from families —for elimination purposes."

He was about to explain, but there was no need. Her expression told him she understood he was talking about murder victims who'd died in their home.

"Oh." Startled and saddened, Caroline cuddled up to him, her head on his chest. "How sad."

"I'm sorry. I didn't mean to throw a damper on today." His shrug lifted her up and down. "Let's focus on the good news I just heard— my transfer was approved. As of next month, I won't be assigned to the Boston field office."

Her head jerked toward him. "And how do you feel about that?" she asked in a cautious tone.

Isaac considered his next words, but when he spoke, it was from his gut. "It's not enough."

Caroline's lips parted, something like panic creeping into her expression. He put a hand over her heart. "No need to worry. It's just that maybe I don't want to be an FBI agent anymore."

She hadn't expected that. "Are you serious? But you've worked so hard to get where you are. Wouldn't you rather stay an agent?"

"I thought I was going to be a Mexican Sherlock Holmes, running down leads and solving intricate cases with my partner, but the reality is a hell of a lot different. More paperwork for one…" He traced a line down her cheek, momentarily distracted by the deep shadow between her breasts. Forcing his gaze back to those crystal blue eyes, he shook his head. "And I'm not sure I want the red-tape life anymore, not if it means working hellish hours while never seeing you and whatever kids we might have."

Caroline gaped. He'd thrown her. Eventually, she found her tongue. "So, what would you be doing if you weren't an FBI agent?"

Isaac grinned, running his hand up her skirt. "I'll give you a guess…"

She bumped him with her shoulder. "For a *living*, Isaac. What would you do for a living?"

"Oh, that." The hand patted her, gentling her in preparation for greater intimacy later on. "Well, it turns out that I kind of like being in charge of hotel security. I thought it would be boring, but it changes every day. It doesn't have to be here at the Wentworth either, although I do think I have a decent shot at getting an offer from the boss. Word is she may have a soft spot for me."

Caroline twisted and straddled him, putting her hands on either side of his face. "You don't have to do that. The transfer to San Diego is already a huge concession on your part. I can make this hotel my home base—we can even start looking for a house in the neighborhood. You don't need to give up your career."

A warmth that had nothing to do with sexual heat kindled in his chest. Isaac wrapped his arms around her waist. "What if I want to?"

"Well...then I support that," she said with the air of someone trying to defuse a bomb. "But it's a big decision. I don't want you to regret it...or come to resent me or the maybe baby."

"I don't think that's a real concern, but if it makes you feel better, we can slow this up. We can let the transfer go through and revisit the idea again in a few months."

"Yes," she immediately agreed before subsiding, sheepish over her own eagerness.

His brows drew together. "Is your worry over me giving up my job or is the idea of working together so closely the real problem? Because I do think I've got this thing down. I'm fairly sure I can get a position at any big hotel now. I don't have to be in the same one once this case is closed. "

"No." She shook her head emphatically. "I love having you nearby. Believe me, even if we work in the same hotel, spending enough time together is only going to get harder once I'm comfortable leaving the Luxe on its own—which is ironically much closer thanks to you and the rest of the staff. You may regret doing such a great job when I got sick."

"No," he said, shaking his head. "My job—my real one from now on—is to make your life easier in every way I can."

His hands cupped her head. "I'm going to keep an eye on you, on our family, and on all the other families who stay here. And let me tell you—career-wise, that's a damn fine upgrade."

# CHAPTER THIRTY-ONE

Janet gave Caroline a coy look as she dropped a box in front of her before handing her the folder she had asked for.

"Someone looks happy," Janet observed. Smirking, her assistant sat on the front of the desk. "Tired, but happy."

A flush crept up Caroline's neck. She closed her laptop, then reached for the folder in Janet's other hand. Isaac had kept her up late last night, but remembering the events of the evening, she had no regrets.

"No comment," she said.

Janet pouted. "Oh, come on. You know I have no social life ever since I broke up with Stephan—again. I'm living vicariously through you."

Caroline looked up from the financial papers the accountant had sent over, a concise prospectus for each hotel for the coming year, broken down by department. It took her a minute, but what her assistant had snuck into her words eventually registered. Caroline frowned. "What do you mean *again?*"

The younger woman winced. "Uh, well...we sort of got back together a few months ago."

Caroline stuck out her tongue, making a production of biting it.

Janet snorted. "It's all right. You don't have to say, 'I told you so' aloud for me to hear it."

"What went wrong this time?" Caroline asked, concerned. Men steamrolled soft personalities like Janet's or took them for granted. Her assistant was too sweet for her own good.

"He promised he'd be more open this time. No more being out of touch or mysterious phone calls. Stephan did well for a few weeks, but, after that, it was the same old thing." Janet shrugged, trying to downplay her disappointment. "I broke up with him again—this time for keeps."

Caroline stifled the impulse to say something critical of the man. She may not have liked Stephan, but he was an employee. She couldn't allow her personal feelings for him to be known. "I know you cared about him. I'm sorry it didn't work out."

"Very diplomatic, boss." Janet winked, aware of the constraints Caroline imposed on her speech. "But you were right the first time. He was too secretive."

Sighing, Janet dropped into the chair on the left. "He insists all his private phone calls aren't to other women, but I don't care anymore. I won't be around, getting in the way of his precious privacy."

Caroline leaned forward. "I'm sorry. I know it's hard, especially when you work together."

"You don't seem to have a problem with a workplace romance." Janet flopped over in the chair, her dramatic posture that of a dying fish. "Seriously, if I don't get some details, I may burst."

Caroline sighed, genuinely sorry because Janet was more friend than employee. "I want to confide in you, I do, but it makes me anxious. As long as Isaac is here undercover with the FBI, we need to keep things quiet."

Janet pouted, but Caroline stood firm. She adored her assistant, and Janet *was* discreet under normal circumstances. But she was also too nice and liable to cave under pressure if anybody grilled her. It wouldn't have been the first time Luxe employees extracted a juicy tidbit from her assistant.

But both were aware of Janet's flaw, which was why Caroline could tell her nothing. "Think of it as plausible deniability," she added.

"All right, but the day you are finally able to spill, I am first in line," Janet warned before heading to the door.

Laughing, Caroline reached for the box, only to find it taped shut. "What is this?"

"Maintenance sent it. They said you wanted it." She was gone before Caroline could ask for clarification.

Not able to recall anything she could have asked for, Caroline took her letter opener and sliced through the packing tape. There was an unsigned note.

*You asked for all of these to be collected. We missed one of these in the sweep.*

Removing the bubble wrap, she reached inside and pulled out a—a head.

"*Shit.*" Startled, Caroline laughed, nearly dropping the object in her hands. It wasn't a head. The object was too flat, green, and the spaces inside the eyes and the lips had been painted gold.

*A mask.* Shaking her head, she lifted it above her shoulder. *Damn.* It must have been carved out of stone because it had some heft to it. But it was obviously fake. The surface was too smooth and shiny. Turning it over, she could see where the coating—the faux-stone finish of the plastic—had bubbled where it met the attached metal base.

Caroline swung around experimentally a few times, testing its weight.

"Hey, you're going to brain someone with that, starting with yourself."

She turned to find Isaac coming inside the office. He closed the door behind him.

"I could take someone down with this," she agreed, swinging it around again. "It's heavier than it looks."

Isaac plucked the mask out of her hands. "No kidding." He held it closer, turning it over to see the back. "Did you buy this?"

Shaking her head, she sat behind the desk, dragging her papers closer. "No. I think it's one of those unapproved pieces that was meant to go back to the decorator. Some wires must have gotten crossed in housekeeping. They sent it up here instead of the manager's office. I'll take it to Anna in a bit."

Isaac seemed intrigued by the piece. "It's not a bad reproduction. Looks almost authentic."

"Maybe." She shrugged, trying to focus on her report.

The news it summarized was significant—and a relief. The Luxe was officially the most profitable hotel in the chain. The other two recently renovated hotels were also doing very well, but the changes had been less extensive at those properties. That was good, but one of the other older locations showed signs of losing steam, and that could become a problem next year.

"Babe?"

Caroline jerked her head back up. "I'm sorry. What were you saying?"

He held up the mask. "Do you want to keep it?"

"Oh. No, thanks." She paused, pointing at his arm. "Unless you want it? It reminds me of some of the faces in your tattoo—the Aztec deities."

Isaac cocked his head at the carved stylized features. "It seems more Machu Pichu, or Peruvian-like, to me. It *is* cool, but we don't have to keep it. I wouldn't want to muddy the waters with your return."

She kissed him on the cheek. "If you want it, it's yours. Trust me, that decorator owes me after what she tried to pull."

He smiled. "We can put it on the bedside table."

The corner of her mouth pulled down. "Or a shelf…maybe the one in your office?"

His eyes lit up, widening. He handed her the mask and picked her up, encouraging her to straddle his waist.

Flushing, she did. He opened the connecting door to the bedroom with one hand. Isaac set her down on the bed, then pointed to the small shelf behind it. "We can put it right there. It can guard us while we sleep."

She pasted a smile on her face. "Sure, honey. Whatever you want."

Isaac burst out laughing. "Okay, for future reference, I'll know that you use endearments on me you're lying through your teeth."

Pursing her lips, Caroline wrinkled her nose. "You've been pulling my leg?"

Isaac set the mask on the bedside table with a thunk. "I can tell you don't like the thing."

She put up her hands. "I would if it were in a museum, or even a living room shelf—which we don't have at the moment. But it reminds me of a display of death masks I saw once." Caroline shuddered. "I don't want one over the bed. It makes me think of dead people watching me."

Isaac grinned. "It's just a replica, so no dead people ever touched it, but that doesn't matter. If it gives you the creeps, consider it gone."

Caroline put her hands on his chest, sliding them up. "FYI, you're spot on about the endearments."

He grinned. "So, if you call me honey or sweetheart, it means you are pissed at me?"

"Yes, but it's 'sugar' you really have to watch out for. If I call you 'sugar,' you better run."

"I'll remember that." He pressed a laughing kiss to her mouth before making a purring sound as she cuddled closer. "If no endearments are safe, how will I know when you are happy with me?"

Working her arms between them, she tugged the hem of his shirt. After he helped with a grin, the polo shirt was soon hanging around his neck. "I'm not the kind of woman to keep a man in suspense. Trust me, you will know."

Hungry hands stroking his muscled back, she leaned forward to press a kiss to his bare chest. "Allow me to demonstrate…"

❦

Reluctantly, Caroline woke up after another delicious night with Isaac at the insistent beep of her bedside clock. Her body was sore but in a sated, pleasant way.

"Time to get up," he said in her ear, poking her in the side.

"Not yet," she protested, her voice still husky from sleep.

It was Wednesday, the hotel's slowest day and their new day off thanks to Isaac. Working with Janet, he had maneuvered, bribed, and cajoled until they'd cleared his and Caroline's schedule for the entire day.

Another gentle poke. "Then you should have turned off the alarm last night. We forgot."

Groaning, she put the pillow over her head. But that wasn't enough to shut out the annoying buzz of her alarm.

Reaching out blindly, she tried to turn it off, only to encounter cold hard stone.

She peeked out from under the pillow, jerking her hand back when she saw the mask in place of her alarm clock. The bed shook as Isaac laughed silently.

"You think you're so funny."

His face was buried in the pillow, his shoulders vibrating as he continued to laugh.

"All right," she mumbled sleepily, grabbing the pillow. "You asked for it…"

Caroline only managed a few strikes of fluffy revenge before she was easily disarmed.

"That is not fair," she panted, trying to look stern and failing. "I'm sure the FBI taught you all sorts of hand-to-hand fighting techniques."

"Funnily enough, pillow fighting is not on the curriculum." He grinned at her smugly, tossing the pillow aside. "However, fortunately for me, I wrestled in high school. Here. Allow me to demonstrate," he said, echoing her words of last night.

Pouncing, Isaac pinned her to the mattress. Gasping and giggling, she struggled, putting up a mock fight she had every intention of losing.

He let her get away, but only for as long as it suited him, which was a little less than thirty seconds.

Taking hold of both her legs, he flipped her over and pulled her closer so quickly that a little yelp escaped. Thanks to last night, she wasn't wearing anything under her nightgown, which gave him exactly what he wanted—no barriers between them.

He settled between her legs, his mouth going straight for her pussy. Falling back in a boneless heap, Caroline throbbed as he delved deep, licking and flicking his tongue along her folds.

A dreamy red hazy swamped her vision as she writhed, making no effort to stay composed. Giving up control was far more pleasurable. And strangely enough with Isaac, that was effortless. She trusted him on a level so deep she didn't have to think about letting down her guard. She just did it.

"Make more of those little sounds," he breathed as a moan escaped her, his hand working her clit hard and fast as his tongue penetrated her.

Whimpering, she clutched his head, pumped her hips up in a vain effort to get closer to his mouth. Making a soothing sound, he inserted a finger, pumping in and out as she writhed, out of control. But that didn't matter. Not here, not in this bed. Caroline didn't care how she looked, or that she sounded like a lust-crazed gibbon, hooting and moaning.

Isaac wouldn't have tolerated any walls between them in any case. She knew that without asking.

Rocking in time to his rhythm, she let the orgasm flow over her, the throbbing ember between her legs igniting like flames igniting before rippling over her skin. Gasping his name, she reached out blindly, seeking hot male skin.

But she wasn't given time to bask in the aftermath. Taking her hands, Isaac urged her to turn around and get on her knees. But he stopped her before she could put her hands down. Instead, he gripped her neck in his dominating fashion, wrapping his free hand around her waist. His mouth sucked at her neck, destroying whatever control she had left.

"I'm going to fuck you now," he murmured with an impossible masculine burr that set something deep inside vibrating in an echoing response. His deft fingers parted her lips, his palm abrading her swollen clit. "Open up for me, baby."

Obeying, she opened her legs a little wider. Nudging her forward, he fit himself behind her, entering her in one smooth, slow stroke.

Reaching behind her, she cradled the back of his head, the other on his forearm as he continued to stimulate, occasionally moving up to cup and squeeze her breasts.

Closing her eyes, Caroline let her head fall back, giving herself over to the experience. It wasn't the frenetic hungry conflagration that characterized most of their lovemaking. This was a slow, sensual ride where the pleasure built not in a steep crescendo but in a lazy climb.

Layer by intricate layer, each penetrating thrust brought her closer and closer. And then she was there, jumping off the peak only to find she could fly.

Isaac carried her down to the bed, holding her through the endless spasms, continuing with measured determined surges until he tightened his arms, cock throbbing. "I love you," he gasped, driving in with a last deeply grinding flex.

She was too out of breath to tell him she loved him back. By the time she caught her breath, his phone was ringing.

"Don't answer," she pleaded.

He looked at his phone and groaned. "I have to. It's work."

"The security office or…"

"FBI." Patting her naked backside a few times, he stood, grabbing his pants. "I'll take it next door in your office. Go back to sleep."

Deciding it was in her best interests to obey, Caroline snuggled under the comforter and closed her eyes.

Isaac burst into the room a few seconds later, startling her. Bolting upright, she reached for her shirt.

"No, it's okay," he said. "I just have to go. We found a body."

"What? Where?" Caroline followed his rapid progress. "And how is finding a body *okay?*"

He grimaced, tugging on his jeans. "I didn't mean it like that. But it's not someone who works here, but someone on our watch list. One of the vendors may have had a heart attack or a stroke and died. But they weren't found right away so I have to go check it out."

He finished throwing his clothes on, retrieving his sidearm from his portable gun safe. He slipped it in the shoulder holster along with his other gear with fast, practiced movements.

"Isaac."

Head jerking up, he stared at her blankly. She pointed to his chest.

Looking down, he blinked at his FBI shield, which he'd slipped around his neck on autopilot. "Oh, right."

He tugged it off, tucking it into a pocket. Shrugging, he added a second gun to the ankle holster.

"I'll be back soon, maybe even before you get out of bed."

A quick wave and he was out the door. Caroline didn't even have time to lay back down before he returned, leaning over and grabbing her shoulders to share a long, hot, blistering kiss.

He put everything he had into their connection—his love, his lust, and the aggressive dominance he no longer bothered to filter or tone down.

Devastated, Caroline swooned for the first time in her life, flopping over on the bed. She couldn't have lifted her arms from the mattress to save her life.

Isaac straightened his tie. He cleared his throat, feigning nonchalance despite the high color on the crests of his cheek. "Okay, that should hold me until lunch."

He hurried back out again without another word.

# CHAPTER THIRTY-TWO

Isaac took one look at the body and swore.

"Who the fuck said this was a heart attack?" he fumed.

Agent James Brody was crouching over the poor woman's head, examining it with his gloved hands. "Don't look at me."

Juan Acevedo, one of the San Diego field agents, checked his notes. "I think it was the uni who called it in."

Isaac raised his head to glower at the small cluster of local cops at the other end of the living room.

They had been the ones to find the body. A patrol car had stopped to do a welfare check at the request of the woman's sister after the victim failed to turn up at a family dinner. But because Isaac had put a flag on all the Luxe's staff and their third-party vendors, the local bureau office received an alert as soon as the death was in the system.

The youngest of the uniformed officers—the pale, sweaty one—piped up. "Her lips weren't blue. That's why I thought it was a heart attack or some sort of seizure. I didn't see any signs of foul play."

*Un-fucking-believable.* "The woman is *black.*"

Not to mention the fact the woman's tongue was sticking out, and there was clear petechial hemorrhaging in the whites of her eyes. She had been strangled, but because of her dark skin, the most obvious signs had been missed—like the dark ring of bruises that were only a shade or two darker than her natural skin tone.

Brody did the rookie cop a favor by herding him and his partner to the hall. Isaac straightened, taking in the rest of the scene.

The living room of the high-rise apartment was small but well-appointed. A matching white leather couch and loveseat dominated the space. In front of them, a delicate oval coffee table was propped up by the thinnest metal legs he'd ever seen. On either side of the couch were matched end tables, each topped with blue frosted glass lamps that echoed the color of the bay visible outside the window.

A plate of congealed pasta rested on the coffee table, with a mostly empty wineglass next to it. Just one. The victim had been interrupted in the middle of dinner.

"It's small, but a nice place," he observed. "Who is she?

Acevedo checked his notes again. "Name is Gillian Jones, age forty-six."

"No, I got that. Brody said she was a vendor for the hotel, but what company was she with?"

"Oh." He flipped pages. "Luma Interior Design."

Isaac twisted, eyes squinted. "The decorator?"

The other agent shrugged. "That's what it says."

Isaac put a hand to his chin, scraping his whiskers with his nails. "Why the hell would they kill the decorator?"

No one answered.

Brody finished his examination of the body. He ripped off his gloves and tossed them aside. "The connection to the hotel could be a coincidence. Strangulation speaks of anger or jealousy. This could be a crime of passion by some rejected lover or rival."

He pointed to the door, walking through his take on the crime. "She's eating, the doorbell rings. She opens, recognizing the perp, and lets him in." Brody gestured to a spot on the floor. "They talk here, it gets heated, and she ends up getting strangled on the spot."

"It's plausible," Isaac conceded. "But I think if it had been personal, there would have been more of a struggle."

He walked the length of the short hallway at the entrance and paused. The body was lying on the clear stretch of carpet in front of the coffee table. A chest and several tables took up the rest of the room, but all the surfaces were covered with something—a vase, a stack of interior design magazines, catalogs, etc. The room wasn't crowded, but there was little open space, as if the owner hadn't been able to resist filling it with her favorite things.

He put out his arms to demonstrate the crowded conditions. "I can't shake the feeling that an argument would have ended in more things knocked over or broken. She died quick, else she would have done something, offered him a drink, or walked away. But she died right at the entrance of the room. He came at her hard and fast."

Brody was skeptical. "Why target someone who chooses curtains and vases for a hotel? Unless she's somehow tied to one of those human traffickers you tagged."

Isaac grunted. "It's too soon to say, but her name has come up too recently for me to believe it's a coincidence. Maybe she was involved with one of the cartel members or something. We'll put the pieces together once we go through her correspondence and phone data."

He stepped back, including Acevedo in the conversation. "I have to make a phone call, but, while I do, please start turning this place over. If there's anything illicit or out of place, let me know."

Hitting number one in his speed-dial, Isaac tried to reach Caroline. When she didn't answer, he texted her a brief message. Then he called Robbie Rhodes, sending her to the Luxe a few hours ahead of schedule. After, he circled the body, taking it in from all angles. But no new insights jumped out.

*Why would the decorator be targeted?*

# CHAPTER THIRTY-THREE

Caroline picked up the yogurt smoothie she'd set on the edge of the tub and sipped, sinking deeper into the hot water. She straightened a leg, bringing it up above the water level to admire the iridescent bubbles sliding down her skin.

She hadn't had a day off in—well, she couldn't remember the last one. The flu did *not* count. It was a shame Isaac had been called into work. He'd only been gone a few hours, but she already missed him.

It was truly incredible how much he'd come to mean to her in such a short amount of time.

*And he loves me back.*

She knew it with her whole heart, which was nothing short of miraculous in itself. Caroline had never felt so certain of another person's feelings before. Caught by a sudden idea, she laughed aloud, but it had an edge.

*Not even with my father was I this sure.*

Gene Wentworth's love hadn't been conditional. But it had still felt that way a lot of the time...especially in her teens. The weight of Caroline's anxiety during those tumultuous years had been like a suffocating blanket. The incidents Isaac had mentioned during their first meeting—the stalkings—hadn't helped. Not at a time when a motherless girl was trying to figure out who she wanted to be.

In the end, it had been easier to be who her father wanted her to be.

Caroline downed the rest of the smoothie, wishing she'd poured herself a glass of wine instead. Thinking about her father always made her tense up despite herself. There was just too much history to unpack there.

On the bright side, Isaac's family had been very welcoming. She and Sonia chatted on Facebook frequently, and some of those conversations had included Mirna. Isaac's mother was of an age where she didn't like to type or text, but she had no problem dictating her questions to Sonia. Despite the nosy nature of the questions, Caroline had hope that they could have a cordial or even warm relationship.

They'd even sent her a picture of Isaac at ten, dressed like Sherlock Holmes—his hero—on Halloween. According to Sonia he'd loved the costume so much he'd worn it for years, only stopping when he finally outgrew it.

Caroline had been half-afraid Isaac's mother and siblings would compare her to his ex and find her wanting, but that didn't seem to be the case. As past relationships went, Isaac's baggage was more than manageable. Not that the acceptance of his family was a dealbreaker. At this point, she accepted that he was her happily ever after with or without their approval. They were going to make beautiful babies together. Although that made her think...did they need to have them right away?

As recently as a few months ago, she would have balked at the idea of delaying. She had longed for motherhood with her entire being. She would see families that came to stay at one of her hotels—see the babies—and would want one of her own so badly she was physically jealous of those mothers. The fathers she could easily dismiss. None, not even the most handsome, had ever figured in her daydreams.

Not until Isaac. But he was a fantasy all on his own.

That burning desire to have a child was no longer all-consuming. She was honest enough with herself to admit it had been an idea born of loneliness. But what she wanted now was time with Isaac, just the two of them. And although he was definitely enjoying their baby-making sex, she didn't think he would mind if she put off their efforts to conceive for a while. At least, she didn't think he would.

Her mouth quirked. Asking him to don protection now *would* be cruel. She enjoyed his flagrant access to her body without any barriers between them. A call to the Lahore clinic, to ask for birth control, might be in order.

Deciding to talk to him about it when he came back, she managed to drag herself out of the tub before she started to prune. Caroline was debating getting dressed—the idea of waiting for Isaac in bed had a lot of appeal. A nap would also be nice. She didn't get a chance to nap very often.

Two short sharp raps at the door derailed her plans. Throwing a robe over her naked body, she opened the door after Robbie Rhodes identified herself.

"What's happened? What's wrong?" Robbie wouldn't be there unless there was a problem.

"Agent Rivera is going to be longer than he thought. He wanted me to start my security shift early, to make sure things stayed quiet on the home front."

Caroline's stomach dropped. "So, it wasn't a heart attack?"

The junior agent's eyes widened a fraction. "No, I'm afraid not. But that wouldn't have been all that likely at her age."

"*Her* age." Caroline's hand flew up to her mouth. "*Oh God. Who died?*"

Agent Rhodes frowned. "I thought you knew the identity of the victim—you knew the initial cause of death was mistakenly called as a heart attack."

Caroline shook her head. "Who is it? Can you tell me?"

Robbie hesitated. "Well, Agent Rivera will probably tell you anyway. It was Gillian Jones."

Caroline's stomach sank. "The woman from Luma Interior? And she was killed. It's a—a homicide?"

Robbie's face was wiped clean of all expression. "I'm sorry for your loss," she said mechanically, clearly unused to comforting anyone. *It isn't part of FBI training.* But it should have been if only to teach the agents how to deal with it.

"Agent Rivera said he called and texted to let you know that he would be tied up and I would be coming in earlier."

"Sorry, I haven't checked my messages," Caroline murmured, her mind on poor Gillian. "I was in the bath."

"Yes, I can see that." Agent Rhodes gestured to her bathrobe. She stuck a thumb behind her at the reception desk. "Are you expecting your assistant today?"

Caroline pulled the sides of her robe closer together. "No, she has the day off."

After nodding, Robbie said, "Why don't I set myself up on her desk for today, instead of the security office? I can coordinate anything I need to from here," she said, holding up one of the secure laptops Isaac had set up.

"Sure," Caroline said distantly, still wondering what had happened to Gillian. "I'm going to get dressed. I may as well get some work done."

"In your office?"

She nodded.

"Good." Robbie smiled suddenly. "I have to say—you are hands down the easiest bodyguard detail I've ever had."

Caroline's laugh was a touch sardonic. "Well, I wouldn't want to make life difficult for someone protecting mine. Why don't I call the kitchen for some coffee?"

Rhodes guffawed and waved her hand. "Okay, now I know why Agent Rivera is determined to put a ring on it."

Blushing, Caroline went to get dressed. The coffees were delivered ten minutes after that. Settling down to work, she made and returned calls and emails. But the question of who killed Gillian and why kept coming back.

She knew better than to interrupt Isaac at work to ask him. If he found a connection, he would tell her about it when he could. She just had to give him time to investigate.

The office of Luma Interior design was a fancy showroom up front and shelves and shelves of plain brown boxes and wooden crates just behind.

"Bad news, boss," Brody said, holding up a clipboard holding a manifest. "It looks like this is only part of the inventory. The rest is at some self-storage place in National City, spread across several units."

Isaac looked up from the too-neat desk. "Why all the way out there?"

Brody shrugged. "Let's ask the assistant. We called him in over an hour ago. He should be getting here soon."

"How many other employees are there?"

Brody checked his notes. "Four, including the victim, are listed as full-time front office people. Then there are two others who move shit around for them, but they are part-time employees."

Grunting in acknowledgment, Isaac went back to checking the computer records. "I can't make head or tails of this invoicing software. When the assistant gets here, have him pull up everything related to the Wentworth Hotel chain."

Vowing to be patient, Caroline worked through dinner on autopilot. Dinnertime came and went. She wasn't hungry, but she could not assume the same about Agent Rhodes. The junior agent's consummate professionalism might keep her from calling for something to be brought to her. Caroline knew she wouldn't leave her post.

Deciding to check she opened her door to find Melvin, the daytime assistant manager, about to knock.

"Hi," she said, stopping short. "Aren't you off duty?"

"I am," Melvin admitted with a buttery smile. "I stayed late because the wife was going to meet me for burgers on the beach in the café. But the sitter canceled so I'm going to head out now. But before I do, we found more of those knock-off things you wanted rounded up."

He gestured behind him in the general direction of the manager's office. Following the gesture, she saw Stephan appear at the far end of the hallway.

"I left them under my desk and wanted to know if we should box them and ship them all back," Melvin continued. "Or should we wait to see if more turn up so we can save on shipping?"

Caroline paused, leaning against the doorjamb. *It couldn't be anything to do with those things, could it?*

"Let's hold on to them until we're sure we have them all," she decided. "Bring them here to Robbie."

"Sure." He left with a little bow, nodding at Stephan as he went.

The concierge stepped forward as if he'd been waiting his turn. "Hey, I saw a few calls come through the switchboard here when I was in reception. I thought it might be Janet."

"No, she's not in." Caroline nodded at Robbie. "Miss Rhodes is just keeping me updated on things from here."

"Okay," he said, shrugging before turning and walking away.

Robbie watched him go. "What's with the kicked-puppy look?"

Sighing, Caroline rubbed the back of her neck. "He and Janet are on and off. Currently off and likely to stay that way."

"Really? He's kind of cute," Robbie mused.

Caroline couldn't resist giving her a warning. After all, Agent Rhodes wasn't her employee. "If he can't make it work with someone as sweet as Janet, there's something wrong with him."

"Could be, he's just oblivious," Robbie observed philosophically. "Most men are denser than a box of rocks. The real question is are they trainable?"

Caroline suddenly smiled. "Not all need to be trained."

"So smug." Agent Rhodes laughed. "Try not to gloat so much in front of us single ladies."

Personally, Caroline thought she had earned the right, but she wasn't going to press that to a woman trained to fight by the FBI.

"What was that about knockoffs?" the agent asked, turning to the computer on the desk.

"Melvin meant a set of faux-artifacts put in the rooms by Luma Interior Design."

The other woman sat up, eyebrows at attention. "Gillian Jones' company?"

"Yes, but I don't think it's anything to get excited over. They're tacky fakes she wanted to add to give the rooms some 'flair,'" she said, putting air quotes around the last word. "It was a minor part of our overall purchase. We sent most back already."

"Could it some sort of fraud thing?" Robbie wondered. "How much did she pad the bill?"

"As far as I know, she stayed within her budget." Caroline had made sure. When it came to the renovations, she had kept a vigilant eye on the bottom line. "There could be a surprise bill in the mail, however. Anna was following up, but I guess we know why Gillian wasn't returning any of her calls."

"Yeah. Sucks. Did she have any kids?"

"If she did, she didn't mention them." Caroline made a mental note to check. "I was coming out to ask if you wanted anything from the kitchens?"

"I'm fine for now." Robbie leaned back, putting her boots up on Janet's desk. Since Janet did the same thing when they were alone, Caroline didn't object.

She went back to her office. But getting any more work done was beyond her, so she indulged in a new shopping interest—local real estate. She and Isaac were going to want at least three bedrooms for their future family.

# CHAPTER THIRTY-FOUR

Caroline rubbed her dry eyes before checking the clock on the wall. It was close to midnight and she had been staring at her computer screen for far too long.

So much for the premium blue-light filter she had added to the screen. It was supposed to reduce eye fatigue, but Caroline didn't think it helped at all. Or the one she had bought was defective...

*Except you don't care about the damn filter.* It was late, yet Isaac hadn't called. She had texted him once after speaking to Robbie, but she'd refrained from doing it again until he replied. And he hadn't.

*He is fine.* But the concern she had felt all evening was coalescing into worry. Panic was only an hour away—two tops.

*Well, this settles it.* If Isaac mentioned leaving the FBI again, she wasn't going to talk him out of it out for fear he'd resent her. No, Caroline was now team Mirna. If he was willing to work for the Wentworth chain, she was going to offer him a ten-year contract as head of hotel security on the spot. She didn't want to live with this anxiety on a daily basis, not when he'd spoken of his desire to leave.

*Ten years might come off as too desperate and needy.* Five would do. Even if they put off conception for a while, there was no way they wouldn't have kids by the five-year mark. She was fairly certain Isaac wouldn't want to go back to the bureau once they had a child.

Devious plan decided, Caroline rose to check on Robbie one more time before going to bed. Even if Isaac was incommunicado with her, the junior agent might have heard something from one of the other agents.

However, Robbie wasn't at Janet's desk, but there was a note taped to the monitor.

*Went to grab box from M. BRB.*

Had Melvin forgotten to bring the box? Irritated and annoyed, Caroline walked down the hall and past the lobby to the manager's office. It was deserted.

There were still people around—the night crew at reception, maintenance, and kitchen hands for the twenty-four-seven room service. Figuring there were enough staff around to satisfy Isaac, she headed to the security office.

The night security guard rose to his feet when she walked inside.

"Hi, Tony. Have you seen Robbie?'

"I think she went down to the basement with Melvin," Tony said, pointing to the monitor in front of him. "Something about some box being put down there on accident. But that was a while ago. She's doing rounds."

"Are you sure? Isaac wanted her at Janet's desk."

Tony frowned, showing his teeth. "Oh. I didn't get that message. I assumed that's where she was. That why I haven't been walking the grounds."

He rose, taking a walkie from his desk. She watched as he called Robbie, but there was no answer.

"I'm not sure she has hers on her," she said, gesturing to the device. When she had come to guard Caroline's office, all Robbie had on her was the laptop.

"She probably went to grab a coffee in the kitchen. I'll go check before doing a circuit around the property. Do you want me to walk you to the basement?" Tony offered.

"No. It's all right." Perhaps Robbie had found something in the box and was somewhere holed up on the phone with the FBI. She struck Caroline as a curious and tenacious individual. "I'll text her from my phone. Go ahead and do your rounds."

Nodding, Tony left. Caroline stayed behind a moment, writing Robbie a note and leaving it on the desk the agent shared with a daytime guard.

She had only gone a few steps down the hall when the basement door swung open and Melvin emerged, his plump face sweaty and red.

"Melvin? What are you still doing here?"

He started, then laughed at his own jumpiness. "Oh, hi, Caroline. I got stuck. Car trouble."

That was odd. Melvin never drove a car more than two years old, leasing a new one every other year. "And Robbie? She left a note that she was going to get the box in your office, but there was nothing there."

"No, that's because I gave it to her earlier. She came and picked it up before I had a chance to bring it to her."

Caroline's head drew back. "Then why did Tony say you two went down to the basement to get the box? He claimed it had been put down there on accident."

Melvin put up his hands haplessly, his round face gleaming. "I don't know. Must be crossed wires."

Then what had he been doing in the basement? Chest tightening with sudden suspicion, she began to edge away. "I see. Well, I'll let you go now. Your wife must be wondering where you are. Goodnight."

Schooling her features into impassivity, she turned, intending to call Isaac right away from the safety of her office.

Rushing footsteps signaled danger. Without turning around, Caroline broke into a run, reaching into her pocket for the panic button Isaac insisted she keep on her at all times. But Melvin only let her get a few steps before he tackled her, knocking her into the wall.

The button flew out of her hand.

Pain exploded across her shoulder and face as she hit the hard surface, but she didn't get a chance to cry out because he was on her, shoving a sticky-sweet-smelling towel in her face.

Caroline kept fighting, managing to drive one of her heels into Melvin's toes. But his hold was too strong.

Vision blurring, she tried to get to the main hallway in hopes that someone at reception would hear the struggle. But despite the fact Melvin was out of shape and had a visible paunch, he was still taller and stronger than she was.

The world went dark before she could summon help.

# CHAPTER THIRTY-FIVE

Isaac knew he shouldn't be hovering over Gillian Jones' assistant. It was making the kid sweat, but he couldn't help himself.

"Are you sure there's nothing else?" he asked as the young man went over the invoices and contracts the guy had printed out for him. His neck was itching, his instincts on full alert despite the fact this part of the investigation was routine.

The kid looked up, a hint of exasperation on his face despite the fact he was clearly intimidated. "The only other thing is our initial bids, but all that information is included in the invoice."

He pointed to a set of wooden filing cabinets along the wall.

Jaw clenching, Isaac passed a hand over his face. "When I said get everything, I meant get *everything*."

Even minor discrepancies were significant.

Cowed, the assistant scrambled to obey, digging through the cabinets and bringing back sheaves of papers along with rough, hand-drawn sketches and a few computer-generated diagrams, schematics of hotel suites with furniture and decorations marked.

"Where is the mention of the stuff that was returned recently?" Isaac asked, flipping to the most recent invoice. "The boxes of Egyptian and Atlantean shit?"

The assistant scratched his nose. He appeared confused, but it cleared quickly. "Oh, wait. I know what you're talking about—"

He gestured to the back room with his thumb. "I took that delivery in a box from the Wentworth. But we went through it, and that stuff wasn't ours. But Anna, the manager, insisted that it was. She wouldn't calm down until Gillian personally assured her those things weren't on their bill—like Gillian would ever mess with an account as big at the Wentworth Hotel."

Isaac's instincts were screaming at him now. "So, none of those knickknacks or masks were from Luma?" he asked. "You're sure?"

"Yes, I'm sure," the kid said, tone snippy. "There must have been some sort of mix-up with another firm. Sometimes, big hotel chains have more than one. I know a few that hire premium firms like ours for their luxury rooms, and more economical ones for their standard rooms."

He broke off, shoulders sagging. "Gillian said not to worry about it. That it was a mistake in our favor, and we could probably use the stuff in another job if the other firm didn't claim it."

"The Wentworth Luxe had only one decorator." Isaac was certain about that.

"I don't know what to tell you, man." The guy was wilting. "My boss is dead, and you're harping on the weirdest shit."

He paused as if waiting for an apology.

Isaac crossed his arms. "And I'm trying to figure out who fuck—who killed her. Every detail is important."

The kid reached for a tissue.

"Can you at least tell me where you put the boxes?" Isaac asked, reining in his frustration.

Nodding, the assistant walked him to the back room.

But the boxes were gone. "I swear I put them right there," the kid said. "I'll go check to see if anyone moved them."

Scowling, Isaac called over two more junior agents. They turned the place over, but they found nothing.

A few phone calls determined that none of the other employees knew where the boxes had ended up.

And then they discovered that the door leading to the loading dock had been forced open. There were scratches on the lock, but no one noticed because it had been relocked afterward.

That was when Isaac realized he had to get the hell back to the Wentworth.

# CHAPTER THIRTY-SIX

That black that was her world slowly lightened to dark, ominous red. Caroline drifted back to consciousness in pain. One side of her head throbbed. Trying to open her eyes was a challenge. It felt like each lid was weighed down by rocks.

"You're the one who said we couldn't kill the bitch."

A tornado of adrenaline flooded her bloodstream. *That wasn't Melvin's voice.*

Trying to breathe without moving her chest, she counted to ten herself to calm down. Caroline couldn't afford to panic. She had to think clearly.

"What I said is that *she* wouldn't give me the go-ahead. Caroline Wentworth is too high profile, with friends in even higher places. Hell, Russian oligarchs want to make her their mistress. But now, thanks to your stupidity, we have no choice. We have to kill her, and it's going to be your ass. Blackbeard is not a forgiving woman."

*A woman.* The criminal Isaac had been hunting was a woman. Caroline didn't know whether to be terrified or impressed. *Isaac is going to lose his shit when I tell him—if I get to tell him.*

"You're the one who almost ran her down with the van," Melvin spat. "And for what? A girl who dumped your ass."

Caroline's mind spun. What the hell did that mean?

She briefly considered staying where she was, pretending to be unconscious. But she quickly rejected that idea. Whatever was coming, she needed to be up and on her feet in case there was a chance to escape. And when it came right down to it, her best hope was to reason with and perhaps bribe them.

Forcing her leaden limbs to move, she sat up with exaggerated care and opened her eyes.

The first thing she saw was her hands. They were tied together in front of her. Unexpectedly, her heels were still on her feet. She didn't know why that seemed remarkable. It just was.

Her head was splitting. Please let her previously unconscious state have been due to chloroform and not the blow to the head. Her chances of escape dwindled with a concussion.

"Welcome back to the world of the living, Your Highness." A hard hand took her chin. Blinking her eyes sluggishly, she focused on Stephan's face.

"What is going on?" she asked, desperately trying to pretend she hadn't heard anything incriminating. "Did I fall?"

"Nice try, bitch," Melvin jeered, jabbing his finger at her aggressively from behind the concierge. "You almost broke my toe."

He began to pace up and down the length of the room—too fast. Following his movements was a mistake. Caroline squeezed her eyes shut as a wave of nausea rose. "I'm going to be sick."

Swallowing back her bile, she took several deep, fortifying breaths until her stomach settled enough to reopen her eyes. They were in the basement.

At one end of the room were the huge boilers she'd had upgraded early in the renovations. There was also the table Nate, their handyman-carpenter, had made so the maintenance crew could use this space as overflow workspace. It was where they soldered and repaired anything from the old hotel equipment, they deemed salvageable. But it wasn't ever used at night.

*There's a dumbwaiter.* It was a larger than average pulley they used to transport equipment in and out of the basement so they wouldn't have to carry it up the steep stairs. But it would be too slow for her to operate to make it an effective escape path.

"I knew you were on to us," Stephan hissed, holding up an Egyptian statue and waving it in her face, snapping her back to attention. "Why else you would you have called in that FBI agent to take a job in security? Now, where are the rest of these? Because the decorator didn't have them all. We're missing two—a statue of Venus and a mask. Where the fuck are they?"

Her lips parted. Isaac had been wrong. It was never about the cartel and their girls.

"But those are fakes," Caroline protested. She'd held one in her hands. It hadn't been genuine.

"Oh, are they?" Melvin snorted. "Or are they just made to look that way?"

"Tell her every fucking detail of the operation, why don't you?" Stephan snapped, throwing up his hands. "Christ, you are such a fucking moron."

A gun appeared in the concierge's hand. He aimed it at Melvin. "I should just blow your brains out now and save Blackbeard the trouble."

Melvin took a step back, his face sullen. "That other piece must be in her office. One of the cleaning girls dropped one there because they heard she wanted them. It was the maid who fucked things up, *not* me."

"I don't give a shit." Stephan swung the gun to Caroline for emphasis, making her flinch. "Look genius, she is *here*. Why aren't you searching the damn office?"

"What if Isaac Rivera comes back? Everyone knows he's sleeping with her."

Stephan was close to snapping. Red-faced, he spoke from behind gritted teeth. "I told you he is at the decorator's office with the other FBI agents. Now *go*."

Swearing under his breath, Melvin stalked out of the room. As soon as he moved, Caroline saw something that made her blood run cold. *Robbie!*

Agent Rhodes was lying on the floor underneath the worktable. The young black woman was so still that Caroline couldn't even tell if her chest was moving. Was she dead? *Oh my God.* She looked dead!

Stephan caught Caroline's expression. "Yeah, we know all about Special Agent Isaac Rivera and his partner here. Blackbeard has people everywhere. We have men watching the decorators. But rest assured, the minute he gets back here, he's getting a bullet to the brain, too. You won't have to live without him..." He jiggled the gun for emphasis.

Caroline lost all ability to breathe, but when she spoke, her voice was very calm. "That's not necessary—he has no idea what's going on or that you're involved. He's not here for you at all."

Stephan laughed. "Then why the fuck is he at the decorator's?"

She held up her tied hands. "Maybe because I've been complaining about Gillian dumping cheap trinkets on us without my permission. I thought she was padding our bill. And then someone killed her. Of course he was going to go check it out. But he has no clue what you and Melvin are up to—I swear it. He is not even on active duty with the bureau. He took a leave of absence."

"I'm supposed to believe that load of *horseshit?*" Stephan laughed before his face hardened. Lips firming, he pressed the gun to her temple. "I don't even know why I'm listening to you. You've been nothing but trouble since the day I fucking laid eyes on you."

Caroline scowled. "I have no idea where this personal animosity is coming from, but I swear to you that Isaac didn't come to the Luxe on business for the bureau."

"So why is he here?" he asked, punctuating each word with a jab of the barrel.

Caroline cringed, instinctively trying to get her head out of range of the weapon. "To get me pregnant."

# CHAPTER THIRTY-SEVEN

It came out as a strangled whisper, but Stephan stopped poking at her, his face incredulous.

"Excuse me?"

Caroline racked her brain, but this twisted version of the truth was the only explanation she could think of. "It's true. We've been trying to have a baby for months."

"Like you'd let some no-name fuckboy knock you up," Stephan scoffed. "I don't care what Rivera looks like. You wouldn't squeeze out a kid for anyone without their own trust fund and lots of zeroes to their name."

"You don't know shit about me, do you?" Caroline snapped, letting the truth color her words—or at least, a colorful revisionist version of it. "After my last relationship, I didn't want anything to do with any man at all. Then my dad died, and I said fuck it. I was going to have a baby on my own through a sperm bank, but my friend talked me out of it. Jason is also an FBI agent. I met him through my ex—they're related by marriage. Jason was assigned to the same field office as Isaac, the one in Boston."

Stephan was staring at her as if he'd never seen her before.

"You can check this all out," Caroline insisted. "Jason knew I was planning on having a baby on my own. He also knew Isaac got divorced from his wife because she didn't want kids. So, he set us up. We've been corresponding and talking on the phone for months. Isaac took a leave of absence so we can—"

"Fuck each other's brains out?" Stephan interrupted, laughing. He wiped real tears from his eyes.

"Get to know each other," she continued as if he hadn't said anything. "And it went well, so, yes, we decided to have a baby together. More than one, actually. I don't want my baby to be an only child."

Stephan huffed, wiping his mouth before shaking his head. "I hate to be the one to break it to you, but I don't think that's going to happen."

"You would shoot a pregnant woman?" she asked quietly. "Is that who you are?"

Stephan's face contorted, and he swore. "I knew I should have turned that van around and taken care of you months ago, but Blackbeard was against it. Well, she should have listened to me. You're the reason everything is fucked now—especially things with Janet."

So, Stephan hadn't tried to kill her on the smuggler's orders? Caroline shook her head in confusion, but immediately regretted it as a sharp pain made her world swim.

"That doesn't make sense," she said, fighting through the nausea. "You...you almost ran me down because of Janet?"

The grip on her chin became punishing. "Don't act innocent with me," he said from behind set teeth. "I know you were the one who told her to break up with me."

"But I *didn't*."

He scoffed, but she was insistent. "I would never advise an employee on their personal relationship. Janet told *me* she was ending things because you were keeping secrets—sneaking off to make phone calls and then lying about them. Does that sound familiar? Because that is why she ended your relationship. She was convinced you were cheating on her."

Stephan's nostrils flared, but he jerked his head and looked away.

"I guess there was another woman," Caroline said slowly, trying to catch his eyes. "Just not in the way Janet thought."

His mouth firmed, but he didn't reply.

"I think she still cares about you," Caroline whispered. "Janet is the sweetest, kindest person I know. Don't be a man she can't love. Don't become a killer."

Stephan met her eyes then, the flat coldness in them telling her it was far too late for that. But she pretended not to see, trying not to force his hand.

"Where are the missing artifacts?" he asked.

"The mask is in my bedroom—Isaac found it interesting. I was going to keep it so he could put it in his office."

"And the statue?" he pressed. "It's not in the room I put it in."

"It must be in one of the breakrooms," she guessed.

Stephan appeared to consider that.

"It might even be in one of the lockers," Caroline suggested. "If the staff knew they were being removed, someone might have decided to hang on to it. Was it an attractive piece?"

Swearing, Stephan got to his feet, his face contorting. Her logic had enraged him.

He pulled his leg back as if he were going to kick her. Caroline curled into a ball, putting her hands over her stomach instead of her face. When it came right down to it, she didn't know whether she were pregnant or not.

The blow never came. After a long, tense minute, Caroline peeked up. Stephan had moved away. He was rummaging at the tables, stopping when he unearthed a roll of duct tape. Unrolling the end, he looped it over her bound wrists and then twisted it around one of the legs of the worktable.

*Damn it.* The table was bolted down.

When he was done, Stephan raised the gun and poked her breast with it. She sucked in a breath at the unexpected pain of it.

"If you move so much as a fucking inch, I will blow your brains out."

With that final threat, he ran up the stairs.

The minute he was gone, she started pulling and jerking at the tape, but it held fast.

*What do I do?*

She had watched videos of people breaking through duct tape, but this was tape *over* ropes.

Yanking her arms up, Caroline tried to get the tape to slide up the leg of the table. Maybe there was an overlooked tool she could cut the tape with on the surface.

Between the yanking and her heels, Caroline lost her balance. Tears stinging her eyes, she slid back down, bending her knee so she could remove her shoe. The beige sole of the heel blurred in her vision.

Caroline sucked in a breath, hearing Isaac's voice in her head. *You're going to kill yourself on those things.*

He had said that about a pair of shoes just like these. Struck by an idea, she gripped the shoe by the toes. Pulling her tape restraint taut, she brought the heel down like a hammer onto the connecting piece.

It broke after three solid blows.

Wedging the heel in between the tape loosened it enough to get it off, but it had no effect on the knotted ropes binding her wrists. She had to use her teeth on those. But shaking and sweating like a leaf, Caroline eventually worked them loose.

She was next to Robbie in the next heartbeat. "Please be alive, please be alive," she chanted.

Caroline felt for a pulse at Robbie's neck, but she couldn't find it.

*No. God no.* And then Robbie shuddered, and Caroline saw the agent's chest rise and fall. In her panic, Caroline had missed the heartbeat.

*That's fine.* At least Robbie wasn't bleeding. Caroline didn't know what they'd done, but the agent didn't have any visible wounds.

*I wish Isaac were here.* Caroline longed for him with all her heart, but she knew she couldn't wait for him. Melvin and Stephan would be back any minute now. It was up to her to get Robbie and herself out of here.

How, exactly, she didn't know. She couldn't carry an unconscious woman out of here by herself. Robbie Rhodes wasn't much bigger than herself, but she was more muscular and at least twenty pounds heavier. Weight training had never been part of Caroline's exercise regimen. That consisted exclusively of running around the hotel.

Scouring the room, she wracked her brain for a solution. She found it in the form of a broken laundry cart. It had been left because it had a loose wheel, but it hadn't fallen off completely.

Out of options, Caroline tipped the cart on its side. Alternately pushing and shoving, she managed to roll Robbie inside the cart, praying she wasn't damaging the agent more with the rough treatment.

Trying to maneuver the cart to the dumbwaiter was another challenge. Unbalanced, it kept fishtailing. When she finally secured it on the dumbwaiter platform, she gave herself blisters by tugging on the ropes because she couldn't find gloves.

By the time the platform reached the first floor, Caroline was soaked with sweat, the muscles in her arms twitching out of control. There was no way she was going to get it to go up another level—if it even went up to the second floor. Caroline wasn't sure. She hadn't even realized the dumbwaiter opened up to the outside.

"What do I do with you?" she asked the cart, expecting Stephan to materialize out of the dark night.

*The pool!* There was a cabana behind the safety gate that held clean towels for the guests. She could hide there.

Caroline pushed the damaged cart, trying to reach her destination, but her progress was too slow. She gave up on the path on the other side of the fence.

*Close enough.*

Punching in the code at the gate and again at the cabana, she grabbed towels by the armful. Caroline nearly twisted her ankle on the run back, but she kept her heels, unwilling to shred her feet on the gravel.

Working as fast as she could, she covered Robbie, doing her best to make it appear as if the cart were full of used towels that a careless pool attendant had forgotten to pick up.

When she was done, she looked around for a place to hide. This part of the hotel was deserted. Going back to her office was not an option. And she didn't think it was safe to go to the lobby for help. If both Melvin and Stephan were a part of Blackbeard's operation, then any of the night crew could be as well. At least one of the maids had helped—someone with easy access had placed those illicit goods in the rooms. It made Caroline sick thinking about it.

What if she pulled the fire alarm and blended into the crowd? Images of her sleep-dazed guests being mowed down by machine guns was enough to discard that idea.

*Walk down the beach until you hit another hotel.* Except there were stretches of isolated beach on either side. In the daytime this stretch was typically crowded with tourists and locals alike, the next hotels a few minutes' walk away. But at night, the distance seemed endless and ominously dark. If she were spotted, she might outrun Melvin, but Caroline wasn't sure about Stephan.

*"She has to be here."*

Caroline whirled around at the sound of the concierge's voice. The question of where to go was moot. Stephan and Melvin were close, almost right on top of her.

# CHAPTER THIRTY-EIGHT

Caroline peeked over the edge of the roof, biting her lip and swearing internally. One of her favorite Jimmy Choo heels laid on the ground at the edge of the walking path to the pool, the creamy color glowing like a beacon in the moonlight. It had slipped off as she climbed to the roof using the fire escape.

There was no way Stephan and Melvin would miss it.

Caroline held her breath as the two men moved below her. Her heart was beating so hard she couldn't hear what they were saying. Additionally, they were speaking in low voices, presumably to avoid being overheard plotting her murder.

Caroline jerked back when Melvin stopped right by her shoe.

*Shit, shit, shit. They're going to know where I am.*

Forcing her heavy chest to move in and out, she strained her ears, listening for the rattle of the fire escape that would signify they were climbing up after her.

She had thought herself clever, using the windowsill of the ground-level window to climb up instead of pulling down the ladder. But then she'd lost the damn shoe in the scramble up, negating all her efforts at stealth.

*I may as well have hung a neon sign that says, 'I'm right here'.*

Sweat dripping down her spine, Caroline began to count. But she was still alone when she hit one hundred. Chancing another look, she leaned over the edge just far enough to see the path.

It was empty.

Collapsing on the flat roof like a deflated balloon, she stayed quiet.

*I just have to wait.* Isaac would return, and he'd immediately start searching for her. Stephan wouldn't shoot him out in the open. *Isaac will know it's him. He'll take one look at Stephan and Melvin together, and he'll know.* She had to believe that.

Caroline remained in that prone position, staring at the stars and listening for trouble, until her sweat cooled and she grew cold. Despite the heat of the days in San Diego, it was chilly at night with the breeze coming off the ocean in the fall. Without the adrenaline to keep her warm, she began to shiver.

*Also, how did I not realize the gravel up here was so pointy?*

Caroline felt each tip of the jagged bits of stone littering the roof and digging into her flesh. It had been here since she bought the property, but she had no idea what purpose it served. *Did it help drainage?*

Deciding it was safe enough to move, she sidled sideways until she was far enough from the edge that she could crouch without being seen. Her single shoe was too tall to walk on without unbalancing herself, so she slipped it off. Holding her Choo in her hand, she padded across the sharp gravel, wincing with every step.

She headed to the big, square vents that protruded, intending to sit on the other side to get out of the wind.

Caroline stopped short. Melvin was at the roof access door, bending over and trying to catch his breath.

Very quietly, she stepped behind the vent, hoping he hadn't spotted her.

"I see you, you *bitch*," he panted, his breath ragged from the exertion of climbing the stairs.

Whimpering, she ducked behind the vent, expecting a bullet at any moment.

# CHAPTER THIRTY-NINE

Isaac almost broke the door to the bedroom suite he shared with Caroline. She wasn't there either.

"Caroline," he shouted, throwing open the connecting door to her office. Empty.

"*Fuck.* Robbie was supposed to be here with her. I gave her specific orders to keep watch over Caroline and to *stay put.*"

"What about the mask thing?" Brody asked, yanking open the nearest drawer.

Isaac had laid it all out to his colleague on the drive over—the decorations that weren't supposed to be there and how Caroline had ordered they be removed. *And Gillian Jones died so some fucker could take them back.*

Brody and four of the other agents had come back with him when neither Caroline nor Robbie returned their calls. They had split up in search of the pair.

"I don't know." Isaac wanted to howl as he tore the sheets off the bed and threw them to the floor. "It should be here, and it's not. And if it's not here and Caroline is not here, that means whoever is behind this clusterfuck has them all."

Brody paled, turning a little green. "Are you sure they're not in the kitchen or something?"

"It's after midnight," Isaac snapped. "The other agents would have mentioned if they'd seen them. I have them going through all the public spaces."

"And what if they're in one of the rooms?"

Fuck, how *were* they going to search the rooms full of guests? Isaac put his hands on his head.

"Caroline will kill me, but we have to get everyone out. We can pull the fire alarm. Then we can do a room-to-room."

"We're going to need more agents for that—we need to make sure no one slips away in the crowd."

"Make the call. Get them here," Isaac ordered. "I'm going to the security room to check the feeds. After you are done, come find me there. I rigged up some laptops for Robbie and me that can access the feeds on the go. Robbie should have hers on her. We can try to trace it."

But when he turned on the GPS from his office, he didn't find the signal for the laptop, which could only mean the whole thing was shut off, or too trashed to send a signal. He booted up the other one, then began to scan the security camera footage as the other agents started to trickle in.

There was no sign of Caroline or Robbie, but they had found Tony, the night security guard. He'd been beaten bloody, then shoved in a storage closet.

When Isaac heard the news, he went deadly still, shutting down as he blocked the panic trying to choke the life out of him. Caroline was in mortal danger.

Jaw so tight opening his mouth was going to rip muscles, he turned away, ignored the other agents as he kept flicking through the feeds. Distantly, he registered Brody delegating orders. They dispersed to the lobby to question the night staff as he methodically scanned every camera they had.

Isaac caught his breath when he saw something he never would have imagined. Melvin Dunne was *running*. Up a flight of stairs, no less. Isaac scanned the ID of the camera, identifying its location.

No fucking way Melvin was running to the roof for an innocent reason. Not at this hour of the night. The man was day staff.

Isaac sprinted out the door, too fast to even shout for the others. *Please don't let me be too late.*

❧

Caroline clutched her shoe in her hand as Melvin charged like a bull. Screaming, she tried to keep the circulation vent between them, but the man didn't dance or hesitate like villains in the movies. He rushed her like some rampaging animal, his face contorted in rage.

Dodging his arm, she accidentally slammed into him with her shoulder. The force of it almost knocked her down, but Melvin was the one who slipped, his loafers skidding on the gravel. He fell with a crash, but sprang right back up, huffing and puffing like an angry boar.

Reacting blindly, Caroline struck out with the only weapon she had—her shoe. The blow dug into his skull, scraping down the side with enough force to break the skin.

"I'm going to fucking kill you," he seethed, spitting. He reached out, going for her throat this time, but she brought her knee up, kicking him away with as much force as she could.

Melvin lunged again. Hissing, she struck out heel-first with her shoe as hard as she could, going for his eyes.

Her aim was better than she thought.

The heel of the Choo drove straight into the soft liquid sphere. There was a moment of resistance, a brief one, then the heel was slicing through like a hot knife and liquid spattered on the gravel.

Melvin froze. Caroline gaped in open-mouthed horror. They both started screaming at the same time.

"*I'm going to—*" he screeched.

But Caroline didn't hear the rest. She twisted away from his hands, kicking out wildly. Her vision blurred as he tripped, grabbing at her as he fell. Caroline was pulled down with him, but they didn't hit the ground. Somehow in the struggle, they had moved to the edge of the roof. Her shoe had fallen off his face, but Melvin was now hanging over the edge, his hold on her arm the only thing keeping him from going over.

"Let go," Caroline cried, her shoulder in agony. It felt as if he were tearing her arm out at the joint, but she couldn't pry off his vice-like grip. *"You're breaking my wrist."*

And then there was a flurry of motion and footsteps. Caroline was crying, her vision obscured. Thinking it was Stephan, she closed her eyes, expecting a bullet in the back of the head.

But it wasn't Melvin's partner.

*"Here."* Isaac grabbed Melvin's arm, wrenching it off hers. Clutching her arm to her chest, Caroline rolled away from the edge, blinking to clear her vision as Isaac hauled Melvin's overweight body back on the roof with one arm.

"Thank—"

Melvin's words were abruptly cut off as Isaac pulled his arm back, punching the other man so hard he slumped over unconscious without another sound.

Shuddering, Caroline stared down at his prone body, cradling her wrist.

*"Baby."* Isaac's hands were frantic, but he was gentle with her arm. "Did he hurt you anywhere else? Because I can throw him over the roof before anyone else sees."

A weak laugh through her tears made Caroline wince in pain. Everything hurt. "Isaac, he's not working alone. It's Stephan, too, the concierge."

He swore. "I knew I hated that piece of shit."

There was a popping sound and Isaac looked down, his face contorting. Caroline hit the roof again, her lover's bodyweight carrying her down.

"Call me a piece of shit one more time!" Stephan screamed.

Jerking, Caroline whirled around. Stephan had come up the fire escape after all—in the fight with Melvin, he had snuck up right behind them.

Isaac was covering her head, pulling her into his chest with one hand, but Stephan was right on the edge of the roof and he wasn't watching her. Stephan kept his eyes on the threat.

Wordlessly, she pulled away from Isaac, ramming Stephan with her shoulder.

The younger man was caught off guard. He began to fall. There were more bangs—these were louder, almost deafening. Ears ringing, Caroline closed her eyes instinctively. Stephan disappeared between one blink and the next.

The gun in Isaac's hand wasn't smoking, but the smell of gunpowder was acrid. It burned her nose. She jerked to the edge, looking down at the ground below.

"*Isaac.*" She started crying. "I think it's over. He's not getting up."

Neither was Isaac. He rolled over on his back, breathing fast. "Caroline, you have to go get help," he said, panting alarmingly.

"*What?*" Tearing at his shirt, she went looking for a bullet wound.

"You're wearing a vest," she cried in relief.

"*Caroline.*" Isaac's voice was weaker now. "Go call…call."

Horrified, she put her hands on the vest, trying to find the fastenings. "Isaac, what's wrong?"

"It went thr—" His thick lashes fluttered closed, the muscles in his face going slack.

"*No, Isaac.* No!"

Caroline started screaming, staggering up and running for the stairs. She was met halfway there by a tall man wearing an FBI jacket with a shield around his neck.

She reached out, grabbing at the man with her good arm. "Please, help. The bullet went through his vest."

# CHAPTER FORTY

Caroline winced as the doctor shined a penlight into her eyes. "Can you tell me how Agent Rivera is doing, please? Is he out of surgery?"

"I'm afraid I don't know. We'll have to wait for an update. I'm sure there will be one soon." The man put the penlight down. His hands gingerly probed her jaw, tilting her head so he could examine the laceration on her scalp. She hadn't even realized there was a trail of blood going from her scalp down the front of her blouse until they'd reached the hospital.

Caroline didn't care about her injury. All she wanted to know was if Isaac was still alive. He had been shot with an armor-piercing round. He'd been in surgery for at least two hours, and people wouldn't stop asking her questions instead of answering her own.

Tuning everyone out, she concentrated on praying for the man she loved.

But people kept talking. Nurses wanted to take her clothes. One kept urging her to try to stretch out her injured arm. But the lights and the pain were too much. Caroline shut down, her mind greying out despite the fact she stayed upright, sitting on an examination bed with her eyes wide open.

Another FBI agent—Juan something—gamely kept questioning

her, but his voice was distant and tinny, only marginally louder than the ringing in her ears. The other agent—the one from the roof who had identified himself as Martin Brody, had disappeared when she told him about Robbie lying under the towels in the laundry cart. Luckily, she had remembered to tell him before Isaac was taken away in the ambulance.

They hadn't let her ride with him.

Hands touched her face. Caroline blinked, her dry eyes focusing with effort. "*Sonia.*" Isaac's sister had forcibly nudged everyone away.

"We're here," Sonia soothed, touching her gently despite appearing to want to hug her.

Mirna was also there. Isaac's mom said something in Spanish over her shoulder to Brittney. Isaac's youngest sister was in front of the door to the exam room, waving her arms and talking animatedly with a man in scrubs. But despite the volume she was speaking with, Caroline couldn't make out what she was saying.

"Did they call you?" she asked Sonia, her brows drawing together.

Sonia looked back at her mother, widening her eyes in concern. She turned back to Caroline. "Your assistant called us. She said you told her to."

"I did?" Caroline had a vague recollection of being handed her phone in the car by one of the FBI agents, but she didn't remember using it.

But that didn't matter. They were here. "The doctors won't tell me anything, but they'll tell you—you're next of kin. Please make them tell you how Isaac is doing."

Sonia cupped her face. "We already asked, and they don't have any news. But we know the bullet didn't hit any vital organs, and it didn't shatter. You need to let the doctors take a look at you. They think you might have a concussion. Isaac will be upset when he wakes up if he finds out you didn't let the doctors treat you."

That was an understatement. "He'll be furious," Caroline said, her tongue unnaturally thick in her mouth.

With a look of relief, the man in scrubs resumed his examination, making her flex her fingers.

The agent named Juan took her cooperation with the medical exam as a sign that he could start questioning her again, but he was interrupted by sharply spoken Spanish words from Mirna. Caroline breathed a sigh of relief as the doctors banished him soon after.

When the attending physician was done, he leaned in and lowered his voice. "I would like you to have a CT scan and some X-rays of this arm and shoulder. But before we get started, I need to know if you have allergies to any medicines or if you are pregnant."

Britney made a sound between a choke and snort, but Sonia hushed her. Remembering just how much her breasts had ached when Stephan had poked them with the gun, Caroline looked at Isaac's mother and then down at her hands, heat flooding her cheeks.

"Yes, there's a chance I might be expecting," she admitted, covering her stomach with her good hand. "But I don't want a scan if it might hurt the baby—if I am pregnant. I'm not sure."

"Really?" a new voice asked in surprise. She turned to see Jason White near the door, standing there with another man. Agent Juan had thankfully stayed outside.

"I said no questions from you lot until all her tests are done," the doctor snapped, visibly exasperated.

"We're old friends," Jason explained, jerking his thumb at the other man. Caroline recognized him. Ethan Thomas waved awkwardly.

"Congrats," he said with a nod, his demeanor bemused.

Britney sniffed. "Exactly how close a friend are you of my brother if you don't know he and Caroline are trying to make beautiful babies together? Or that he's leaving the bureau to be with her at the hotel full-time?"

"Because they're not telling people yet, Britney," Sonia sputtered, smacking her sister in the arm. "So, *shut it.*"

Isaac's big sister drew herself up to her full height. She pointed an accusing finger at the men. "Nothing you heard leaves this room."

Her voice rang with an authority that appeared to run strongly in the Rivera family.

Jason held up his hands. "Baby? What baby?" He nudged his partner. "Did you hear anything about a baby?"

Ethan groaned. "The Angel is already irritated at Rivera for asking for a transfer. Imagine what he's going to do when he hears he's resigning."

Caroline winced. "Gentleman, I have a bad headache. Could you stop yelling and tell me what you're doing here?"

Ethan stepped forward. "We think Isaac's case—the other one dealing with the traffickers that he ID'd at your hotel, is tied to a former associate of my wife's father. I've been working with some of the Mexican authorities, and we wanted to talk to him about an upcoming operation."

"All of this has to wait," the doctor interrupted. He touched Caroline's arm gently. "Don't worry about the possible pregnancy. We can work around that area, do a head CT, and restrict X-rays to the injured arm. With these precautions, there's little chance of harm to a developing fetus, but I strongly suggest we get moving—you need these scans."

Caroline was shaking her head, but Isaac's mother stopped her, cupping her face the way Sonia had.

"*Todo va estar bien*," Mirna murmured, transferring a hand to her back and rubbing in soothing circles. She urged her to stand, rising on her tiptoes to buss Caroline's cheek.

"Go with the doctor, *mija*," she added in English, giving her a little push.

"Here." Jason held out his hand. "I'll walk you down."

"No walking," the doctor said emphatically, pointing at a wheelchair that had appeared at her side.

"Then I'll wheel you down," Jason amended, helping her sit. He pushed her out of the room before the doctor could protest.

§.

Consciousness didn't hit him like a train, as was the norm. Waking up today was like swimming up from the bottom of a lake filled with molasses. But there was something urgent he had to do, although his will was strangely muffled, his energy sapped.

When he finally opened his eyes, it was to see his abdomen wrapped in bandages.

"*Fuck.*"

"Hello to you, too."

Isaac turned his head to see Jason White sitting in a chair. "I got shot again, didn't I?"

"Yup." Jason leaned forward, bracing his arms on his thighs. "This one wasn't a little flesh wound in the arm either. The bullet was an armor-piercing round. Blackbeard's people carried only the best."

Isaac swore again. It was all coming back. "*Caroline.* Is she okay?"

"She will be," he said. "She does have a mild concussion and her wrist is fractured, but she'll recover."

Jason's tone was off. Isaac summoned the strength to frown. "What aren't you telling me?"

Jason's lip pulled in. "They're being cautious about how to treat her injuries. Apparently, there's a good chance she's pregnant. Know anything about that?"

"Ah." Well fuck, he hadn't factored that into the scenario. His stomach clenched. Caroline couldn't have serious painkillers, and she would need them after what that piece-of-shit Melvin had pulled.

"They gave her a test to be sure."

He waited, but Jason didn't continue.

"Do I have to beat you with this IV pole to get you to spit it out?" he threatened, pointing to the drip giving him...whatever it was giving him.

"Is she pregnant?" he asked, holding his breath—a painful act.

Jason lifted a shoulder. "I don't know. Fairly sure the doctor gave her the results, but Caroline hasn't talked since. And your sisters are better at cracking hard witnesses than us three combined, so that's quite a feat."

This discussion was making his head hurt. "Three?"

"Ethan's here," Jason supplied. "We've got news on the cartel across the border. But then you went and got yourself shot, neatly avoiding an undercover assignment that could last months, maybe a year..."

Isaac knew from his tone that Jason wasn't seriously accusing him of shirking his duty. "Hey, I was protecting my woman. You would have done the same."

"I know," Jason said with a big grin. "One of these days, you're going to tell me how you talked Caroline-fucking-Wentworth into letting you put a baby in her. That's a pull way above your pay grade—and I don't mean because she's rich."

Isaac sniffed. He knew Jason had added the expletive as a show of respect. "Says the man who talked Mary Margaret Tyler into marrying him."

"Cupid must have been drunk on the day we met. Else, Maggie would have never looked at me twice."

Isaac grunted. "Okay, as much as I'm enjoying this little chat, you better go find Caroline and get her over here if she's able to walk. I need to see her."

Jason held up his phone. "Already on it. I texted Ethan as soon as you started to rouse."

A knock at the door made him turn. Isaac's blood was pumping sluggishly, the probable aftereffects of anesthesia, but the sound was enough to pick up the pace.

"Speak of the devil." Jason rose to open the door. Isaac was alarmed to see Caroline laid out on a stretcher, being pushed into the room by Ethan Thomas.

"Help me with this before someone sees us," Ethan groused as the door closed on the mobile bed, impeding its progress. "If that snippy doctor catches me, he'll bar the entire bureau from the building. He yelled at me earlier."

"*Caroline.*" Oh God, why was she in a bed?

Caroline twisted her head, trying to see him. "Yes! I'm here."

"No, don't get up," she chided when he tried to reach her. "I'm fine. I told them I could walk, but Ethan wouldn't listen. He just commandeered the bed."

As soon as Ethan pulled the stretcher alongside his bed, Caroline twisted, shuffling over. On her knees. One arm was in a cast.

"*Damn it.* I should have hit that son-of-a-bitch Melvin harder," he said, reaching for her. With his help, she tucked herself into his side, her immobilized arm on her other side.

Once her body was nestled into his, he relaxed, something deep inside him unclenching. Suddenly, Isaac felt like crying.

"We have news on Melvin—" Jason began.

"I don't care," Isaac mumbled, pressing his mouth against Caroline's forehead. "Get out."

"Take a look at this first," Jason said.

Something landed at the foot of the bed. Isaac felt them leave. Once they were gone, Caroline scooted down to retrieve the object.

"Ugh." She held up the mask. "If I never see this thing again, it will be too soon."

He held out a hand. "Give it here."

Shuffling back on her knees, she handed him the mask before resuming her spot pressed against him.

Isaac frowned, tracing a split in the back of the mask where the plastic coating had been ripped open. "Are my pants somewhere around here?" he asked. "I have a little penknife in there."

"I think I can use my nails." Working together, they widened the cut, peeling the plastic off to reveal real jade underneath.

"Damn. I can't believe this was under there," he muttered, touching the mask all over.

The low-quality colored plastic had been vacuumed-sealed onto the genuine artifact, thickening the intricately carved facial features until they had been altered to appear like every other knock-off relic sold by art museum gift shops the world over. But the real one was a stunning piece of ancient craftsmanship.

"It must be worth millions to the right collector."

Caroline murmured her agreement, touching the edge with a finger. "It's magnificent—but I still hate it."

Isaac couldn't blame her.

"I wonder if everything in the rooms was like this—a smuggled relic," she said, pressing closer.

Dropping the mask, he pulled her into him, resting against the inclined head of the bed as he thought it over. "I bet they weren't. Some must contain secret compartments," he decided. "Together, Melvin and Stephan were in the ideal position to set up contactless drops. They get word that their buyer is coming to town, they book them a room, and then they put in whatever it is they bought—real artifacts disguised as fakes or hollow knick-knacks with drugs in them."

"And they used my hotel to do it," Caroline grumbled.

He stroked her back. "Probably not just yours. This could be going on all over the place for all we know, although I've always said Blackbeard was on the cutting edge. With luck, no one else has imitated him."

Caroline settled under his arm again. "Imitated *her*. Stephan let that slip. Blackbeard is a woman."

Isaac jerked in surprise. "Well, fuck. And here I thought Stephan might *be* the boss. That'll teach me to be a sexist schmuck."

He glanced down at Caroline. There were tears in her eyes.

"Hey now." He reached out to wipe one crystalline track away. "No tears. We're both alive, and even though I'm pissed that those assholes hurt you, we're both going to be okay—"

He paused, his pulse starting to race. "They didn't hurt you more than this, did they?"

"No, I'm fine. This is the worst of it," she said, indicating her arm. "You were injured far worse than me."

Her lip trembled, and fresh tears spilled from her beautiful blue eyes. "Oh, Isaac. I thought you were going to die."

Isaac rushed to assure her, but Caroline wasn't listening. She buried her face against his chest and wept. He let her cry it out, soothing her with his touch and little murmurs. "I just found you," he told her. "I'm not going anywhere."

He crooked his index finger under her chin, nudging until she met his eyes. "You're going to be eighty years old, reminding me where I left my wallet, while I complain about the music our grandkids are listening to."

That earned him a weak smile. "I like the sound of that."

She took his hand and lifted it to her mouth, kissing his fingers.

She was so gentle—no one had ever touched him with that care and delicacy. Isaac could feel his heart swelling until it felt like he was going to burst. He was too full of the emotion—it was spilling out of him at every seam.

"I heard you had a test," he said, nuzzling her cheek.

"Yes," she whispered. "I'm pregnant."

Joy burst in his chest, giving him a visceral kick. *Thank God.* He pressed a hard kiss to her forehead. "That's amazing. But why do you look sad?"

Her smile was a touch shaky. "Timing. I had just decided we should stop trying to have a baby."

Isaac frowned. "Why?"

She touched his cheek. "I love you—I love being with you more than anyone else in the world. I started to think we should have more time alone before we start a family, the way a normal couple would do it."

Isaac had been starting to worry, but he just laughed and shook his head. "No. Our relationship has never been normal. Why would we start now? I love you, and I want a baby that's part you and part me yesterday—okay, maybe mostly you, gorgeous."

Her answering smile was so pure and beautiful that he could have stared at her all day. Isaac rubbed his cheek against her hair. "I want it all, and I want it now…and you're going to have to forgive me for unintentionally quoting Willy Wonka."

Caroline passed a hand under her eye, wiping the traces of her tears away. "I think it was one of the children who said that."

He shrugged. "We'll figure it out when we watch it with our kid."

She chuckled, but when it subsided, her face was deadly serious. "You're the biggest surprise of my life. Sometimes when we're together, it doesn't seem real. You're like a fantasy I never knew I had."

"I picked the wrong time to get shot," he groaned. "Because there is nothing more I'd like to do than prove just how real I am."

A stroke of her hand left a trail of warmth and heat that he, unfortunately, couldn't act on. But he didn't stop her. He would never stop her.

"I'll take a raincheck on that," she whispered.

Isaac pressed another soft kiss to her hairline. "That's a promise I intend on collecting, My Queen."

Caroline poked him. "I used to hate it when you referred to me as royalty."

"It was said with love."

She harrumphed, but then gave him a cheeky smile as something occurred to her. "You realize if I'm the queen, that makes you my king, doesn't it?"

Caroline was adorable. Wrong. But adorable.

"No. I am now, and forever will be, your knight." Isaac pointed to his bandages. "It's just the armor is a little dented right now."

She cuddled closer. "In chess when you capture the queen, the game is over."

Isaac considered that.

"Funny…" He bent to graze her skin with his lips. "This feels more like the beginning."

# CHAPTER FORTY-ONE

Isaac pushed his aviator sunglasses farther up the bridge of his nose, but they kept sliding down. Taking them off, he wiped the nose pads thoroughly before putting them back on. He was wearing too much sunscreen for someone of his complexion, but his new bride hadn't stopped fussing until he'd been slathered in the stuff.

Isaac hadn't thought he needed that formal tie of marriage. He also hadn't wanted to pressure Caroline. They would do just as well without that piece of paper. But the day after his surgery, the words, 'will you marry me' had popped out of his mouth and she'd said yes.

Isaac dragged her to the hospital chapel that very day, determined to seal the deal before she could change her mind.

Today, he was poolside at the Luxe with Jason White and Caroline, stretched out along one of the plush, double-capacity lounge chairs. There were still bandages around his abs, but they were due to come off later that day. His wife—and he did love calling her that—was not so lucky. Her cast was not due for removal for at least three more weeks. Maybe a month.

"Caroline," he said, trying to grab her before she stepped out of reach. "Sit down, babe. I don't like you serving me, especially when you should be lying next to me."

A fine line appeared between her golden brows. She wore a white sundress at his request. Not only was it sexy as hell, but he'd also been hoping the casual look would inspire her to relax. It wasn't working.

"Are you sure you don't need a bottle of water?" she asked, her hand adjusting his glasses for him. "It's very warm out. I'm going to get you one."

Since she'd already brought him a coffee, a Caesar salad, and a fruity drink with an umbrella in it, he was going to say no. But she was gone before he could stop her.

"Just let her get it out of her system," Jason advised with a lopsided grin when Isaac sighed. "I once got a black eye on the job, and my wife wouldn't stop coddling me until it was gone—I was tempted to recreate it with shoe polish after. Maggie does do coddling well."

"I may not be one hundred percent yet, but neither is she," Isaac groused. "And she's not the only one. The entire staff has gone off the deep end. I had to threaten bodily harm to get them to stop bringing me food and drinks I didn't ask for every five minutes."

"Well, that's your curse for being heroic." Jason snickered. "You saved their boss and therefore their jobs. Throw in the news of the baby—and knowing how quickly news spreads in a hotel, I imagine they knew before you left the hospital, and bam, you're Mr. Popular."

Ignoring him, Isaac kept an eye on the door. When Caroline finally returned with the chilled bottle of water, he caught her undamaged arm by the elbow.

"That's enough fetching," he scolded. "The only thing I need is for you to sit next to me and listen to what Jason was saying about the other stuff in the box you had sent to Luma."

Lush lips compressing in a line, Caroline obliged him with a resigned expression. She toed off her heels and sat, her posture tense and uncomfortable.

"This feels weird," she observed, her eyes darting from side to side.

"Don't you ever come down here to relax?" Jason asked. "It's your hotel. You should enjoy it."

"You, of all people, know that's next to impossible. Correct me if

I'm wrong, but didn't you and Maggie move out of the Boston Caislean?"

"Not because I wanted to, I assure you. I was extremely comfortable there." Jason's grin was wry. "But I suppose you're right. Maggie finds it easier to relax at our condo. But I miss the big pool. I'm trying to talk her into getting a hot tub."

Caroline twisted to him. "I thought you said no shop talk today," she said, watching the folder in his hand askance.

"This is too good," Isaac assured her. "They picked up Blackbeard yesterday."

Caroline sat up. "But you said she was going to get away—that all the communications between her and Stephan were encrypted."

"They were." He smiled. In the end, the capture of his nemesis had been easy and a bit anti-climactic. "But Stephan was one of her top lieutenants. They had face-to-face contact regularly."

Jason took the manila folder from his hands, opening it and handing them a picture of a fashionably dressed woman in her early fifties.

"Meet Mary Oswald, aka Blackbeard. Every few months, on his day off from the Luxe, Stephan would drive up to an accounting firm in Beverly Hills. The office was a front for Blackbeard's operation. This was the building where she would conduct business with the handful of contacts it was necessary to meet in person."

"They were able to scour traffic and bank camera footage from the surrounding neighborhood," Isaac filled in when Jason paused. "They captured enough faces to identify people. Knowing Blackbeard was a woman was a huge help," he told her, giving her the credit she was due.

"Without that bit of information, they wouldn't have been able to focus on the right woman."

Jason nodded. "This is the kicker—Blackbeard's real name was Mary Oswald. The similarity of her name to Mary Ormond, the historical pirate's real-life spouse, inspired her to use the moniker 'Blackbeard's wife' at the start of her life of crime. But she soon learned that many men of the underworld wouldn't deal with the fairer sex. So, she dropped the 'wife' and became just Blackbeard, putting a string of male lieutenants between her and her clients."

Caroline sniffed. "Being a woman in business is hard, but I have little sympathy or admiration for her. I'd like nothing more than to slap her face, even if she told Stephan killing me was not an option."

Stephan had survived the bullets Isaac had pumped into him *and* the fall from the roof. Ironically, Melvin, whom he'd only punched, had died of a heart attack while in custody.

"I still can't believe Stephan targeted you because of Janet," Isaac muttered for the hundredth time.

Caroline glared.

"I mean, she's a sweet kid," he amended, noting the warning look in his wife's eye.

Janet was a nice woman, decent-looking, and well put together. But for Stephan to be obsessed with anyone else when Caroline was around struck Isaac as the most bizarre detail in this entire affair.

"Stephan was in love with Janet and rightly so," she said, indignant on behalf of her young assistant. "Janet is sweet—she was always trying to take care of him, making him lunch or baking him treats. She picked up medicine for him when he got a cold and generally babied him. Janet always puts everyone else first."

Caroline broke off and lifted her good shoulder. "For all his jaded tendencies and criminal past, or maybe because of them, Stephan recognized the worth of a good and loving woman."

"I guess even criminals can be romantics," Jason observed. "Too bad he screwed himself over by blaming you for the fact she dumped him."

"I doubt he was thinking at all when he did that," Isaac admitted. "Trying to hit Caroline with the van was a spur-of-the-moment thing, an impulse. We figured that from the start because Caroline wasn't supposed to be in the parking structure at that moment. Blackbeard reprimanded him after—taking Caroline out of the picture jeopardized the hotel, and they needed it to run smoothly to carry out their operation under our noses."

"Then Janet took Stephan back for a little while, and he forgot about holding me responsible for their break-up," Caroline said. "At least until she ended things a second time. After speaking with her about that, I think the timing fits. Janet broke up with him the second time the day I was pushed down the stairs. He must have seen me go up to investigate the broken pipe and decided to teach me a lesson."

She broke off, staring at the distant shoreline. "Janet feels terrible about that. I don't think she's going to date anyone from the hotel ever again."

"Well, at least this particular creep is never going to see the light of day," Jason promised as she ducked her head down, pressing her face into Isaac's arm. He gave Isaac a significant look over the top of her head.

Jason had already told him the gun Stephan had used was tied to several of the bodies they had traced to Blackbeard, including that of an off-duty police officer who'd stumbled on her operation.

Stephan was going to spend the rest of his life in jail. He wouldn't get another chance to hurt Caroline. Nobody would. Isaac was going to make sure of that.

Another picture appeared in Jason's hand. "I wanted to show you this, too—not all the artifacts were genuine ones in disguise. Some did have drugs like you guessed. They were packaged in thick plastic and then embedded in plaster, the kind that dissolves in water." He tossed Isaac the photo. "One had a cache of diamonds and at least half a dozen had cash, which suggests they were payments for goods delivered."

Isaac nodded, scratching around the edge of his bandage absently, stopping only when Caroline put her hand over his to make him stop.

"It makes sense the buyer would come prepared. This was a pretty sophisticated operation."

"It's still a mess to me," Caroline confessed. "How did the people who bought things get their pieces?"

Sitting up, he laid it out. "The buyer would get instructions, maybe even a kit to create their own dummy artifact. They filled it with cash or diamonds, then swapped it out with the one in the room, which held their product. It didn't even have to be the same object as the one in the room. I doubt many people would notice the artifact was different outside of the maids. I spoke to them. Those who noticed didn't question the changes. They just assumed management was shifting things around. I'm sure Melvin and Stephan never expected you to be so detail-oriented, noticing their additions."

He continued. "And if the contraband in question was too large to be disguised as an artifact, well then, Stephan could just conceal it in a gift basket, the kind the hotel leaves for VIP guests."

Caroline scowled. "That makes sense. Both Stephan and Melvin had access. They didn't even need a maid to drop the object off in those cases."

"Which may explain why none of the maid's background checks threw up a red flag, no matter how deeply I looked," Isaac confirmed. "They either never used one or they did, but the woman quit after planting the first lot. What self-respecting smuggler would want to be a full-time maid? It's hard work."

"I hope you're right and none of the remaining cleaning team were involved," Caroline said. "Melvin and Stephan were bad enough. I couldn't stand it if another member of the staff was part of their operation."

"If they were, they'll disappear, just melt into the woodwork," Jason predicted. "We'll never hear from them again."

That didn't seem to comfort Caroline, but it was best she be prepared.

"We'll keep a close eye on anyone who quits in the next few days," he promised. "It could be no one does."

"Speaking of quitting," Jason grimaced. "I think someone wants to talk to you about that."

Isaac twisted his head to see Robert Angel walking out of the hotel to the pool area.

The Boston bureau chief was wearing one of his fine wool suits. It looked crisp and clean despite the heat.

"Don't get up," the Angel told Isaac when he made a motion to stand. "I just came to congratulate the newlyweds."

Robert held out his hand to Caroline, bending over to kiss it old-world style. "Caroline Wentworth, I've heard so much about you. Or is it Mrs. Rivera now?"

"She's keeping her maiden name." Isaac shrugged, unperturbed at his boss' interest. Caroline was a beautiful woman. But he knew she was his, body and soul. "It comes with the hotel."

"Of course." Robert laughed. He made small talk, admiring the view of the beach and Isaac's new wife for a few more minutes before he got down to business.

"There is a small matter I wanted to discuss with you in private," he told him.

Isaac glanced at Caroline, noting the tightness at the corners of her mouth despite the smile on her face.

"You can use the conference room on the first floor," she said, her soft southern burr deeper than he'd ever heard it.

His impulse was to decline, but he'd been working for Robert for over five years. The man had earned his respect. If that meant listening to him try to talk him out of resigning, then Isaac would do that.

"Don't worry," he whispered to Caroline, trying to tell her it wouldn't work, but her tension remained.

An hour later, he found her in their suite, opening boxes. Caroline saw him, and lifted a tiny onesie that read 'F.B.I. Agent in training'.

"See," she said, her voice thick. "I was never going to ask you to quit. If you want to keep being an agent, you have my full support. I don't have a problem with it."

He loved that she was a terrible liar.

Sitting beside her, he reached out to stroke the satiny skin of her inner arm. "Well, that's too bad, because I am kind of attached to my current position—it has fringe benefits like you wouldn't believe."

He was hoping for a smile, but Caroline had prepared herself for the worst and she wasn't about to budge. "You don't have to shield me. I accept this. I would never want to hold you back."

Isaac pressed his forehead to hers. "That's very selfless of you, but Robert didn't ask me to stay on as a special agent."

Her lips parted. "He didn't?"

"No. He had something else in mind."

Isaac passed a hand through his hair. "It seems that spotting those traffickers here cracked a big case down South. And Robert smells an opportunity. He's fairly good at that sort of thing."

Taking Caroline's hand, he stopped to kiss every fingertip before continuing. "The Angel wants me to stay on as liaison to the hotel industry. Officially, I'd be a consultant. I'd go around to different chains, teaching them how to spot traffickers and other criminals. There would be lots of seminars and meetings with security personnel, etcetera."

Caroline's fingers flew to cover his. "That's amazing. You could do so much good in a job like that. What a great idea."

"It is, isn't it?" Isaac put his arm around her. "And with good planning and some creative scheduling, I can book these events in the cities you need to visit to keep an eye on the Wentworth chain, even if we are primarily based in this one."

"It would be handy," he added when she started. "Being stationed physically in a hotel would help me keep my finger on the pulse, not just on security measures but also on what people get up to in hotels."

Caroline burst into tears, covering her face with her hands. Isaac nudged them off, wiping her tears with the novelty onesie.

"Oh, no, don't mess it up," she cried, pulling the cotton away from him.

"I think the baby is going to take care of that." He laughed, kissing her tears away, covering her still-flat belly with his hand. "Just wait."

"I thought you were going to leave me," Caroline said, sniffling. "I mean, leave the hotel."

"I would never," he said, squeezing her. "I am exactly where I want to be—with you."

She laughed with tears in her eyes. "I can't believe it."

"I know, but that's okay," he said, cupping her face with his hands. "I intend on staying right where I am until I've convinced you, even if it takes years...decades...or the rest of my life."

Raising her head to look in his eyes, she gave him smile that went straight through him, right into his heart. "In that case…I think we can come to an understanding."

# EPILOGUE

"I don't know if I can leave her," Caroline murmured.

Isaac pressed his head against hers, his hand reaching to stroke the soft down on their daughter's head. To Caroline's infinite surprise and shock, their baby girl had been born with a full head of dark black hair—the exact same shade as her papa's.

"I don't want to leave her either, but we're only going to be a short ten-minute walk away."

He and Caroline had bought a large four-bedroom house on Ocean Boulevard, a few blocks away from the Luxe hotel. It was the biggest place he'd ever lived in, although Caroline often referred to it as 'cozy'. But those obvious little disparities in their upbringing never amounted to much. Not when their life was full of affection, heat, and so much love it sometimes startled him. That and Caroline loved their home. She'd spent a lot of time decorating every room, taking his input into account with a generosity that didn't surprise him or his family at all.

His wife loved him and their life.

The tangible result of their love was yawning now, waving her mittened hands as if she were stretching, getting ready for a well-deserved nap. Baby Elise had been named after Caroline's mother, and at two months old, she was the spoiled and cosseted delight of their lives.

But Isaac was eager for a night alone with his wife, and tonight was the perfect opportunity for them to get away. His sisters and mother had come down to San Diego for Elise's baptism. After the service in the morning, they'd had a party on the beach before coming back to the house to grill up a feast in the backyard.

Isaac had been surprised when Caroline had suggested such a casual party when he'd first brought up the baptism.

"I thought you'd want to have a big bash in the ballroom for such a momentous occasion," he'd told her shortly after welcoming their baby girl home.

Caroline had been laying out the tiny little dress she was going to put on Elise—their baby had more outfits than either combined thanks to his wife and family's enthusiasm for shopping. Isaac had severely underestimated how much people loved shopping for little girl clothes.

"These moments with Elise should just be family," she told him, smoothing the dress before picking a pair of matching tiny tights to keep the baby's legs warm.

"Then why is Janet coming and bringing half of the Luxe staff?"

"Not half," she tsked before bustling out to accept their dinner delivery—courtesy of chef Cerise Lions at the Luxe. "And Janet *is* family," she insisted.

But he was glad to have Janet there the day of the party. She helped corral his family with the same efficiency she ran Caroline's life, giving him enough time to sit back and savor the day. She was also his willing accomplice for tonight's plans, along with his family.

He was able to convince Caroline to leave the baby with his mother and sister's help.

"She'll be fine," Sonia assured, cuddling Elise close. "I promise to call you if anything goes wrong—which it won't," she added at Caroline's sudden anxious expression.

"Don't worry," his mother interceded, hugging Caroline. "Brittney and I will be here to help Sonia. Nothing will go wrong. Now run along. Get your alone time while you can. It's only going to get harder."

"She's right," Isaac said, tugging Caroline out before his gorgeous, overprotective wife could marshal another argument to stay.

They walked down to the hotel along the beach, holding their shoes, making their way to Caroline's old suite via the back route to minimize chances they would get stopped.

"Oh no," Caroline cried when he opened the door.

The bed had been stripped, and it was covered in plastic. The smell of new paint—a soft pink—was overwhelming. The other furniture was gone.

"I forgot about this," Caroline confessed with a grimace. "I was trying to make this room more baby friendly, so Elise can have a nursery here."

"Well, I'm glad you kept the bed—for future use—but this does toss a spanner in my plans for the evening," he said, kissing her neck. He tugged her into the office, closing the door after them to avoid letting in the fumes.

"It's not a problem," he told her, not wanting to give her an excuse to go home to the baby. Isaac rounded the desk so he could call the front desk when Caroline's hands flew to her mouth.

"Oh no!"

Startled, he put the receiver down. "What's wrong?"

She grimaced and held up a hand. "Don't get mad."

He frowned. "Why would I get mad?"

She pursed her lips, her entire face contorting. At first, he thought she was going to cry, but then she burst into laughter. "I am so sorry. I was going to tell you about this—I swear."

Moving to the couch, she peeked around the back, moving from the right to the left side to push something he couldn't see.

His jaw dropped as the couch began to fold out into a queen-sized bed.

"I'm sorry!" Caroline squeaked, her shoulders at ear level.

"All that time," he scolded. Isaac had never complained about the foldaway cot he was forced to sleep in at the start of his investigation, but she'd gotten an earful since.

"I knew there was a reason you looked so guilty whenever I mentioned that damn cot." He scowled, stripping off his shirt. "Get ready to get spanked so hard."

Laughing and squealing, Caroline kicked off her heels and made a break for it, but he caught her easily.

He stripped off her clothes and turned her face down, but he only managed a single spank before getting distracted by the satin feel of Caroline's skin. Even after having a baby, her body was still the most beautiful thing he'd ever seen. It had changed subtly. Her hips were a touch wider, her bust and derriere a little fuller. Always greedy for more Caroline, he couldn't have been happier about the changes.

But they hadn't made love since the baby was born, and Isaac was ready to explode.

Caroline was still laughing when he turned her over. "My hand to God, I was going to tell you, I just kept forgetting…"

"Sure, you did." But he was grinning as he bent down to kiss her. "I love you, my sweet little liar."

She put her hands on either side of his face. "I love you, too. And, in my defense, you talked your way into *my* bed so fast, you didn't really suffer all that long."

"True," he admitted, still grinning like a fool, pinning her arms to the cushion. "But it's the principle of the thing, you see. I'm going to have to teach you about keeping secrets from your man."

Pushing her arms against her sides, he put his mouth on her breast, taking one rosy tip into his mouth and sucking.

Caroline melted into the mattress, a hand flopping weakly at her side. "I don't have any secrets from you," she breathed as he turned his attention to the other nipple, his hands parting her legs.

Settling between her creamy thighs, Isaac stroked her cheek, pressing his face against her neck to nip at the spot where her pulse was beating like a hummingbird. "You're as much a mystery today as you were the day I met you."

She put her arms around his neck. "I don't believe that's true for a second, but if it were, then it's a good thing you're such a great investigator."

Flexing his muscles, he made them bounce, pressing her deeper into the mattress. "An agent is only as good as his last solved case," he informed her, parting her legs so he could stroke the satin of her inner thighs. "That's something I once heard as a rookie, and I decided it applied to other aspects of life...including this one."

Caroline's breath caught as he settled against her softness, pinning her arms to the mattress. "I know the last time we made love might be a little fuzzy for you, given our long, enforced abstinence, but you don't have to worry. I plan on taking my time, to make sure I have *all* the facts."

His wife began to pant as he palmed her breast, flicking the rosy bud at the crown with his tongue. "I promise, I won't overlook any detail...because some things might have changed since the last time. But a skilled investigator takes nothing for granted, and he approaches each new puzzle from every angle."

This time, Caroline cried out his name as he slid his thick length home, pumping into her gently as she learned to accommodate his body all over again, and then harder and faster when she urged him on in breathy whispers.

He guided her legs until they were wrapped around him and he thrust hard, grinding into her softness until she splintered, her nails digging into his back. Then he let go, throbbing inside her with a ragged sigh.

"Isaac," Caroline began, her breathing fast.

"Hmm?" he murmured, rolling to the side so he wouldn't crush her.

She ran her palm over his chest. "Sherlock Holmes has nothing on you."

Laughing, Isaac pulled Caroline close. "And I'll always happy to be at Her Majesty's service."

The End

Knight Takes Queen is the third installment of a spin-off series. If you want more romance read the award-winning Singular Obsession books. Or you can order the next installment of Rogues and Rescuers today!

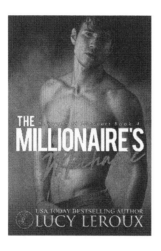

*Can the shy mechanic fix his broken heart?*

Millionaire Rainer Torsten just wants to do his job and lay low. After his trust is violated by a woman, he's leery of letting anyone get close to him. But Rainer's fat wallet and chiseled hard body makes him the object of many people's desire—and envy.

When mechanic Georgia Hines overhears a scheme to kidnap the wealthy CEO for ransom money, she knows she must do something to help the soft-eyed philanthropist. After the kidnapping plan goes awry, Rainer and Georgia hole away in a secluded cabin, looking for sanctuary. As danger looms and snow falls, the heat between the businessman and mechanic intensifies. Can Rainer save them both and finally open his heart to Georgia—or is his past too broken for the mechanic to repair?

Available Now

# ABOUT THE AUTHOR

*A 7-time Readers' Favorite Medal Winner. USA Today Bestselling Author. Mom to a half-feral princess. WOC. Former scientist. Recovering geek.*

Lucy Leroux is the steamy pen name for author L.B. Gilbert. Ten years ago Lucy moved to France for a one-year research contract. Six months later she was living with a handsome Frenchman and is now married with an adorable half-french 5yo who won't go to bed on time

When her last contract ended Lucy turned to writing. Frustrated by a particularly bad romance novel she decided to write her own. Her family lives in Southern California.

Lucy loves all genres of romance and intends to write as many of them as possible. To date she has published twenty novels and novellas. These includes paranormal, urban fantasy, gothic regency, and contemporary romances with more on the way.

www.authorlucyleroux.com

 amazon.com/author/lucyleroux
 facebook.com/lucythenovelist
 twitter.com/lucythenovelist
 instagram.com/lucythenovelist
 bookbub.com/authors/lucy-leroux

Printed in Great Britain
by Amazon